PRAISE FOR MICHAEL SALA

Winner of the New South Wales Premier's Award for New Writing, 2013
Winner of the Commonwealth Book Prize, Pacific Region, 2013

THE RESTORER

'This is powerful, poetic, extraordinary fiction…Sala never falters.'
AUSTRALIAN

'Unputdownable…Sala creates an atmosphere of simmering
tension with an undercurrent of unpredictability that seeps into every
exchange. [He] is a brilliant writer.' *SATURDAY PAPER*

'Michael Sala's prose is clear and unadorned, the setting exquisitely
rendered, but it is his characters—all of them flawed and complex and
deeply, deeply human—who will stay with me for a very long time. I would
defy anyone to read this story and remain unmoved. *The Restorer* is an
incredibly powerful novel and, I believe, an important one.' HANNAH KENT

'A beautifully written novel about growing up, starting again—
and how the riptide of personal history can pull us further and further
from safety, no matter how hard we fight.' CHARLOTTE WOOD

'Builds and breaks like a summer storm—
just as beautiful, just as brutal.' FIONA MCFARLANE

'Closely observed, with the visceral force of truth,
Michael Sala's heartbreaking novel captures the tender hope
of love and its terrible cost.' KATHRYN HEYMAN

THE LAST THREAD

'Michael Sala has a rare gift: in prose that takes your breath away,
he tells a story of heart-rending sorrow without a trace of sentimentality.
His debut as a novelist is one to celebrate.' RAIMOND GAITA

'A confronting and compelling story of a family. Sala captures
perfectly the puzzled silence of the ⎯⎯⎯⎯⎯prehending child in a
narrative swollen with unspoke⎯

'Skillfully written…Sala expl
damaging saga of family myth-mak

D1112984

Michael Sala was born in the Netherlands and first came to Australia as a child in the 1980s. He lives in Newcastle on the New South Wales north coast. His critically acclaimed debut novel, *The Last Thread*, was winner of the New South Wales Premier's Award for New Writing and regional winner of the Commonwealth Book Prize in 2013.

MICHAEL SALA

THE RESTORER

TEXT PUBLISHING MELBOURNE AUSTRALIA

textpublishing.com.au

The Text Publishing Company
Swann House
22 William Street
Melbourne Victoria 3000
Australia

Published by The Text Publishing Company, 2017
Reprinted 2017 (three times)

Cover design by Sandy Cull, gogoGingko
Cover photo by Jarrad Hemphill
Page design by Jessica Horrocks
Typeset by J&M Typesetting

Printed in Australia by Griffin Press, an Accredited ISO AS/NZS 14001:2004 Environmental Management System printer.

National Library of Australia Cataloguing-in-Publication entry
Creator: Sala, Michael, author.
Title: The restorer/by Michael Sala.
ISBN: 9781925355024 (paperback)
ISBN: 9781922253606 (ebook)
Subjects: Man–woman relationships—Fiction. Families—Australia—Fiction.
Dewey number: A823.4

This one is for my mother

Author's note

This story is set in a real place, at a particular moment in history. It draws on the author's experiences of that time, and also makes reference to some real-life events, such as the earthquake that hit Newcastle in 1989, but the characters in it are entirely fictional.

Before

He heard it for the first time from a long way off, the engine's noise cutting through the hum of the city and harbour, and when the station wagon rounded the corner, trailer in tow, Richard guessed where it was headed. The car pulled to the kerb just past where he sat on the steps leading to his front door. There was a man at the wheel, a woman beside him. A young boy pressed his face to the rear passenger window nearest to Richard, and there was someone on the other side whose head wasn't turned. The trailer was loaded with cardboard boxes, a fridge, a table, the whole lot of it held in place with mismatched lengths of rope. From the look of it, he supposed it was everything they had, but it wasn't much. At least someone was moving into the place. He'd been living next to an empty house for too long.

The door at his back creaked on its hinges. Richard threw down the rest of his coffee. It had been a hot, windless summer day, but the sun was gone. In an hour it would be dark. A breeze had sprung up from out on the ocean, and it was growing stronger. A storm was piling up beyond the terraces that blocked off the sea—he could hear it, could taste the briny scent of energy gathering to break itself across the city. The storms along this part of the coast were fierce, and Newcastle always caught the brunt of them.

The engine of the station wagon was still running. The front passenger door opened and the woman climbed out, face tilted upwards, her brown hair drawn into a ponytail. She crossed her arms and looked at the house beside Richard's as if she were about to get straight back into the car. The next gust of wind pressed her dress—a pale, flowery wisp of cotton—against her slight frame, but she didn't seem to notice. Then the engine cut out, and the driver came around the side of the car. He was broad, muscular, with stains under the arms of his T-shirt, and a way of moving like his hands were the heaviest part of him—the kind of man Richard enjoyed looking at, but only from a distance.

As the man jumped onto the trailer and started undoing the ropes, a girl emerged from the far passenger door. She stretched her arms behind her, took several steps, and came to a standstill on the road. She was as tall as the woman, with the same pale skin, but not as slight. Her hair was like the man's—thick and dark, almost black—and it hung halfway down her back. The boy got out last. He put his entire weight against the door nearest to Richard to shut it and then made his way to the girl. After a moment, the woman joined them on the road. She gathered them in, her hands around their shoulders, and the three of them stared up at the vast three-storey terrace. She spoke to them, but Richard

2

couldn't hear what she said. The man on the trailer, the ropes slack in his hands, followed their gaze.

There was something about them, the way they were standing, that Richard would remember later, in the gloom of an early morning, with the jostle of neighbours and the blue and red lights washing across everything.

But for now there was no one to see but him. The woman had turned away. The boy kicked a discarded soft drink can along the gutter. The man glanced at him, then leaned down from the trailer and held the keys out to the woman.

'Maryanne,' he said. 'Can you open up the house?'

She took the keys from his outstretched hand.

Richard tried and failed to catch her eye as she walked past and let herself in the front door. He rose to his feet and approached the man.

'Hey.' He extended his hand upwards. 'Welcome to the neighbourhood. I'm Richard.'

There was something restless in the man's deep-set eyes, but the rest of his face hardly moved. 'Roy,' he said.

He returned to undoing the last lengths of rope around the table.

'Nice to meet you.' Richard dropped his hand back to his side. He could feel the children behind him, watching. 'Need some help?'

'We're good.'

'Sure? Saves the kids breaking their backs.'

Roy looked down at him again. 'Well,' he said at last. 'If you want.' He began to slide the table off the trailer. 'You ready?'

Richard took the legs of the table and grunted with the unexpected effort as the weight met his hands. 'Woah, it's heavy. I love the wood, though. Is it oak?'

Roy held his end of the table easily. 'Blue gum.'

'Where'd you get it?'

'Built it myself.' Roy's tone was less guarded now, but detached, as if his mind were somewhere else. 'Easy enough, if you know how.'

'That's great.' Richard let himself be guided along the path and up the three steps to the door. 'I've always wanted to do that. Never had the talent. Suppose you cut the tree down yourself, did you?'

'Yep,' Roy said. 'That'd be it.'

Richard couldn't tell if he was being mocked. 'Where you from?'

Roy showed his teeth, a smile of sorts, but his eyes made it a warning. 'We're here now. That's the main thing.'

Richard was the one to break the stare. A flush suffused his face and neck, a prickling unease that reminded him of being singled out at school. That feeling never truly went away—you just forgot about it sometimes. He cleared his throat. 'Well, you've got your work cut out for you, anyway, with this place. Wasn't sure what'd happen to it after the fire. Good for the buyer, I guess. Isn't it meant to be a buyers' market?'

Roy didn't answer. It took them a while to manoeuvre the table through the doorway, Roy issuing short, terse instructions that Richard tried to follow as best he could. Then they carried it past the front room on the left and down the hall, their footsteps resonant on the floorboards. The layout of the house was the same as in Richard's, only a mirror image: two rooms off the hall, with the entry to the second room just opposite the foot of the stairs, and the kitchen at the back. The place was a dump—he was shocked at its condition. There'd been a fire a few years back, accidentally started by squatters. They'd at least had the good

4

sense to knock on his door before they'd run off, and Richard had called the fire brigade, but no one had been in there since, not that he knew of. It looked and smelled worse than he'd imagined.

'Bet you picked this place up for a song,' he ventured.

'Here,' Roy said, as they swerved round the stairs, and jerked his head towards the open door of the second room. They turned the table on its side, and Roy edged in backwards, Richard shuffling after him.

They put the table down and Richard looked around. The room was connected to the kitchen at the back by an open doorway. He could see through it into the kitchen, and then out through the back door to the courtyard. The woman was standing out there, her back to the house. She didn't turn around.

Roy was already making his way out to the street again. Richard followed him. He glanced in at the front room as he passed it, curious. That was where the fire had started, from what he could tell, right in the middle. A hole had been burnt in the floorboards down to the basement below. A single candle, that was all it had taken.

Out on the road, Roy was lifting a couple of boxes from the trailer.

'What next?' Richard asked.

'We're good. Thanks.'

Roy walked past him, staring straight ahead, and mounted the steps to the front door again. Only a slight twist in his mouth indicated that he knew Richard was still there. Richard returned to his own steps and picked up his empty coffee cup. The breeze was cooler now.

The girl came past carrying a cardboard box. There was that awkwardness in her that girls her age often had, a leaning inward. Her eyes were almost the same as her father's, the same colour as

5

his, and guarded, as if she did not expect much from anything or anyone. Richard lifted his empty cup in a half-salute, backed into the comfort of his own house and closed his door before the wind could blow it shut.

1

Freya paused at the foot of the steps to look up at the house, at the window she could see on the top floor, then she tightened her grip on the cardboard box and walked inside. A draught brushed her face. It smelled of old fire—a sharp, cloying tang of burnt wood and chemical and plastic—and underneath that, rotting wood, urine, things long since dead.

The high ceiling in the first room off the hallway was ornate in an old-fashioned way, but sagging and blackened with smoke stains. The wallpaper was filthy too, and separated here and there from the walls in folds and curls. In the middle of all this, beside a charred hole in the floorboards wide enough to fall through, stood her brother.

'Daniel,' she said.

Her brother's face was slack, the tip of his tongue resting against his upper lip as he leaned forward and peered into the hole. He looked like he might topple in with the slightest push.

'Daniel,' she said again, a little louder.

The wood creaked under him as he gathered some spit in his mouth and released it.

'Daniel.'

If her brother didn't answer this time, she'd push him in herself.

His large eyes fixed on her, and his lips, more like a girl's than a boy's, broke into a smile. Without a word, he stepped back from the hole, picked up the small box he'd been carrying and came towards her.

'We're not supposed to come in this room,' she said. 'Remember what Mum said?'

He followed her down the hall, just past the stairs, into the next room, where Dad was sliding the heavy table against a wall of raw brick. The room had a single window, narrow and cracked, boarded up from the outside, but dim afternoon light seeped in through the doorway to the kitchen.

Dad looked up. 'Not in here,' he said. 'Take those to your mum. And don't waste time. It's getting dark. The sky's going to open up any second. Okay?'

'Okay,' Freya said, and went through to the kitchen.

Daniel was close behind her. When she stopped, the box he carried prodded her in the back, and she cursed under her breath.

'What?' Mum said. She was on her knees, wiping down the kitchen cupboards.

'My head hurts,' Daniel said.

Mum got to her feet, took the box from him and put it down

on the bench. 'It's the weather. It happens with your father's knee too.'

Daniel came in close and rested his head against her ribs. Freya put down her own box. The benchtop was damp and shiny from having being wiped over with a wet cloth, but the stains hadn't gone away. Outside, through a row of windows, she could see a wall hemming in the courtyard, and the rooftops of neighbouring houses. At her back, Dad's heavy steps clomped through the hallway and out the front door.

'Do you like the house?' Mum was speaking only to Daniel, her hand running through his hair.

Daniel nodded against her dress.

'I knew you would.' Mum kissed him on the top of his head and released him with a slight push. 'And Daniel?'

Daniel turned back to her.

'Just try to listen,' she said. 'Really listen. Okay?'

Daniel hesitated.

'Say yes, Daniel,' Mum told him. 'You have to say yes when people talk to you, so they know you heard. Remember that.'

'Yes, Mum.'

'Go help your father.'

Mum watched him walk off, then her voice changed, now she was just with Freya. 'You know we can make this a beautiful home, don't you?'

'I guess so.'

'But what do you think, Freya?'

Freya had never liked saying what she thought, not since she'd figured out that people didn't usually want to know. 'I think it's fine.'

'It'll be more than fine, Freya. You'll see.' Mum put a hand on her shoulder.

Freya gave the smallest smile she could, and stepped back so that Mum's hand dropped away from her. Mum sighed, picked up the wet cloth, and began wiping down the cupboards again.

The wind was picking up outside, blowing in the open front door and right through the house. Dad was in the dining room again—she could hear him—so Freya went from the kitchen out through the hall instead.

As she passed the door to the basement, tucked beneath the stairs, it was banging against its frame. Freya opened it further: a set of steps descended into the darkness. She started down, but the awful smell stopped her—like there was something solid in the air, thickening as she moved through it. The floor below was hidden under garbage, plastic wrappers, empty bottles and bits of rotting newspaper.

'What are you doing?' Mum said from the kitchen.

Freya came back up the stairs and shut the door behind her. 'Just thinking.'

'About what?'

She shrugged. 'Wondering how many people died in this place. Smells like a lot.'

'Don't be horrible,' Mum said. 'Remember what your father said.'

'I can't believe you let him choose a house without you, Mum.'

Mum didn't meet her eyes and kept cleaning. 'That's just how it worked out.'

When Freya went out to the trailer again, the day was gone. Time was like that, though—one moment an open sky that stretched and stretched and you were bored and waiting, and hungry in a way that you couldn't describe, not knowing what was going to happen next or what you were supposed to do. And then. Clouds from one end of the sky to the other, shot through with flashes of lightning, the low rumble of thunder, the first drops of rain spattering and fading on the footpath and the warm road, and all of a sudden, this sense of urgency.

Freya resisted it. She stood on the road beside the trailer and looked up at the window on the top floor again. She wanted to go up there, to look out that window, so she could make out the shape of the land, discover what lay past the buildings, perhaps find the ocean, see whether it was anything as wild as she imagined it, but another part of her wanted to remain right where she was, outside, and pretend that the house wasn't hers, that she was just a passer-by, that none of this had anything to do with her. A drop of rain burst against her forehead. She opened her mouth and put out her tongue. The next drop, against her cheek, was heavier. Then there was no waiting at all.

~

The last boxes they brought in were soaked. The rain was pelting on the roof. Mum was peeling away the wet cardboard of each box to reveal the things inside. The lights were on in the kitchen and the dining room—naked, dusty bulbs that didn't quite find every corner.

The smell of rain swirled around them, full of the odour of sodden leaves and ocean and warm road that hadn't been wet for a long time. The front door slammed shut. Dad was stamping his feet in the hall and coughing. A flash of lightning blazed through the kitchen and a rumble shook the ground.

'Jesus,' Dad said as he came into the room, pleasure in his tone. 'That was close.'

With the rain beating down, and the world outside gone, they sat around the table and ate a hurried dinner of sandwiches and salad that Mum had brought with them in an esky, and then kept unpacking. Another crackling boom rattled the windows, and a gust of cool air billowed up around Freya's legs from under the floorboards.

Daniel was hugging Mum around the waist.

'It's okay,' she said, prying him loose. 'We're inside. We're all safe.' She opened another box, dug around inside it. 'There!'

Mum held the candles up just as the next crack of thunder exploded outside. A burst of light filled the room and Freya saw everyone as if in an old black and white photograph—Dad wiping his hands uselessly on his sodden T-shirt, his eyes shadowed by his forehead, Mum beside the table, Daniel buried again into her side. Then the house, like the world beyond the windows, dropped into darkness.

Everything became louder. The house pressed in close. The rain sounded like it was crashing down on her skull. Her brother whimpered. Dad coughed and cleared his throat. A rustle came from somewhere in front of her, a metallic rasp.

'For God's sake,' Dad said. 'My hands are too wet to light this damn thing.'

'Give it to me,' Mum said.

'Where are you then?' Dad said.

'Here,' Mum said. 'Give me the lighter, you take the candles.'

Freya couldn't see them, but she heard their movement, the rasp of the lighter. Sparks, and then the sparks condensed into a flame that brought Mum's hands into view, and then her face, and Dad beside her. Freya thought of a story in the book she'd been reading in the car, a book Nan had pushed into her hands that afternoon, in Sydney, just before they'd left. *Greek Mythology*. Prometheus stealing fire from the gods, Zeus chaining him to a rock, an eagle eating away at his liver, the liver growing back each night. She'd read about Prometheus and thought of Mum, the strange mixture of hope and suffering with which she lived her life, how she never gave up on anything, even when it hurt her.

Mum cupped the glow of the flame with her palm and held the lighter to the candle in Dad's hands. When the flame took hold, Dad put the candle on the mantelpiece. Mum lit another candle behind him.

Daniel stood there between them and reached for the next candle.

'Not you,' Dad said as he turned back.

'Roy,' Mum said.

'He's eight,' Dad said. 'We don't want the house burning down, do we?'

'We can risk it.' Mum lit the candle and gave it to Daniel. 'Just put it on the table.'

Everyone watched Daniel walk to the table and put the candle down with trembling hands. After a moment, Dad walked over and shifted it to the other side of the table.

'The draught,' he said, without looking at anyone.

The rain filled the courtyard on the other side of the kitchen windows with a dull, constant roar. They placed more candles around the room. The flames shrank and danced while her parents set out the foam mattresses, two side by side, at either end of the table. They stayed up for a while, sorting through things by candlelight, but the power didn't come back on, and there wasn't much that could be done without it.

'Go to bed now,' Mum said at last. 'It's been a big day. We'll get up early.'

'I'm not tired,' Daniel said.

But he was asleep as soon as his head settled on the pillow.

Freya lay down beside him. She pretended to sleep too, and

perhaps she did, because when Dad's voice lifted through a lull in the rain, it startled her.

'Those scented candles of yours finally came in handy. I can't believe you've still got them, after everything.'

'I was smart enough not to leave them with you,' Mum answered.

Dad laughed, but not for long. For a moment the rain took over.

'God, I'm tired,' Mum murmured. 'But I don't think I can sleep.'

'You don't know how to relax.'

'Do you blame me?'

'Never, love. It's usually my fault.'

Freya was facing the other way, but she saw from their shadows on the wall that they were close together. She heard them kiss, saw the shape of his hands merge with the shape of her neck. Then they separated, and Mum began sorting through a box. The metallic rasp of Dad flicking at the lighter again cut through the rain, and the smell of tobacco filled the room.

'I know I promised,' he said, 'but I can't go outside. And I really need a smoke.'

Mum's voice came back at him. 'Can you at least do it in another room?'

Freya heard his footsteps, and then the door closing behind him.

The rain intensified. Mixing into the sickly odours of the house were more familiar ones: Mum's incense, her candles, her floral perfume, Dad's tobacco and that smell he had that Freya couldn't describe but it was his alone and it reminded her of an animal that did not belong in a confined space.

The house was a drum being beaten by rain. The whole world

outside was sinking. For a while she let herself imagine that she was alone, and drifted in and out of sleep until Dad returned and lay down on the mattress beside Mum. Only a single candle burned on the table.

'I want water,' Mum said.

'Well, you've got that,' Dad answered. 'Plenty of it.'

'I meant hot water. Tomorrow, I want a shower. I hope there's going to be hot water.'

'I'll make it happen.'

Then Freya couldn't hear anything but the wind and the rain. A picture sprang into her head of Nan, standing by the window earlier that day, arms by her sides, not waving, not smiling, as they'd pulled away and started driving. It had been a hot, still afternoon, no hint of a storm. She thought about the school she had left, and her friends, and whether anyone there would ever know where she had gone, or why.

A few hours, between all of that—and this.

Sometime after midnight the rain and the wind stopped. The room filled with the sound and smell of the ocean, both amplified somehow, as if it were about to pour through the windows, full of storm debris—ground-up shells, rotting wood, seaweed, the husks of marine animals, endless other fragments suspended in the salt water, all of it caught in the roar of the waves. But by then there was no one awake to hear.

2

One bird was calling to another. Bright morning sun lay on her face. An object crashed to the floor in the other room, and Dad's curse carried through the wall. She had been sleeping on her hand, and it ached. Freya rolled onto her back and massaged the tingling skin. Light was streaming in through the doorway from the kitchen. Mum was washing dishes, humming a tune. From a distance, the second bird answered the first—a sonorous, reverberant cry that made her think of lonely streets and empty suburbs. Two weeks now of hearing that sound, always in the morning, always at this hour. She took a deep breath, and the house, its presence, its smell, filled her.

They had spent the first few days down in the basement, shovelling piles of rotting newspaper and rodent shit and rusty nails and all sorts of barely recognisable rubbish into thick plastic bags. Though they'd scrubbed the concrete floor, dousing it in disinfectant and liquid sugar soap, the odour seemed to have soaked into everything—the wallpaper, the brick, the exposed wood. She could still taste it in the air, laced with cleaning agent: the sickness and the cure inseparable.

Dad began moving around again in the living room. He was ripping up the fire-damaged floorboards—she could hear the splintering crack of wood being wrenched free. The new floorboards sat already in a pile in the hallway. Soon there'd be two rooms on the lower floor to sleep in, and sometime after that— she didn't know how long—their bedrooms would be ready.

But for now it was the last day of January, and the first day of school. She stared at the paint curling in flakes off the ceiling and let the thought consume her. They'd gone there a few days ago, to enrol her. Afterwards, as they'd driven away, her and Daniel in the back of Dad's steaming-hot car, tools sliding across the metal bay behind them, the windows wound down, Mum had turned and said, 'Doesn't it look good?'

Freya glanced back at the old brick buildings and empty sports fields behind a long line of brooding Moreton Bay figs. Sure, she'd answered. It looked great. She would have said anything to make Mum stop trying to win her over. It was bad enough that she had to go there, let alone that she had to be grateful for it.

She rolled off the mattress and rose to her feet, then went to the narrow window and leaned forward, her forehead almost touching the cracked glass pane. The sky was clear. The breeze that trickled in through the crack in the glass smelled good. Heat was already rippling across the rooftops of nearby houses. The bird closest to the house called out again. God, it was loud. After a pause, the one in the distance answered. Maybe they weren't calling to one another. Maybe they were calling to the same silent listener. Or maybe in all of that sound there was just a simple message to the other: hey you, buster—stay away.

~

Daniel was sitting at the small table in the kitchen, legs swinging back and forth. He glanced up from his comic book, open at the first page. His face was blank for a moment, then he smiled.

'Have you made it to the end yet?' Freya asked.

'I don't want to read the end,' he said. 'Only the beginning.'

Mum turned from the sink. 'Finally, you're up. You'd better get ready for school. Don't want to be late on your first day, do you?'

'I could live with that.'

Something passed across Mum's face. 'I'll make you some eggs.'

'I'm going to have a shower.'

Freya pulled a towel from the coat rack in the corner. The stairs to the next floor creaked under her feet. The grout between the bathroom tiles was the colour of rust. The showerhead leaned from a corroding pipe over a bathtub chipped and rusting at the edges and around the drain hole. Leaking droplets spattered against the enamel. Freya let her clothes fall to the tiles. She stepped into the bath.

The pipe gave a shudder when she turned on the water. A groan came from deep within the house, followed by a hard knocking sound that faded as she turned the tap further. She stepped back and adjusted the heat.

The ceiling was pregnant with moisture, swollen into warped undulations peppered with mould. With both hands, she touched her hipbones, the curve of her belly, the beginning of her ribs, as if they belonged to someone else. Her feet were long and uneven, just a little, but once she'd noticed, she couldn't stop thinking of it—they were like Dad's feet. And she didn't have any breasts. Nothing. Or almost. And she was fourteen. No girl would have less than her, not in year 9.

When she stepped out of the shower, she wiped away the fog on the mirror and looked at her face again. She grimaced, then bared her teeth more fiercely at her own reflection: you, buster, stay away.

~

Two glistening, perfectly poached eggs were waiting, arranged on two pieces of brown bread, the butter soaked away around them, yolks like cloud-filtered suns, with the steam rising from them in coils.

'—must have been in the living room,' Dad was saying.

'How can you tell?' Mum asked.

'Food,' Dad said. 'An apple core. He must have thrown it down through the hole in the floor. Like he couldn't even make it to a bin. After all the cleaning we've been doing down there, he thinks we need to do a bit more. Seriously.'

'It was an accident,' Daniel said.

'So it was you. Then why didn't you go down to get it?'

Daniel didn't answer. Freya knew why. He was scared of going down there, but he wouldn't admit that in front of Dad.

The phone began ringing.

'Daniel,' Mum said, 'why do you do these things? You know you weren't even meant to be in the living room yet. It's not safe until the floor's fixed up. Look at me.'

Her brother stared back at Mum over his comic. Mum was beautiful, usually—everyone said that—but today she looked tired and drawn, her pale skin blotchy, circles under her eyes, which were a little red, like she hadn't slept, like she didn't know where she was.

'Say you're sorry, Daniel.'

Her brother said he was sorry.

'Say you won't do it again.'

He said he wouldn't do it again.

The phone was still ringing. Dad walked into the hallway to answer it. Freya caught Daniel's eye and winked. His face didn't change. He went back to reading.

'The uniform looks nice, Freya,' Mum said.

'It's ugly,' she said. 'I don't like blue.'

'Blue looks good on you.'

Freya made a face. 'Not this blue. Not with white. I look like a sailor.'

'I like my uniform,' Daniel said solemnly.

'That's good, darling,' Mum said, smiling, but then she turned back to Freya. 'The blouse fits you okay?'

Freya cut her egg with her knife. The sickly yellow insides spilled out and spread across the white plate. 'I guess.'

'Well, do that button up. I can see your bra.'

Mum stood in front of her and waited. Freya did the button up.

The phone clattered back into its cradle. 'No one there,' Dad called.

Mum was standing behind her now, her firm fingers against Freya's scalp, tugging at the hair hard enough to make her wince.

'Such a waste. There are so many knots—do you actually brush it? As in move your brush through your hair?'

'Of course I do.'

'Looks like you just wave your brush in the air and hope for the best,' Mum said. 'It's not a magic wand, you know. If you're going to keep your hair long—'

'You know what you need to do?' Dad said from the doorway. 'Relax while you've got the chance. She'll worry about how she looks soon enough.'

'It's not her I'm worried about. What'll people think of us?' Mum returned to the sink. She stood there with one hand against it and kept looking at Freya sitting at the kitchen table like there was no one else there. Dad went back out to the living room and started working again. Freya shoved half an egg into her mouth, forced the lump down with a gulp of milk, then burped.

Mum was still watching her. 'Oh, for God's sake, Freya, on top of everything else, do you have to eat like that too?'

'Yes, Mother,' Freya said, imitating Mum's tone, meeting her eyes. 'I do. Thanks for asking.'

Mum's mouth sank at the corners. Her chin became, briefly, completely ugly. 'Don't call me Mother. It makes me sound old.'

'Well, aren't you?'

'You'll be this old one day. And I'm only thirty-four.'

'I didn't mean that.'

'What then?'

'Forget it.'

A piece of wood crashed to the floor in the hallway behind them.

'You're impossible sometimes.' Mum turned to the sink and began washing up with a kind of furious motion, clattering each dish into the rack as she finished with it.

Dad walked into the kitchen again and swept his large arms around Mum's waist from behind. 'That makes her pretty much like you, doesn't it?' He kissed her neck. Mum stayed there, hands unmoving in the water, as if she were playing dead. He pulled her in closer, peered out through the window above the sink.

'Look,' he said.

'What?'

'Not a cloud in sight. First time in a week. Ever seen anything so pretty?'

'You shouldn't use words like that,' Mum said.

'Like what?'

'Pretty. They never sound right coming from you.'

He kissed her neck again, held her more tightly. 'I can't help it. Not around you.'

'Oh, stop it.' But she finally relaxed into the embrace.

Dad looked back at Freya sitting there at the table. 'It does look good, sweetheart, the uniform. But not too good. You don't want it to look too good. Not with all those boys around.'

He grinned. It made him look much younger, more like a boy himself. He had a straight, broad nose and a wide mouth with the ever-present shadow of stubble etched darker at the corners, his big clean teeth made brighter by his olive skin. There was a spark in his eyes when he was being charming—especially bright when he knew you didn't want to be charmed. Before she could stop herself, she smiled back.

~

The sun sat a good distance over the sky and the street radiated warmth. It was going to be a hot day. She'd be riding to school on a bike. It was a second-hand one that Dad had picked up cheap from the paper in Sydney and restored with her in mind, back when she'd thought they'd never see him again, when Mum had refused to say his name. A classic, Dad had called it when he'd given it to her.

There wasn't a speck of rust anywhere, and he'd given it a new coat of paint. It had a thick, nicely curved frame, a white wire basket at the front, a back-pedal brake, no gears. She unbuttoned the top button of her blouse, threw her bag in the basket and set off. The chain creaked in protest as she pushed the pedals. She rode along the main street, shopfronts to the left, the railway line blocking off the harbour to her right, the corrugated aluminium flank of a Sydney train gathering pace as it pulled out of the city. The cars overtaking her came close enough to touch, the air full of their exhaust. It mingled with the briny odour of the nearby harbour, and, as she passed it, wafts of baking bread from the Vietnamese bakery. A car slowed alongside her and a flat, reddened, boyish face leaned out.

'Show us your tits!'

The boy drew back inside the window. A burst of laughter came from deeper in the car before it accelerated and swerved around the corner. She kept pedalling and stared straight ahead.

~

Near where she sat with a group of girls for recess, under the shade thrown by huge Moreton Bay figs that lined the quadrangle, the boys put on their displays. They wore their collars up and their shirts untucked, shoved each other to punctuate sentences, tossed fuck and shit and cunt into laughing exchanges. When they weren't playing handball, they sat mainly on the tables, feet on the seats, facing outwards, so they could perve on the girls, and keep an eye out for the teacher on duty.

The girls sat at their own tables, facing one another over neat assortments of food that they picked at.

'So where in Sydney are you from?' one asked.

Freya told them. Someone asked her why they'd come to Newcastle, and she felt herself tense up.

'Because of Dad's work,' she said.

'What does he do?'

'He was a foreman. I don't even know what that is.'

'Was?' one of the girls said. 'He dead then or something?'

'Ally,' another girl exclaimed. 'Don't be so rude.'

Ally's reactions seemed slightly delayed, like she put a lot of thought into arranging them. She pouted. 'What's wrong with asking that?'

'What if her dad really is dead?'

'I wish,' Freya said quickly.

They all laughed, and half of them said they thought the same thing about their dads, but they didn't really mean it, she could tell. The conversation trailed off.

In that quiet, Freya thought of Nan, and the last time she'd seen her. In the kitchen, back in Sydney, Mum and Dad had been waiting outside at the car and it had been just her and Nan standing there. Nan had to look up at Freya when they stood close. She'd gripped Freya's arm tightly—as if one of them at least needed to be supported—and given her the book about Greek mythology.

'My phone number is inside,' Nan had said. 'On a piece of paper. Don't lose it, don't tell your mother, and definitely don't tell your father.'

Freya hadn't known what to say. A blush had risen into her when she'd stepped out to the car, but no one had noticed. She wasn't sure if it was bad luck to have that phone number, hidden from Mum, and especially from Dad, if it was like inviting something to happen. But the book was there, in her suitcase, under a pile of clothes, waiting.

'So where do you live now?' one of the girls asked.

'Newcastle East,' she told them.

'Heaps of druggies there.'

'And a brothel.'

'Don't walk around there without your shoes. You'll step on a syringe and get AIDS.'

Freya took an orange out of her bag and started peeling it. She didn't tell them that she was sleeping on a foam mattress in a dingy living room because most of the house was a ruin. The day after they'd moved in, Dad had taken her up to the top floor of the house, to see what would be her room at some unimaginable point in the future. The staircase led up from the second floor landing into a kind of attic. It had large windows looking out over the street to the harbour beyond, and a small one overlooking the courtyard out the back. The underside of the tile roof was exposed, the two sides pitched together high over the middle of the room and then swooping low.

'It's a gable roof,' Dad had told her. 'You'll have to watch your head when you get out of bed, but you get used to it. Before you move in, I'll put up insulation and plasterboard, and I'll paint it, so it'll be a nice, clean finish.'

They'd gone to the window together. 'Look at that,' he said. 'How lucky are you? You can see everything from up here.' Newcastle East, he told her, was the heart of the city, where everything happened. It was an exposed heart, laid out on a long, thin triangle of land jutting out into the sea. The southern side was all beach and cliff, and the other—he pointed out the window, swept his hand in an arc—was the harbour. Past the harbour was Stockton, and further up the coast, way out in the distance, lay the wreck of the *Sygna*. He talked about how the bulk carrier had run aground on its maiden voyage in a huge storm fifteen years earlier and had been left there to fall apart ever since. Dad had been happy, animated, boyishly excited, full of hope, like he always was at the beginning of things.

Shouting erupted nearby. A boy was swearing, a meat pie slathered with tomato sauce and gravy dripping down his shirt. He jumped over a sprawled chair and grabbed another boy in a headlock. The two of them wrestled each other to the ground. The first boy began punching the other in the head. The other boy was throwing punches too, but his fists weren't hitting anything. His shirt was halfway up his back. Dust kicked up as they scuffled. People came running from every direction, making a circle. A roar of noise lifted from the crowd, jeering and shouting, and chanting *fight*, *fight*, *fight*, and then a teacher barged his way through, and the boys were pulled apart and led away.

Freya finished peeling the orange. She broke it open with her thumbs and put a segment in her mouth. It tasted bitter, and she tossed it in the bin with the peel. A wind picked up through the nearby trees. The air was so warm and dry it made her throat itch. Brown leaves spiralled down and scraped and swirled across the asphalt, propelled by sudden mad gusts that disappeared as quickly as they came. The girls were talking again, and she threw in a smile sometimes or a nod, to show that she was listening. She didn't always get the timing right. The bell rang out for the end of lunch. No one showed any sign they'd heard.

Out in the middle of the quadrangle, in the bright sunlight, some older boys were arguing over a game of handball in raw voices, whether a ball had been in or out. One boy pushed another in the chest. Out, he was saying. Someone raised another jeer, but there was no energy in it—no expectation that it would lead anywhere. The game started again. It was only then that she recognised the second boy, his flat, red face, as he smacked the ball away with his hand. Show us your tits. When he looked her way, his eyes slid over her in one motion.

~

Wheeling her bike out of the school alongside Ally, she could hear raucous shouting at her back—*You stupid fucking fag!*—maybe the beginnings of a fight, no, just more play, followed by laughter that seemed to change direction like a lunging flock of birds. *Sweetheart, you can ride me instead.* She kept walking. It might not even have been directed at her. Every step she took felt jerky, as if she were in a spotlight, as if she weren't quite in control of her limbs. Boys were hurtling past on bikes, spraying gravel in the air, weaving between the cars that passed the school gates.

'See you tomorrow then, hey?' Ally said.

They had ended up together, after lunch, in a double period of maths. If anything was going to bring two people together, it was that sort of pain.

'See you,' she said.

A couple of other boys walked past throwing a football between them, making it whistle through the air. It rushed by close behind her, but she didn't turn. She didn't get on her bike until the school was well behind her, until there was no one anywhere that might be watching, and then she rode alone through leafy side streets across the inner city towards home.

~

Dad pulled up in his station wagon just as she approached the house. He got out, slid a cigarette into his mouth, and leaned back against the car. He was wearing a blue T-shirt that clung tight around his biceps, the material dark with sweat under his arms and on his back. The angle of the afternoon sun had thrown the footpath where he stood into shadow.

'How was school?' he asked.

'Fine,' she said.

Dad nodded, the cigarette dangling from his lips. 'That's probably the most you can expect from it, trust me.' He had a way of staring ahead, glancing at her side-on when they spoke, as if he didn't want to admit that he was having a conversation. 'Bike working all right?'

'Yeah.' She began pushing it to the front door.

'Freya.'

The muscles in his shoulders shifted. He studied her. His dense, dark eyebrows made his eyes look like copper or gold at the right time of day.

'You good?'

She knew what he was asking, how he was trying to reach not just into the day that had passed, but into everything. He didn't want to know—he wanted to be reassured, to feel right about the things he'd done.

'I'm good.'

Something relaxed in him, and he took the bike from her, gripping it with both hands, then walked up the steps and lifted it into the house. She came in and stood alongside him. He smelled of body odour and smoke.

'Thanks,' she said.

Dad nodded. 'I remember when I got my first bike. A second-hand job too. I might have been seven. Had to climb on a wall to get on, and getting off was a bit tricky, but the second I got on there, I didn't really care about anything. Something about the wind hitting my face and being able to go anywhere I wanted. I could picture you riding to school—that's why I did it up. I knew I'd get a chance to give it to you. It's a good feeling, isn't it, riding a bike? Beats walking or catching the bus.'

'Yeah,' she answered.

He glanced at her. 'Let me know if it needs anything. Anything at all.'

'Okay.'

'Go on then,' he said. 'Your mother'll kill me if she catches me smoking inside.'

Freya wheeled the bike down the hall to the kitchen and then out the back door into the narrow courtyard. She leaned it against the wall, between the outside toilet and the gate, and chained it to an exposed water pipe. Whenever she sat out there over the next months, she'd glance at it and watch the unused tyres sag into flatness, the ivy claim the frame, the rust creep out from the cracks and functional angles and spread across every bare metal surface. They didn't speak of it again, not her, not Dad. It would stay there until long after they were gone.

3

And then February was halfway through, and they'd been in the house for a month, and the heat grew heavier, and settled deeper, and they were in the part of summer where it didn't seem possible that it would ever end. The four of them were sitting around the dining table, eating steak and salad. It wasn't long after six. The front door was open, and the falling sun sent a blaze of light along the hall.

Dad had replaced the floorboards in the living room, and he and Mum slept in there now, while Freya and Daniel still slept in the dining room, on either side of the table. The colour television had been moved to the living room, but they had a small black and white one in the dining room, sitting on a milk crate in the corner. It was on as they ate, and showed a grainy image of a column of tanks crossing a bridge. The Russians were leaving Afghanistan, or they'd already left.

'I reckon it's because of Rambo,' Dad said.

'Really?' Daniel said.

Mum shook her head. 'Your father's joking. He does that sometimes.'

'I don't know.' Dad caught Freya's eye and winked. 'I think he must have knocked off half the Russian army in that last movie.'

'I hate Rambo,' Freya said.

Dad made a face. 'What's wrong? Don't you like big muscles?'

'He doesn't even open his mouth when he speaks,' she said. 'I hate idiots.'

Dad pretended to look sad. 'So does your mother.'

'Can I watch it?' Daniel said.

'Can you?' Dad laughed. 'You wouldn't make it through the first five minutes.'

'They wanted to see me,' Mum said, 'when I came to pick Daniel up.'

Dad kept eating. 'What's he done now?'

'He hasn't done anything. They say he's musical. He's got perfect pitch.'

Dad ran a hand across his stubbled chin. 'At least he's got perfect something.'

Mum's mouth pressed inwards in an impatient way. 'They want him to join the school band. Do you think we could manage that?'

'How much is that going to cost?'

'Nothing.'

Dad picked up his knife and fork, cut a piece of meat and looked at her as he chewed. 'So it's free—that's what you're saying?'

'We only have to pay for the lessons. Ten dollars for half an hour.'

'Not free then. Lessons for what exactly?'

'The clarinet.'

'Do you really think now's a good time to be doing that?'

'Doing what?'

'Paying for things we don't need.'

A small sigh escaped Mum's lips. 'We're building a life here, aren't we?'

'What good will playing an instrument do him when he leaves school?'

Mum gave a quick, slight shake of her head. 'We don't know what he'll need or what he'll want to do when he leaves school. He's not even in high school yet. All we can do is our best, right now, don't you think?'

They looked at Daniel, who kept eating without lifting his eyes, as if he were sitting alone at the dining table.

'Forget it,' Mum said at last. 'It doesn't matter.'

'No,' Dad said, 'if that's what you want. If you want him to play an instrument, he can play an instrument.' He levelled his fork at Daniel and spoke softly, a faint smile still on his face, his words slow and precise. 'But you'd better look after it. Don't make me regret it.'

Daniel nodded.

'What do you say?' Dad asked him.

'Thank you,' Daniel said.

They kept eating.

~

After dinner, they went to the beach. It was startling in the open air after the dim, dirty confines of the house. The sun, sagging towards the horizon, filtered red by a muddy pall of smog that hung over the distant steelworks, was lost from sight as they turned the corner and began walking along the street that led straight to the sand.

Down by the shore there was hardly any wind. The waves came smooth and clean, barely disturbing the water's surface until they broke. Dad dove in just as a wave lifted towards him.

'Come on,' he shouted as he surfaced, shaking his head.

Freya followed. She always felt free under water, out of sight of anyone. She plunged underneath a wave, let herself lift towards the sky, and burst through the surface near Dad. He floated there, the water up to his tanned neck. His hair was slick and black, and water dripped down the straight, hard line of his nose.

'What?' he said.

'You look so clean,' she answered.

'I clean myself up every now and again,' he said.

'Not that often.'

He laughed.

They turned to face Mum and Daniel, still there on the shore. Mum was sitting on the sand, her hands clasped over her knees, and Daniel was squatting by the water, drawing in the sand with one hand.

'Your mother's a good swimmer,' Dad said. 'Why doesn't she ever come in?'

Freya didn't answer. She dove back under, found the bottom, ran her hands through the fine sand and lifted it in front of her, watching it spill through her fingers and dissipate on the current. She stayed under the water, could hear the intricate sound of small shells scraping against one another, and the soft, gathering rush of the next wave building towards her. The view stretched away from her, its clarity dissolving into gloom, and nothing moved in it, and it was full of a life she couldn't see. When she broke the surface, Dad was on the beach, towelling off, and she was alone in the water, shivering, her feet not quite reaching the sandy bottom beneath her. She swam in.

The air was growing hazy. They walked to the ocean baths at the northern end of the beach, climbed up to the top of the terraced blue wall that ran along one edge of the lap pool and surveyed the rock shelves and the coast on the other side. The sleek fins of dolphins carved up and down through inky waves. On the other side of the rock shelf a stretch of sand made a tapering arc towards a saltbush-covered headland at the mouth of the harbour—Nobbys Beach and Nobbys Head, Dad said. Nobbys Head was flat on top where a white lighthouse caught the luminous end of the daylight. A breakwall emerged from the base of the headland and cut across the sea—Freya wasn't sure for how long, maybe half a kilometre—its darkening line broken by lifts of white sea spray. A single red light blinked on and off just at the dim point where the breakwall vanished into the ocean.

'What's that light?' Mum asked.

'A warning,' Dad said, holding her hand. 'For the ships. As they're coming in. So they know where they're going and don't run into trouble.' He gave her a sidelong glance. 'A bit like you and me.'

'Which one of us is the light?'

'I reckon it depends,' Dad said, letting go of her hand, turning back the way they'd come.

The lights were coming on all along the concrete esplanade that overlooked the main beach. There was still a lone lap-swimmer traversing the baths behind them—Freya could hear the metronome slap of hands against the water. Between the rocks and the ocean, some children were splashing around in a wide, shallow circular pool. It was full of murky water at one end and sand at the other.

'There used to be a map in there,' Dad said.

Freya followed his glance, but she couldn't see anything. 'Where?'

'See how it's oval, the pool? That's because there used to be a map of the world in there, back in the fifties, made out of slabs of raised concrete. Someone was telling me about it at work. It was for kids. The British Empire was red. The rest was green, I think. They made it so that the water would come in with the tide half a metre deep. You could swim in the water and jump up onto the continents.'

'What's the British Empire?' Daniel asked.

Dad stared off into the distance. 'It's long gone now.'

'Where's it gone?' Freya asked.

'The British Empire?'

She shook her head. 'The map. I can't see it.'

'The sand and the water,' Dad answered as they stepped back onto the beach. 'Those two can destroy anything. It's because they never let up. With every big sea, the place used to fill with sand. The concrete kept needing to be repaired. It was too hard to keep the whole thing from falling apart, so they demolished it and took the pieces away.'

'What a shame,' Mum said.

'I don't know,' Dad said, staring at it. He looked thoughtful. He was holding her hand again. He winked suddenly at Freya. 'Run up ahead. Be kids or something. Give us a bit of peace.'

'Come on,' she said to Daniel, 'let's put our feet in the waves.'

They ran down the edge of the water. The sand had a pink glow to it now. That'd be gone in a matter of minutes, and the fine blue of the sky would bleed into darkness. But for now, clouds, luminous white, edged in brilliant amber, moved around their feet in the film of water left by each wave, as if they were walking on a pristine mirror.

Daniel picked up a piece of driftwood and carved a wavering line into the wet sand. 'Freya,' he said. 'Do you ever think about Pop?'

'What? I guess so.'

Daniel had stopped moving, and stood there with the stick in one hand. 'Do you think he's looking after us, like Nan always says?'

'Do you even remember him?'

Daniel nodded.

'I thought you'd be too young. You were only four when he died.'

'I'm not too young,' he said at once. 'I can remember everything.'

'What colour was his watch then?'

Daniel's face tightened. 'I'm not telling.'

She laughed. 'Because you don't know.'

His voice turned thick. 'I just don't want to tell you.'

He turned from her and—in a gesture that was both violent and helpless—flung the stick as far as he could across the water. It did not go far. To tease him, she could have told him then that he threw like a girl. Dad would have said it. With the next wave the stick came floating back towards them.

'It's silver,' she said. 'The watch. Nan's keeping it. For you, she told me. For when you grow up. You're the only boy in the family, you know.'

His face relaxed. 'Will we see her again?'

'Nan? Of course.'

How long had it been since they'd seen Nan? A month. She thought again of the book Nan had given her, sitting there in her suitcase. Freya turned a slow circle, took in the floodlit beach, the ocean baths to one side, and to the other, on a bluff, the hospital where Mum worked. Past the bluff, cast into darkness, was another, smaller beach they called South Newcastle, and beyond that more rock shelves and jagged boulders under high, sheer cliffs. Further off, she could just make out the nearly black outcrop of another headland, the endless march of the land away from her, disappearing into the evening.

'Are they fighting?' Daniel asked.

She turned back to him. 'Who?'

'Nan and Mum. I heard Mum say she hated Nan.'

'Mum says stuff like that sometimes. She doesn't mean it. You should hear some of the stuff she says to me.'

'Like what?'

'Like nothing.' She paused, studied his face. 'Of course Pop's looking after us. We need someone up there, right?'

'Does Dad have a dad too? Or a mum?'

'No. His mum died when he was little.'

'What about his dad?'

'A lot later.'

What was it like for Dad, to not have a mother anymore, or a father—anyone really, outside of them? She'd never ask him something like that.

Mum and Dad had kept walking along the beach. They were up ahead, standing facing each other, arms hooked around each other's waists. They looked like they'd just kissed. Dad lifted Mum suddenly, easily in his arms. Mum laughed and shrieked as he walked into the water up to his ankles. He made a show of staggering, but he was never, ever going to fall.

~

It was completely dark by the time they got home, the open sky an echo in her thoughts, the laughter and the lightness left behind at the beach, and no breeze in the house, though the windows were open. The place still looked and smelled like a ruin, and it was worst when you first came in.

They had an old chocolate-coloured couch in the living room now, a red shawl thrown over the backrest to hide a stain, and matching armchairs they'd bought from the Salvation Army. Mum and Dad sat together on the couch, Mum with her feet in his lap. They were watching a movie called *Vertigo*. The music set Freya on edge, but nothing really seemed to be happening, or at least nothing that made sense, just a man watching a woman, going where she went, but never so she noticed he was there, more like he was a shadow, waiting for something—what?

Daniel went upstairs and had a shower. Freya retreated to the dining room and sat cross-legged on her mattress while she waited for her turn. Ahead of her lay school, and then the rest of the week, and the week after.

In the other room, Mum said something and Dad laughed. They had fallen back into their rhythm, together again. They were her parents, and this—this was the new world. She was not sure yet whether it would settle into something more solid or fall apart again, but it was somehow better not being sure. At least that way she was ready for anything.

4

In the narrow lane behind the house, a dog was barking. Maryanne had heard it a few times in the last week. It sounded trapped, furious at the world, helpless. Its voice seemed to tear with the strain of the barking, but it wouldn't stop. She took a breath, let it go. The kids were at school, Roy at work—it was just her, getting ready for her shift, listening to the dog that was going mad.

She closed the kitchen windows, checked that the back door was locked, and went out into the hallway, with its dirty floorboards and dusty wallpaper. The place hadn't grown on her yet. These were the quiet sorts of moments where she didn't even have to pretend.

The look on her daughter's face when she'd walked in on that first day had nearly broken her heart, because she'd known that look. She'd been feeling it too. So she'd begun talking in the usual way, trying to convince them both that it was better than it appeared, not that either of them had bought it. But what could you do? You made the most of it—that's what. It was theirs now. And maybe—in all its abandoned desolation—it suited them.

She did like the hospital where she worked. There was something gorgeous about the way it sprawled there across the bluff by the sea, and rose over the park as you walked towards it, especially at night, when the salt air made the evening lights hazy, and the noise of the waves and wind in the background was like the hum of life. There was a feeling too with the people who worked there, an easy camaraderie she'd never really encountered back in Sydney. Something about being on the coast, maybe, with the open windows and the sunlight and the fresh air and the sounds of the lifeguards on the beach drawling their instructions at anonymous swimmers.

But the house, oh, the house. This ruin that they'd staked their lives on. The worst house on the best street you could afford—that was the mantra, right? And you pushed yourself, you suffered for it. If they made the most of it, they would come out ahead, sell it with enough left over from paying off the loan to really make a start on something else. That was the secret to getting ahead. But God, the work it would take! Why did it always feel like she was on some treadmill? Why was she always trying to make the most of things? Not just this house, but everything? She had so little to show for the last ten years.

She pulled her watch from the front pocket of her uniform. Time to go, more or less. Really, she didn't have to go straight away, but she wanted to. She wanted more than anything to get out of the house.

The phone began ringing. She dropped her bag where she

stood in the hallway and listened. Her mother didn't have her number. It couldn't be her. Did she *want* it to be her, though? The dog was still barking, muted now by the closed window but no less grating, and the phone kept ringing. Something was building inside her.

She shook herself, took several steps, and picked up the receiver. 'Hello?'

Roy's voice came at her through a faint static hiss. 'Expecting someone else?'

'I wasn't expecting anyone, to be honest.'

'Shouldn't you be at work?'

'I'm going now. Did you call to check on me?'

He laughed softly. 'Do I have to?'

'Only if you want to. I've left dinner in a pan in the fridge. Just heat it up.'

He was silent a moment. 'I just wanted to say I love you.'

'I love you too.'

'Are you sorry yet?'

'No, Roy. Of course not. Why would I be sorry?'

'You hesitated.'

'I didn't.'

'I was joking. Don't be so sensitive.'

'I'm not sorry.'

'You don't even know what I'm talking about.'

'I do know,' she said. 'The house. Everything. This leap into the dark.'

'A leap into the dark? Is that how you see it?'

'Don't you?'

'I'm never the one that doubts our relationship. I'll wait up for you tonight.'

Before she could say anything else, he'd hung up. He liked

that, to get in the last word, to leave her off balance. She placed the phone back in the cradle. No. Sorry was not a word she would use. Not again.

As soon as she stepped outside, as the door closed behind her with a resolute snick of the lock, she remembered her bag, sitting in the hallway where she'd dropped it. She cursed and reached into the pocket of her uniform, but realised as she grasped at nothing where her keys were. In the bag, of course.

She slumped with her forehead against the door. Being locked out wasn't a big deal—it wasn't—but whatever had been gathering inside her climbed up through her lungs. She was crying, she suddenly realised, big, convulsive sobs. She wasn't sure what she was crying about, and she didn't care who saw her.

'Hey,' a voice said beside her.

She turned. The next-door neighbour was there, standing at his front door. Of course it had to be the next-door neighbour.

'Are you okay?' he said.

He had very light eyebrows. His cheeks were slightly pockmarked. There was something papery about his skin, like it would tear easily.

'I just—' She wiped her face quickly with the backs of her fingers. 'It's nothing. I just locked myself out of the house. I don't even like this house.' She laughed in spite of herself. 'I don't know why I told you that.'

He stepped closer, looked from her to the door. 'Can I help?'

He was maybe in his late forties. Tall but not broad, stooped slightly. A long-sleeved shirt rolled up to the elbows, sandals, his hair thinning, the face overall a little ruddy—a drinker—and lots of lines around his eyes, as if he was used to smiling a lot, not that it meant anything at all. Plenty of arseholes were used to smiling all the time.

Maryanne shrugged. 'Look, it doesn't matter. It's only my bag in there.'

'But you want your bag,' he said wryly. 'I can tell. Why don't we look around the back, see if you've left any windows open? That's what I always do.'

It meant going around the block to the lane that ran behind the terraces. He was already in motion, and she had to catch up. She found herself taking two steps for every one of his as they walked together around the back. She felt embarrassed, vulnerable, her face still flushed from crying. She wished she had her sunglasses, but they too were in her bag, and as they reached the gate, she shielded her eyes with one hand.

'God, it's bright out here.'

The man laughed. 'I know. Daylight. You don't realise when you're stuck in these gloomy old terraces. I'm Richard, by the way.'

He held out his hand and she took it. It was large but surprisingly soft and smooth, and slightly damp.

'Maryanne.'

'Like in that song by Leonard Cohen,' he said.

Maryanne smiled politely. She hooked her hand inside the gate and unlatched it. She didn't close the gate but rested it, fully open, against the bike that Freya had locked to the water pipe. The bike was a nuisance just there, but there really wasn't anywhere else for it to go.

'There,' Richard pointed. 'It looks like you've left the door to the balcony open. I can get up that way and let you in.'

'I don't want you to break your neck,' she said. 'I'll just call my husband.'

Richard shook his head. 'You're going to work. You don't want to be waiting around.'

Maryanne hesitated.

'It's all right,' he said. 'I've had to climb onto my own balcony plenty of times.'

Before she could say another word, he hoisted himself up onto the brick wall that separated his courtyard from hers, made his way to the small balcony—it was easy to reach from the top of the wall, she realised—and hauled one leg and then the other over the railing.

'Don't worry,' he said, looking down at her with a grin. 'I'll just let you in the back door and be out of your hair.'

He disappeared inside the house.

A minute later, he emerged from the back door into the courtyard. 'There you are.'

'Thank you.' She stepped into the kitchen, glanced at him over her shoulder. 'I'll just get my bag.'

When she returned, he was still there. She pulled her cigarettes from her bag, put one in her mouth and offered him one, which he took. She lit both. He had a manner of leaning forward, a shape to his mouth when he exhaled the smoke, that made her think maybe he was gay. She thought of Roy and hoped so.

'So,' he said, releasing a plume of smoke from the corner of his mouth. 'What brings you to this charming part of the world?'

'I need a reason to come here?'

He showed his yellow, slightly crooked teeth. 'Everyone needs a reason to come to Newcastle. I'm not saying it's not worth it.'

'You know,' she said, 'I have no idea.' She let herself smile. 'Love, I guess.'

He looked at her a moment longer than he needed to. 'Well,' he said, 'it's an easy place to get used to. I'm sure you'll enjoy it. And the sea, right there—what's not to love?'

'I guess so.'

'If you need anything,' he said, 'let me know. These walls are thick, but I'm only a door knock away.'

'I'll remember that,' she said.

And then he was gone. She left by the back alley this time, past the dog, which started up again at the sound of her footsteps, but she did not slow down, and the wind straight off the ocean, coming at her between and over the houses and apartment blocks, buried the world behind her.

~

Work passed quickly. One minute she glanced out the window and it was daylight; the next it had been dark for hours, and the moon was big and yellow, looking as exhausted as she was as it slouched over the water near the ocean baths. Then her shift was over, and it was time to leave.

Roy was watching television when she got home, his large feet slung out before him on a coffee table that he'd made himself.

'How was your day?' he said.

She thought of Richard, and was about to say that she'd locked herself out, and that he'd broken into the house for her, and how easy it was to get onto that balcony at the back, but it sounded too strange once she'd started arranging the words in her head. She opened her mouth and closed it. Roy was watching her curiously.

'The usual,' she said. 'What's on?'

'Just the late news. You know that Salman Rushdie bloke?'

She stared at him blankly.

'You know,' he said, 'that writer. He wrote a book and now the Arabs want to kill him. The Ayatollah's offering three million bucks to anyone that'll do it. God, I'd do it at that price. You reckon I could pull that off? It might be less work than all this.'

'If you put your mind to it. How long have the children been asleep?'

He looked at his watch. 'Daniel for ages. Freya, an hour maybe.'

'It'll be good when they have their rooms.'

'I'm working on it as fast as I can.'

She smiled at him. 'I know. How was your day?'

'Long.'

'Me too,' she said. 'I got a padlock for the back gate.' She put a key for him on the coffee table.

He picked it up, chuckled softly. 'Worried Freya's going to make a run for it with some boy in the middle of the night?'

She shook her head. 'It's other people I'm thinking about. I don't like the thought of them just being able to walk into the courtyard off that dirty alley. They should at least have to go to the trouble of climbing over the wall.'

He was stretched on the couch. The singlet he wore lifted at the front to reveal his belly—hairy, softer and fuller than it had once been. Just a bit of grey in the dark hair on his chest. But his legs were muscular, his calves knotted and thick, and there was still a feel to him as if he might burst into energetic motion at any moment, the king lion under his tree. He slapped the couch with one hand.

'Come here,' he said.

She approached him, stood before him.

He pulled her down next to him by one wrist. 'Did you save any lives today?'

'A few,' she said.

'Of course you did.' He unbuttoned the top of her shirt, pushed one warm, rough hand in between her bra and her breast. His other hand brushed the inside of her thigh. 'Speaking of which…'

'I don't know if I can relax,' she said. 'Especially with the kids just in the other room. I need to get in the mood, maybe have a shower.'

'You'll relax just fine,' he answered, already on his feet, lifting her up, carrying her to the mattress. 'You'll get in the mood.'

5

On the last Wednesday afternoon of summer, Freya found herself in a press of others, spilling out of a school bus at the ocean baths. They were there to practise for their Bronze Medallion. It was sunny, but there was a cool wind up, and it stripped the warmth right out of her bare arms and legs when she left the change room. A few men in speedos lounged on the stone steps built into the wall by the lap pool, out of the wind, parading the sag and bulge of their old, hairy, gleaming bodies.

In the other direction some surfers were walking with their surfboards along the walkway between the baths and the kids' pool. A few of them let off piercing whistles at the girls and one thrust his hips and jeered when a teacher walked towards them. The teacher turned back and shook his head. The surfers began hopping one by one from the rock shelf. They dropped from sight, then appeared out past the rocks, paddling on the swell as it ripped and tilted towards the shore. The last surfer lingered on the rocks, his body straight as he stared back across the baths, and Freya had the sensation that he was looking directly at her, before he too jumped in, vanishing from sight.

'Come on, boys and girls—it's healthy, the salt,' Mrs Lanigan was shouting as she paced back and forth between them. 'Just get wet. Do you the world of good.'

Turning to the choppy water of the pool in front of her, Freya couldn't make out the bottom. A wiry, tattooed man with no hair and half his teeth missing squatted by the dark water and cleared out his nostrils, one after the other. He shook his fingers before dipping them in the pool, muttering all the while, as if he were the last man in a desolate world.

A whistle screamed behind her, and Freya shuffled forward with the others. She tried not to look at her feet. Mum was the one who had once said, in passing, that they were Dad's feet. That was a year or two ago now, but she thought of it every time she looked down. Dad's feet, the asymmetry of the left and the right, the shambling path they cut.

All the students stood in rows. They had to plunge in and swim across the pool, hit the other side and come back, then do it all again. Seagulls drifted and veered away above them. A plastic bag floated on the water over near the rock shelf. Now Mr Graham blew his whistle. Jump. Wait. Jump.

Boys pushed each other, jostling for position, pulling in stomachs or leaning into themselves, trying to hide what they didn't have, most of them with flat or sunken chests, a few more muscular, and holding themselves like they knew it. She liked the skinny ones better, the ones full of doubt. With each gust of wind, spray leaped in at the edge of the rocks beyond the baths and filled the wind that cut through her swimmers.

'There's a party on Saturday,' Ally said behind her. 'Coming?'

'Where?'

'Sarah's parents are away for the weekend. They always leave her with money for the week. She spends it all on the first night. Everyone's invited. There's going to be heaps of people there.'

'Sure. Sounds good.' Freya made herself give a quick smile.

She pulled her crossed arms in closer against her chest and let her eyes stray to the hospital up on the bluff, its angled structures towering over the beach, level upon level of windows and white balconies gleaming under the sun's glare. Mum was working there right now. Freya didn't know where exactly, just somewhere inside all of that.

Mum had been the first to leave that morning, but she'd sat down on Freya's bed before she'd walked out the door. 'Try to look ahead,' she'd said. 'Don't brood. Just live. There's so much to get excited about. You and I both have to learn that.'

The last girls between her and water had plunged in.

'Go on,' Ally said behind her.

The hairs on her forearms were standing on end. She straightened her hands, leaned forward. The water lapped up against her toes, the concrete slick beneath her feet. The wind threw spray up against her legs. Her swimmers were biting into her bum. She sensed the other kids behind her, heard some boy make a laughing comment that might have been about her, the words slap and arse in there.

She hoped her bum didn't wobble when she hit the water, but it probably would. She was skinny everywhere but somehow still had a bum that could shake when it hit the water. That was probably worse than having feet like Dad's. She imagined the boys behind her looking, waiting to see. She was like a combination of all of Mum and Dad's worst features, the mutant survivor of a nuclear war.

'Go on. Jump in.' Ally made a face and stuck her fingers down her throat. 'Don't make me look at Mr Graham any longer than I have to!'

Mr Graham was standing a few metres to the side, one hand on his hip, the other clutching a whistle, his greasy reddish brown hair fluttering in the wind. Nothing embarrassed or backward about him. His nipples were like sagging erasers at the tips of pencils. Freya could see the press of glistening blue speedos against his crotch, and strange patches of pale skin on his otherwise tanned brown hairy legs. He had heavy eyelashes, like a labrador, not that you'd want to pat him or anything.

In PE he always used girls for demonstrations. He would trace his hand along their legs to adjust their postures and show the proper techniques for sports that none of them cared about. He turned now, fixed her with a vacant stare and blew his whistle again. She dove in, imagined the ripple pass through her, all the boys looking on.

The water smacked her face. The cold shot into her ears, swished across her scalp and radiated into her chest. For a moment she couldn't breathe, could only float in the sensation, her heart racing, then she took control of her limbs. Ribbons of seaweed swayed through a silty landscape on the bottom. An old bandaid floated past. A school of silvery fish, bright and glittering as painted fingernails, flicked away beneath her.

She sliced one hand through the surface, then the other, kicked her legs. Turning her head, she pulled in the air, tasted the salt water, spat it out, kept swimming. She pushed smoothly through the turbulence of the other kids—that was all they were, turbulence, and she could get through it, get past them. With each stroke she caught a blurred glimpse of the boys standing there on the edge, jeering and laughing, but whatever they were saying was lost. As long as she focused, drew out each breath, made her hands cut through in steady, unshakeable time, swimming was the calmest thing in the world.

~

In the late afternoon, with school behind her, she stepped from the bus, waited for it to turn the corner, then bent down and took off her shoes and socks. There was plenty of day left—the hot, bright sun hung a good distance in the sky.

Somewhere behind her she could hear the grinding metallic squeal of a train pulling out of Newcastle Station. The park was to her right and, looming over it, the hospital where Mum worked. Past that, out of sight, the sea. Home was only a couple of blocks away, but she veered into the park instead. There was a fountain near the edge, in the shade of the surrounding Norfolk pines, a glistening circle of black tiles, flush with the grass, from which five bubbling columns of water took turns towering into the air before dropping down again. A gust of the breeze carried a fine mist against her face. A couple of children were playing, running from one column of water to the next. They'd scream and laugh as the water rose around their legs, their waists, their heads, and they'd be gone, their screams muffled, until it fell again. She came close to the water herself, let it rise up around her feet, her shins, her knees—then stepped back as it climbed higher still.

She walked home barefoot, enjoying the feel of the concrete against her soles, and the cool memory of the water like an echo in her bones. Some of the houses along the street were shuttered up and abandoned, patches of the walls crumbling, pieces of their roofs missing. They looked a thousand years old. A stream of cars filled the road, most of them heading in the opposite direction. They were heading home too, back to the spread of the suburbs. Sometimes she'd sense the cars slow alongside her or the drivers turning to look, and she'd steel herself, but it was nothing. It was usually nothing.

Their house was empty. All the windows were shut. The air was stifling—brooding and dank. The old smell wasn't so strong anymore, but it was still there, especially when the place had been locked up all day. The makeshift curtains Mum had thrown together with her old sewing machine were drawn. She went around pulling aside the curtains and opening windows. She started in the living room, where Mum and Dad slept, then the dining room, where her mattress lay a short distance from Daniel's, and had just gone into the kitchen when a soft creak and bang of wood drew her back to the hallway.

The basement door was open again. Before she shut it, she turned on the light and looked down the stairs, she supposed to make sure that the basement was empty, even though she knew it was. Who would bother staying down there anyway, when they had the whole house to hide in? A knife-wielding maniac, maybe, out of one of those movies: the kind that waited until girls were getting undressed, and never broke into a run and yet always seemed to catch up with you. You could laugh at them because they weren't real, but then sometimes the silence and emptiness came at you in a way that made you not want to laugh. The grey concrete floor still looked dirty, but at least she could see it. There were a few boxes of Dad's things, his workbench, and some of his tools laid out on a canvas sheet at one end of the floor. Nothing else. She wrinkled her nose at the faint smell, turned off the light and shut the door.

She went to her suitcase, took out the stash of paper and tobacco she'd stolen from Dad the day before and rolled herself a cigarette, practising doing it with one hand like Dad did, but she had to use two in the end and the cigarette wasn't perfect. She smoked it in the courtyard, listening to the sound of the neighbourhood over the murmur of the sea and the distant, wind-cut clang and boom and whine of machinery from the harbour, waiting for the telltale slam of the front door.

The sky was framed by the brick wall that separated their courtyard from the next one along. She imagined she was sitting at a dead end, like in that movie with David Bowie. *Labyrinth*. If she got up and pushed the wall, it would fall over, and there'd be goblins or monsters on the other side. There was moss in the brickwork, and a crawl of vines speckled with white flowers that carried a heady scent around her. Jasmine. A few clouds just made the blue of the sky bluer. She stared up at it, watching the thin smoke of her cigarette wither into nothing.

Pop had smoked a pipe. As far as she knew, it still sat on the desk in his study, back in Sydney. Nan hadn't taken anything out of his study since he'd died. She just went in and dusted it sometimes, like it was a museum exhibit. Looking at it, you could imagine him wandering around somewhere else in the house, talking to himself, teeth clenched on the pipe—but he was gone. Daniel had always been in there, even though he wasn't supposed to be. Freya had only ever stood on the threshold.

A brilliant man, Nan had called him. Brilliant. She often said she'd been incredibly lucky to end up with him, lucky to have even known him. That's why she kept the room the way it was, to remind her of that luck.

'Hopefully you'll be lucky too,' she'd told Freya last year. 'They say it can skip a generation.'

Mum, who had been sitting in the living room too, had stood up and left.

'All of this,' Nan had said, 'and I'm not allowed to make a little joke?'

There was a loud bang as the front door slammed shut. Mum had come home, as if summoned by that memory. Freya heard her short, sharp steps in the hall and stabbed the cigarette into a pot plant, waving the smoke away from her face. A moment later she heard her in the kitchen, clattering the breakfast dishes in a way that said, *Would it hurt anyone else to wash these when they came home?* That anyone else being Freya.

Daniel came out into the courtyard and stood in front of her, waiting. He was holding a black case.

'What's that?' she asked.

He sat down beside her without a word and opened the case.

'A clarinet,' she said.

He nodded.

'Play something,' she told him.

He stared down at the pieces. 'I don't know how. I just got it.'

'Can you make a noise at least?'

After a moment, he took out the clarinet, fumbled with the pieces, fitted them together and lifted it to his mouth. He kept it there, in place, his large grey eyes fixed on her.

'What?' she asked at last.

He lowered the clarinet a fraction. 'I can't with you looking at me.'

'Okay then.'

She faced in the other direction. After a moment, he blew into the instrument. A squeak came out. He tried again. This time he played a single, clear note that trembled away into silence.

'That's good,' she said, looking at him over her shoulder.

'That's like the start of a song.'

Something like a smile came onto his face. 'I can do more.'

Then a voice called from the alley. 'Hey!'

A head poked up over the top of the wall. Blond hair, the upper half of a pale face, blue eyes that met hers before the head vanished. Freya jumped onto the pipe next to the wall, the one her bike was chained to, and peered down. The boy in the alley stepped back.

'Hey yourself,' she said.

He grinned up at her. His light blond hair was swept back from his face. His arms were skinny and his shoulders sloped ahead of his chest. He was wearing a pair of board shorts patterned with multicoloured skulls and a Guns N' Roses singlet. A small silver ring pierced the middle of his lower lip, and another went through his eyebrow. There was one in his left nostril, too. She didn't mind that. It reminded her of some of the boys she'd known in Sydney.

'What are you doing?' he said.

'Nothing,' she said. 'You?'

'Not much.'

She rested with her elbows on the top of the wall. 'Do I know you?'

The boy lifted a hand to shade his eyes. 'I sit behind you in English. Whenever Mrs O'Neill says she won't go on until the class stops talking, that's usually me.'

'Oh.'

'It's all right if you didn't notice me. I notice you all the time, but you know.'

She liked his eyes. 'Mrs O'Neill's kind of mental.'

'Yeah, isn't she.' He grinned, showing his teeth. He had braces. More metal.

'So, what are you doing?' Freya said.

'Going to the beach,' he said. 'Want to come?'

'I don't know.'

He took a packet of cigarettes from his pocket. 'I saw you the other day at the beach. I thought about coming over then, but I didn't. But now—well, here I am. It's a nice arvo. You keen?'

She glanced behind her. Mum wasn't in the kitchen anymore. 'Okay,' she said.

Daniel was still standing there, the clarinet in his hands.

She climbed up onto the wall. 'Tell Mum I went for a walk, okay?'

'I want to come too,' Daniel said.

'Next time. I'll be back soon.'

His face dropped in a way that made her feel guilty, but before Daniel could answer, she swung down the other side of the wall and into the alley beside the boy.

They walked to the corner and stepped out onto the street that led towards the beach without saying a word. She was happy, happy at the thought that each step was carrying her further from Mum, and from the house.

The boy gave a short laugh. 'I lied about it being a nice arvo.' He smiled at her again.

'You still haven't told me your name,' she said.

'Sorry, I'm Josh.' He lit a cigarette, put it to his mouth and squinted as he sucked back on it. He handed her the cigarette, their fingers brushing. 'What do you think of it?'

'What?'

'This place. Newcastle.'

She held the smoke in her lungs, exhaled out of the side of her mouth. 'It's all right.'

'Yeah, I hate it here too. How long have you been here now?'

'Six weeks.'

He bit his lip. 'Give it six months. Then you'll really be ready to get out of here.'

She laughed. 'I'm ready now.'

'Me too,' he said. 'I think about it all the time. Anyone with a brain does.'

They crossed a road, continued along the street past a decrepit wooden building with a red light hanging over the front door. Two storeys high, its wood was cracked and peeling with paint, its windows shuttered.

'That's a brothel,' he said without looking at it.

'Yeah,' she said. 'Opposite an ice-cream shop. Perfect.'

The beach made a fat crescent with cliffs and saltbush at either end. There were hardly any people down on the sand, and the sun had disappeared behind the hospital at their backs. Clumps of seaweed and broken bits of reef littered the shoreline. The waves were large and thick, and turned to rusty foam as they broke. Several surfers drifted near the rocks beside the baths. Every now and again one of them rode a wave all the way in to the shore, then ran along the sand with a springy step and jumped again off the rocks. She sat with Josh on one of the seats that lined the concrete along the edge of the beach.

'Did that hurt?' she asked.

'What?'

She pointed to the piercing in his lower lip.

He shook his head. 'Dad's a dentist. He's got great needles. It was like a bee sting.'

'A bee sting on your face?'

'Maybe less than a bee sting then. Maybe a mosquito. Somewhere between the two.'

'Your dad was cool with letting you use his needles?'

He shrugged. 'I just took them.'

'He didn't notice?'

'He's got things on his mind. You know how it is.'

'I guess,' she said.

'I can pretty much do whatever I want. School went on about the ring in my eyebrow—said they were going to send me home—until my dad came in and spoke to them. They left me alone after that.' He gave her a sidelong glance. 'Hey—I can do you if you like. I mean, you know, pierce your face. Your lip, maybe. That'd look good, I reckon. If you want.'

He coughed. They both looked at the water.

'At least there's the beach here,' Freya said. She brushed the hair away from her face, though it wasn't really in the way—more like just something to do.

'What?' he said.

'The beach is cool.'

He nodded. 'Yeah, for sure.'

'My mum works there,' she said, with a nod towards the hospital. 'She's a nurse.'

The wind blew flecks of cigarette ash back in their faces. Shadows were lengthening across the sand.

'I'd better get home,' she said.

They didn't speak again until they reached the corner of the street and the alleyway, the ocean a dull roar at their backs, a bulk carrier entering the harbour ahead of them. They could see only the top of the ship from where they stood, the hull and the harbour hidden by the shape of the land.

'You should come over sometime,' Josh said. 'I live just around the corner. Alfred Street. The place with the red front door. My room's in the basement. Got this window just at street level. Just call down into it. I'm usually home.'

He turned down the street without waiting for an answer.

~

As she crossed the courtyard towards the kitchen, she heard Dad's voice from inside the house.

'Daniel. Speak properly. Open your mouth. Did you do it? Answer like a normal person.'

Freya paused in the kitchen, Dad's shadow ahead of her in the hallway. Then she heard quick, sharp steps on the stairs that could only belong to Mum.

'Roy,' Mum said.

'What?' Dad answered, but his voice was different, now that he was talking to Mum, like he knew exactly what she meant.

Mum came the rest of the way down the stairs and walked straight past Freya and out into the courtyard. Dad came past too, hands in pockets like the boys she saw sometimes at school, when they were in trouble, but not like that at all, either. Freya stood beside the open door, so that she was out of sight.

'I was just having a conversation with him,' Dad said.

'Just a conversation?' Mum said. 'With your son?'

After a pause, Dad answered in a quieter voice, 'You say it like he isn't.'

'Oh, shut up about that. I saw how you were standing over him. What would you have done if I wasn't there?'

He muttered something.

'Right,' Mum said.

Dad said something else, but Freya still couldn't catch it.

Mum sighed in an exasperated way. 'Do you realise how you sound?'

Dad's words came out in an explosion of breath. 'I know how I sound! He's still my son, as far as I know, and you're not going to make me feel like shit every time I—'

Her voice cut through his. 'Just say the word, Roy—say it.'

'Don't even joke about that,' he said.

'Or what?' she said, something fierce and eager creeping into her tone now. 'Come on. It's been a while since you've made a good threat—let's hear it.'

'It's not like that.'

'What's it like then?'

Freya leaned across the kitchen counter, just enough to see what was happening through the window. Mum's arms were folded across her chest, her face angled up to Dad. His hands hung at his sides as if he didn't know where to put them. Freya's belly tightened, and there was a beating inside her head as she watched Mum put her hands on Dad's chest and push him back.

'What?' Mum demanded. 'What are you going to do?'

Freya picked up a glass from the sink, held it over the lino floor. She would drop it. She would drop it and everyone would come running in. Everything else would be forgotten. She couldn't feel the glass—it was as if she were holding nothing, just heat in her fingertips. The beating in her head grew stronger, like there was a bird trapped inside her skull, trying to break out. The silence outside filled with the thrumming of cicadas, the sudden long blast of a ship's horn, the distant wrestling of the sea and the shoreline.

'Okay,' Dad said at last. 'Okay, then.' He took a step back.

'What?'

'I'm sorry.'

'You're sorry.'

He coughed. 'Yes, I am.'

'For what?'

'I'm trying, you know. I'm trying.'

'You're sorry for trying?'

'No, of course not.' His voice had softened. 'I'm sorry for being an arsehole. There, I said it. I'm an arsehole. But I'm trying—you don't know how hard.'

'Yes, you certainly are an arsehole sometimes,' Mum said.

'Didn't I just say that?'

'A real arsehole.' She pushed him lightly on the shoulder.

He looked at her, his face motionless, his arms taut, then he began laughing, and Mum started laughing too, the laughter brief, a little shrill. They laughed and then they were quiet again, still facing one another.

'I'm trying,' he said. 'I am. And I'm sorry.'

'Right.' Mum took a pack of cigarettes out of her pocket, tapped one into her hand. As she lit it, she studied Dad. Her eyes remained on his as she exhaled, but she was smiling again, the smile hard, like she was amused at something that might make another person feel sad. 'Let's see how long you stay sorry.'

'Maryanne.'

'What?'

'I don't want you to leave again.'

'You made a promise. What happens is up to you.'

'Well…' Dad said, but he didn't finish.

He came back inside and went upstairs without even a glance towards Freya. She listened to him moving around upstairs above her head. Daniel had turned on the television. *Doctor Who* was on. Mum was still in the courtyard, smoking her cigarette. It was humid and stifling in the kitchen. Freya realised that her hand was still clenched around the glass. She put it back on the sink. Dad had started hammering again—hard, precise strokes at measured intervals—and Freya stood alone in the kitchen as that noise filled the house.

6

Roy's hammering had set the dog down the alley barking again. Stupid animal. Maryanne ground the stub of her cigarette against the brick wall and lit another. She made herself breathe slowly but she could feel her heart beat, the flicking pulse of her blood, and the new cigarette trembling between her fingers.

The house loomed over her, its edges growing vague against the sunless sky, but the blistered paintwork on the windows, and the salt-pitted brickwork, the roof with half its gutter hanging loose, were easy enough to make out. She could imagine it all collapsing on top of her. It did not feel like home, or even like she belonged here, or that any of them did. It felt like something in the house was set against her, had been from the start. Something that was becoming more obvious even as Roy threw himself into it heart and soul—and he was good at this, had always been good at this, working with his hands.

She pushed the thought away, returned to the moment that had just passed. The way he'd confronted her just now, the look of him—the tightness in his body as he'd stood over her, his fists clenched, that cord of muscle sprung up in his neck, and his eyes, the light in them—it hadn't felt real, like a memory more than something happening there and then. A small, fierce part of her had wanted him to lose it then, to make it all simple. But how close had he really been? Was she just afraid that he would, and was it simply her own fear she'd seen?

Maybe it was something in her he was responding to, that dangerous residue of anger that remained even after they'd both agreed to let go. It wasn't right to hold on to it now. At least not if she wanted to make this work—and she had to make it work. She'd allowed him back in. No one had held a gun to her head. There'd been an opportunity to finish it for good, and no one would have blamed her if she had, but she hadn't. She'd gone back to him.

Not that anything was ever so clear-cut, not when you were in the thick of it, not even when you looked back on it later, not with a man like Roy, who was all charm when he wanted to be, larger than life, and you wanted to see that side of him too, and did anything you could to keep seeing it, because what was the world when that was taken out of you, that hope, that desire? And there were Freya and Daniel to think about, too. Once you had children with someone, you couldn't ever step back from that. There was a connection, and you made of it what you could. Roy was in her life and would always be, one way or another, no matter what else the future held. She twisted her wedding ring and slid it up against her knuckle. The ring felt heavy, as if she might break her finger, snap the bone, by pulling a little more firmly on it. But her hands were stronger than they looked.

After what had happened, after what he'd done, nearly a year ago now, she'd returned to her mother's house with the children. She'd walked into the bedroom that had once been hers, wrenched the ring off, and thrown it against the wall. The ring had rebounded and disappeared in a flash of gold. She'd searched for it the next day, and the day after, but with no success. How could you lose something in such a confined space? She'd wanted to find and get rid of it properly, to end the relationship with a proper gesture. There were only so many places you could look in such a room. Every minute, every hour that she couldn't find it, felt like a defeat. Her mother cleaned every room in the house once a week. She couldn't find it either.

Maryanne had eventually stopped looking and stayed there, in her mother's house, with her children, trying to breathe, to get through each day. And, as always, alongside the anger and the fear that faded as they always did, Maryanne began to miss Roy—the densely packed heaviness of his body, how it made her feel grounded when it rested on top of hers, even just his hand, those rough fingers splayed across her breast or her belly. Yes, she missed him. And there'd been no one she could talk to about that, least of all her mother.

As the weeks became months, she'd lie there on her bed at night, feeling her own lightness. She had dreams sometimes of floating from her body, drifting out into the night unencumbered. They were nightmares. There was nothing to keep her steady, no sense of purpose, nothing to preoccupy her when she wasn't at work, good or bad, just this emptiness that seemed to be saying, now what? She hadn't counted on that uncertainty, or that the lack of pressure would so often feel simply like a lack, or that under it there'd be the dreadful feeling that things between them were unfinished.

She'd wake up, jaw clenched painfully hard, and get up and close the window, shut the blinds and then open them again, pace up and down with her arms folded across her chest, shivering but not putting on anything warmer because the cold reassured her. She'd stand and stare out at the streetlight half hidden by the leaves of the tree outside, listening to the formless roar of traffic on distant roads, trapped in her childhood bedroom like she was caught in some perverse winding back of her own life.

It was terrifying, that sense of hurtling backwards. Sixteen years since that room had been hers. Sixteen years, and now here she was again, all of that struggle and failure behind her. The posters were gone, but her bed remained, and her desk, and there was still a bookcase beside the desk, though the books on it were no longer hers. The memories here were like a smell that you only noticed when you first came in.

Some nights sleep wouldn't come to her at all. A wakefulness bloomed in her, so intense it was as if something made of needles were trying to claw its way out. She'd watch as dawn spread over the street. She'd check on Daniel in the other room, his frail body hardly taking up the bed, and she would lean in close to make sure he was still breathing, as if he were a newborn infant and not the son she'd done her best, her very best, to look after, for better or for worse, for seven years. She would do better. You could always do better. If you didn't think you could do better, then what sort of parent were you?

Many of the days in her mother's house passed leaving no impression on her at all. She did what she had to at work, kept it together there, because for all its difficulties, work had always been the easiest part of her life, and that was that. She heard from Roy a few times, messages on the answering machine—terse, factual accounts of selling their house and barely breaking even, and getting rid of everything that she hadn't packed into her suitcases on that day he'd come home to find her gone. Others needed those things more than him, and why should he care if she didn't? Then it grew quiet, and after eight months she had almost stopped expecting to hear from him. She no longer felt the absence of that grounding weight at night. One by one, his fingers lifted from her skin.

~

Maryanne hadn't been thinking about him that day he turned up again, but she'd known the instant before she opened the door. His beard was gone and he was lean, the bones of his face more cleanly defined, his eyes brilliant and clear. A dizzying vertigo struck her, as if she were still in high school and he was there again, at the door of her parents' house, to pick her up.

'Maryanne.' He swallowed, smiled unsteadily. 'You look good.'

Her grip tensed on the door. The sense of his body poured into her, the raw vitality of it, the barely suppressed energy, his feet, shod in the usual workboots, the left pointed towards her, right near the threshold. Her mother was at the end of the hallway, watching. Maryanne wrenched herself into action. She began to push the door shut, to close him out.

'Wait,' he said. 'Please. I won't keep you.' The smile was gone. 'Please,' he said. 'Please, don't close the door.'

She felt that if she did close it, something would happen—something massive and irreversible. Or maybe she'd paused because he didn't even try to prevent her closing the door. Or maybe it was the sadness in his eyes. Nothing put on about that—it was real.

'Please wait,' he said again.

She kept the door open.

There was a gift Roy wanted her to have, not for her but for Daniel. Their fingers didn't touch as she took the parcel.

'I wrapped it myself,' he said.

She fingered the package. 'You didn't do a very good job.'

He flinched a little. That made her feel good, and then guilty, as if she were taking advantage of his weakness.

'I want to see you,' he said. 'It doesn't have to be for long. It can be in a cafe or someplace like that. Somewhere where's there's people around.' His voice sped up, the words tumbling over one another. 'I don't want anything else. I just want to talk. I wouldn't do anything else—or expect anything even.'

'I'll let you know,' she'd told him. 'Call me in a week.'

She was happy with how she'd said that, the decisiveness in her tone.

Her mother was waiting for her with crossed arms. 'You're not going to see him again, are you? I hope you understand why that would be a terrible idea.'

Perhaps it was her mother's reaction that had solidified everything, that had pushed her into making a decision too quickly.

'I can see him,' she said, 'if I want to.'

The air hissed out of her mother's mouth. 'Why don't you put the children first for once?'

'You don't think that's what I'm doing?'

Maryanne walked away before her mother could answer.

That night, in the darkness of her room, Maryanne felt more restless than ever, by turns hopeful and sick with worry. The thing that had driven her back to her mother's house had become vague, uncertain, something she could barely bring herself to touch with her thoughts, though she had promised herself that she would keep it clear in front of her for as long as she needed to. Instead, there was the weight of him—that firm, solid, reassuring weight—and she realised that her need for it had never left her at all.

~

They went out for a coffee, and it was early spring with all of the European trees along the street budding into pale green leaves and a pale sun gleaming on the table between them. It was surprisingly good to be there with him, just for an hour—an invigorating break from the judgement and the claustrophobic intensity of her mother's house. They had always shared a chemistry, Roy and her, something primal and fierce that pulled them together hard when they got too close. She'd always thought, always believed, that if somehow they could learn how to handle it, then everything would fall into place, and all the risk and hardship would have been worth it. She'd put in so much effort and suffered so much to keep her marriage to Roy intact—was she just meant to throw it all away?

They sat at a table across from one another, a space between them that Roy was careful not to disrupt with his large, restless hands. A girl came and took their order. Roy barely glanced at her before turning back to Maryanne.

He began to tell her about a house he'd found. It was in Newcastle, only a few hours up the coast, a harbour city, just like Sydney, but smaller and quieter. Yes, there was the steelworks around the upper part of the harbour, and there were the coal-loading terminals too, but the inner-city suburbs were leafy and close to the coast. He'd come across the house by chance when he'd been up that way on a three-month contract. It was nearly a hundred years old, a crumbling inner-city terrace only a couple of blocks away from the beach, half ruined, and that's what had kept it on the market for so long, but underneath the superficial damage it was a treasure, something worth putting yourself into. He'd known as soon as he'd seen it that someone else would jump in if he didn't, and that an opportunity like that wouldn't come again. So he'd made a decision, put in an offer for it, hoping that everything would fall into place.

There was a hospital nearby too, a huge, busy one, right across the road from the beach. Someone like her, with her experience, they'd be sure to snap her up. She'd be able to walk there, it was so close, and look out over the sea while she worked.

And they'd be able to fall asleep to the sound of waves. Before he'd bought the house, he'd used to stand out the front at night, listening to the way the sea filled the street with its noise and swept all around. It made him think of Maryanne, the passion with which she did everything, how rare that was.

'And you know what I couldn't stop thinking, Maryanne?' he said. 'That the house needs you. You can change a place. Most people can't, you know. No matter what I do, a house is still a house. I don't know how to make it anything more. You're the one that knows how to bring the life into it.'

'I wouldn't know about that,' she said.

He gave a subdued laugh. 'You know more than I ever will. Everything important I've ever learned in my life, it's been because of you. I'm not saying it's been easy'—he smiled at her in a knowing way, as if to acknowledge the terrible darkness that set them apart from ordinary people—'but it's been something real. That's life, isn't it? That's what life should be.'

The waitress brought their coffees out. She was young and pretty—fine, blond, shoulder-length hair tucked behind her ears, lively eyes—and she smiled at Roy, pausing for a moment as she turned, her shoulders pushed back a little, the way some women did with an attractive man, but Roy didn't even look up. Maryanne realised there was a jealousy still in her, a part of her that did not want him to belong to anyone else.

As he waited for them to be alone again, Roy's hand crept out towards Maryanne's, but he did not touch her. His fingers were bent, only the tips with their square, broad nails resting on the table. Dark hair grew in tufts between the knuckles, reappearing halfway to the wrist, exploding in dark whorls up his forearms, his skin tanned and smooth underneath.

He was still talking and she looked up to meet the gold-brown flash of his eyes, his broad, smiling face, the teeth white against his olive skin. He was going to do the house up, he said—whenever he wasn't at work. He'd lined up a job, too, a one-year contract with the same people that'd had him up there in the first place. And that was what he wanted: a year to get somewhere, to rebuild. It'd take a year to do up the house at most. If she was there with him, they could decide together what to do next. Maybe they'd keep the house or maybe they'd sell it, but either way, there was a good future in it. He couldn't imagine that future without her, and the kids. Their kids. He waited for her to disagree, but she didn't. His hand remained there, close to hers. And what about her then, he asked. What could she imagine?

~

When Maryanne got home, her mother was in the kitchen, having a cup of tea with a friend. They'd been talking about her—you could tell by the silence that followed her arrival. Her mother stayed at the table, fingers laced around her cup, staring up at Maryanne through the steam that rose from the tea.

'What did he say?'

'I didn't take notes.' Maryanne went back out into the hall, slipped off her shoes and started up the stairs to her room.

'Maryanne!' Her mother had come to the foot of the stairs and was looking up at her. 'Are you going back to him then?'

'I don't know.'

'Oh, I know. It's in your eyes. I know what you're like.' Her mother spread her hands in the air. 'I just don't know why.'

Her mother didn't know why. That was a laugh. Her mother, the bloody Roman Catholic saviour. She was always there in the house, waiting, had saved her a few times, for sure, but she never let her forget it, and no matter how much Maryanne needed to be there, she could never go back without being plagued by the thought of what lay beneath her mother's generosity—the guilty refusal to really talk, to acknowledge what Maryanne's own father had been like.

~

That night, Maryanne had searched through her room for several hours. The ring had slipped into a gap under the skirting near the foot of the bed, just a glint of it still visible, and only if you looked at it from exactly the right angle. She had to tease it out with a knife. When she slid the ring back on, it felt warm, as if it had just come off her skin.

And from there, it was easy. Her mother didn't want any explanations. She didn't want to know where they were going, although she nodded in a bitter, satisfied manner when she heard that it was so far away. And who did that suit then? She did not expect an answer. Maryanne did not offer one.

Her mother became distant after that, resigned. This was a relief to Maryanne. It made everything easier.

~

On the day that Roy came to collect her and the children, her mother managed to avoid saying a word to him. But at the door, when Maryanne was about to leave, when Roy was already in the car, she said, 'Sixteen years of this. It's going to happen again. I think you know that.'

Maryanne got in the car.

'What did she say?' Roy asked.

'Nothing,' she said.

That was the first lie she'd told him since she'd left. She closed the door of the station wagon and felt the heat enfold her. The car seemed to be the one thing he'd hung on to from their old life, a relic from the seventies, from before they'd had Daniel, when there had only been Freya, and things had been less complicated between them. The windows were wound down, but it made no difference. Every surface radiated heat. Even the fabric of the seat was hot under her thighs. The vinyl dashboard, underneath the lighters and discarded cigarette packets and various bits and pieces, was faded and finely cracked. The engine coughed into life. It had some flaw even Roy couldn't fix. It didn't sound right, but the car never broke down. You could drive it off a cliff and it would keep going.

Freya was the last to come out of the house, a bag over her shoulder and a strange look on her face. Her daughter didn't understand yet, but she would. They were a family and they belonged together, and everything else would sort itself out. Freya got in and Roy pulled out from the kerb, the trailer behind them. Maryanne looked in the rear-view mirror at her children in the back seat. Daniel was looking back, waving in Nan's direction. Freya was staring ahead. They drove for a while in silence. With one hand on the steering wheel, Roy rolled a cigarette and, as they crossed the Sydney Harbour Bridge, he put it in Maryanne's mouth, his eyes never leaving the road. And it was in that moment, with that gesture he made—so ingrained, so part of their old routine—that her certainty vanished.

~

How many weeks ago had that been now? Six. Just six. She stubbed her cigarette out against the brick wall. Six weeks. No time at all. The sky was starting to fade into evening. The hammering had stopped and she could hear the sea again, as if it were coming closer with each wave. Maryanne stared up at the window, watched the shadow of Roy's movement thrown up against the ceiling.

He'd certainly oversold the house. Or maybe she had just hoped for too much. Maybe it was true, that the house was solid under all the damage. All of this had happened for a reason. She had to believe that.

Even if it was a mistake.

She made herself look away. She wanted nothing more than to go to sleep, alone, to go upstairs and collapse on her mattress and not get up until it was day again, but there were things to do. Dinner, for a start. The children must be starving. She went back into the house.

Freya was in the kitchen.

'How long have you been standing there?' Maryanne asked.

Freya shrugged. 'Not long. I just wanted to—'

'What?'

'See if you were okay.'

'You want to help me finish making dinner?'

While Maryanne cooked some lamb chops, Freya made the salad.

'It's the last day of summer today,' Maryanne said.

'Yeah,' her daughter said.

'Where'd you go this afternoon?'

Freya hesitated. 'The beach.'

Something in her tone made Maryanne glance at her. 'Did you go with a boy?'

Freya didn't answer. She directed her attention at the carrot she was chopping into ever finer pieces. Maryanne thought of her own mother, probably sitting alone in her house right now, husband long since dead, and only one daughter of her own to worry about and be there for and be loved by.

'It's okay,' Maryanne said. 'I didn't mean to pry. It's good to have a few secrets.'

7

Freya was drunk. She laughed as she stood in some stranger's house, swaying on her feet, and her voice sounded like it belonged to someone else. She'd drunk more than she'd thought, white wine from a cask, not because she'd wanted to, really, but because she hadn't been paying attention. But now, yes, now it was good, and she didn't feel sorry, not for doing it, and not for telling Mum she'd be staying at a friend's place and watching a movie.

Ally had disappeared out the back with some boy, and Freya was alone in the crowded room. Lights glittered on the harbour through the windows. There were tangled limbs in every shadowy corner of the house. Someone was moaning and retching in the toilet. The Cure were blazing through the walls—'Why Can't I Be You?'

Someone bumped her shoulder. She turned and it was Josh. He was wearing black acid-wash jeans and a blue tie-dye Led Zeppelin shirt.

'Hey,' he said.

'Hey.'

'Enjoying yourself?'

'I guess,' she said.

He put his hand on her arm. 'Are you okay?'

Freya nodded. 'I'm fine. I've just had too much to drink.'

Then Ally was there beside her again, holding a beer bottle by the neck, a pale sheen on her face of too much foundation.

'We have to go,' Ally said without looking at Josh. 'It's eleven-thirty. Dad'll be coming to pick us up. We don't want him coming in the house, trust me.'

Josh dropped his hand and stepped back, but he caught Freya's eye. 'You know where I live.'

'Yeah, like anyone needs to know that,' Ally said, as if noticing him for the first time.

They walked out to the street.

'So did you kiss that guy?' Freya asked.

'What?' Ally looked at her blearily. 'Oh, what's his name out the back. Yeah. And then I threw up.'

'You didn't.'

Ally grinned and gave a slow, deliberate nod. 'Yep. Just a bit. I don't think he noticed. I don't care if he did. I don't even like him. I think this is his beer.'

They stood together on the kerb, waiting.

'So what's your problem with Josh?' Freya said.

Ally finished the bottle and hurled it into the bushes. 'Just know trouble when I see it.'

~

They sat in the back on the drive home to Ally's house. The car was huge on the inside, and so clean it was like they were taking it for a test drive. It had power windows that slid up and down with the faintest whir, air conditioning, and a music system with a CD player that made the classical music Ally's father was playing sound as if it were coming from every direction and nowhere all at once.

'You girls have a good time?' Ally's father said as they left the east end of the city behind.

'Yeah, Dad. Just drive.'

He tipped a pretend hat at Ally. 'I'd probably rather not know.'

He had hair only around his ears, a shiny skull. He glanced at them every now and again in the rear-view mirror and talked like he was trying to impress them, like a man practising for when he might actually need it. As they drove up along the coast, the road began to climb. An escarpment rose on their left, huge houses staggered along its flank. They turned from the main street, went up another, and kept following the road until they came to the end, to one last house before the darkness and the sea down below.

Ally led her inside and straight through the house. The rooms were large and clean but there wasn't enough furniture, and all the colours in the house were cold blues and whites. When Freya stepped onto the balcony, she could see across nearly the whole city. She was beginning to know it now, could pick out the distant arch of the bridge that led across the water to Stockton and, closer in, the floodlit cathedral. On another hill she saw a single, thin, luminous white column.

'What's that?' she asked.

'The obelisk,' Ally told her.

'But what is it?'

'I don't know. It's just the obelisk. That's just what it's called.'

'Weird.'

'I never thought about it before.'

They fell silent. Down below, along one of the main streets, Freya could see the blue and red flash of a stationary police car.

Freya said, 'It's a great view.'

'Yeah,' Ally murmured with a faint smile. 'You get over it after a while.' She leaned against the balcony, stretched one arm towards the lights in the city. 'My mum lives down there, near the beach. I'm so glad I'm not there now. She never lets me go out at night when I'm with her. Or she makes me come home really early. When I'm with Dad, he doesn't care. He just wants to be the cool dad. It's pathetic. Most of his girlfriends aren't that much older than me. He never keeps them that long.' She shook her head. 'And Mum still comes over to iron his clothes.'

They both stared out over the city, and Freya felt the buzz of the night beginning to dull inside her. Why can't I be you? Who, though?

'God, I can't wait for this term to be over,' Ally said. 'It's really dragging. I'm so over it. Ever been skiing?'

'No,' Freya said.

'You should come up one year. We usually go at the end of August.'

August. Freya wondered if they'd even be here then, her and Mum and Daniel.

'Sure,' she said.

They went to bed but stayed awake a while longer, Ally talking on in a flat, slightly bored tone about the boy she'd kissed and whether she'd do it again, and about the girls in their group, that one bitch who got paralytic every party she went to, and just embarrassed herself, and another girl who wasn't in their group but everyone knew how she'd let a boy touch her under her skirt while they were watching a documentary in geography. What a slut. She hadn't even been drunk.

Freya mainly just listened. She liked Ally, or at least didn't dislike her, but nothing that Ally cared about really mattered much to her. Maybe that was exactly what she needed, to be around people who knew nothing about her. Ally kept talking, and she answered where she needed to. Longer and longer gaps opened up between what they said. Soon Ally was snoring.

Freya began to doze. She was in the car, watching Nan's face vanish behind the grey reflection of a window. Dad was leaning forward over the steering wheel, Mum beside him, and it was too late to get out, they were already driving, had already come too far. Then she was awake again, Ally still snoring in the bed beside hers. She needed to talk to someone, but there was no one. Such a surge of loneliness crashed down on her that she thought she would drown in it. Gusts of wind were blasting against the windows. The whole house seemed to be trembling, like it didn't belong here, like it wasn't going to last, like it was only a matter of time.

~

The next morning, they walked along the strip of ocean that began at Merewether and went up to the rocks past Bar Beach. It was a perfect autumn day, a huge empty sky, just a light breeze, and the water as warm as the air. A group of boys from school were jumping off the rocks. They were the rich kids from Bar Beach and Merewether and the Junction—the ones who seemed to know exactly where they belonged and where they were going.

As Freya and Ally walked past them, a tall boy with a flat-top stood waiting on the edge of the rocks until he was sure they were watching, then grinned and did a slow, perfect backflip, landing feet first in the deep, green water below with barely a splash.

~

'Well then,' Dad said. 'What do you think?'

They were upstairs, on the top floor, standing at the threshold of her bedroom. Her things were in the room—her mattress, her suitcase, a rack with her clothes. The wooden floor underneath was smooth and lacquered in a dark, gleaming hue. The gabled inside of the roof was hidden by clean, pale grey plasterboard.

'Well?' Dad said. 'Do you like it?'

Mum was watching her too.

'Yeah,' Freya said.

Dad frowned. 'Yeah? That's it? Do you know how hard I've been slaving away up here to get this right for you? They're all solid now, the floors, good as new. I'll get around to putting carpet down eventually, but there's still a lot to do before then—the skirting boards, new power points, paint. For now, though, this is pretty good. You've got your own room.'

'It's great,' she said.

'I love mine,' Daniel said. 'I love it.'

Dad looked only at her, watchful, waiting. 'Do I get a kiss or something?'

Freya slung her arms around him and kissed his stubbled cheek. 'Thanks, Dad.'

'That's better.' He stepped to the window. 'This is pretty hard to open. I'll fix it later. But what a view, eh? You've definitely got the best one.' He peered outside, then turned back to grin at

81

Mum. 'Maybe we should move up here and give Freya our room, eh?'

Mum ignored him. 'It'll be nice when you can start bringing your friends over. You've made some friends now, haven't you?'

'Of course,' Freya said.

~

Josh's house stood on a narrow street of two-storey terraces that huddled together as if sheltering each other from a storm. The balconies threw the footpath into shadow. Most of the windows were protected by cast-iron bars.

She stood in front of the door—it was the only red one along the street. There was a doorknocker, one of those brass ones that looked like a lion. Freya lifted and dropped it. A breeze stirred around her, a sudden coolness in it that hadn't been there before, a promise of winter with winter nowhere in sight.

Footsteps stirred somewhere within the house and came towards her. The door opened, and a tall, thin man studied her from behind a pair of black-framed glasses.

'Well then,' he said. 'And who are you?'

'It's for me, Dad,' a voice called out.

The man stepped back, directing her down the hall with a glance. There was music coming up through the floorboards.

'Good luck,' he said as she walked past him.

'Down here,' Josh called. He was standing at the bottom of a set of narrow wooden stairs.

'I just thought I'd drop by,' she said as she made her way down.

He stepped back as she reached him, letting her past and into the room. He pointed at a window that was higher than either of them, at street level. 'I knew you were coming. I saw your legs.'

'I like the red front door,' she said.

He nodded. 'My mum did that.'

The room was dimly lit. It took her eyes a moment to adjust. An unmade bed was in one corner, next to it a lava lamp. The walls were white-painted brick, but she couldn't see much of them beneath all of the posters plastered alongside one another. Pink Floyd, Queen, Neil Young, Bob Dylan, the Cure, the Smiths, the Beatles. He had a small colour television on a table near his bed. *Rage* was on. The top forty. On the other side of the room, under the window, there was a desk, and next to it an old hi-fi system with two freestanding speakers clad in peeling wood veneer, and a box full of records. Two faded red armchairs on the other side of the room faced the speakers, a carved Chinese camphor chest between them.

'Your dad's interesting,' she said.

Josh made a face. 'I think the word you're looking for is *weird*.'

'I wasn't going to say that.'

'He's weird.'

'All right. My dad's weird too, I guess. What are you up to?'

'Nothing. I was just playing my Commodore 64.'

She sat down next to him. 'What game?'

'Golf.'

'How do you play it?'

He showed her. They sat side by side at his desk for a while playing Golf, which he said he hated in real life, but he was good at it on the computer, then they played California Games, taking turns to surf across a big, blue pixelated wave. She'd never really played computer games before. It was fun, maybe because she was sitting next to Josh, taking turns with him.

'I don't like surfing either,' he said as they played.

'Do you only play games you don't like in real life?'

'Pretty much.'

Footsteps creaked overhead. The front door opened and closed. Josh climbed up on his desk and put his head to the window. He kept peering out until a car door opened and closed and the sound of an engine faded away.

'Dad's finally gone,' he said. 'I thought he was never going to leave. He won't be back now till late. Let's crank the music up. Sit over there, near the record player.'

She sank down into one of the big red chairs.

'Be careful.' Josh began rifling through a wooden box full of albums. 'Those chairs are like quicksand. They're older than we are. It'll take you a while to settle into the cushions, find your place. Just go with it. Don't panic. If you panic, you'll never get out.'

Someone walked past along the street, only their legs visible through the window.

'I've never seen a bedroom in a basement before,' she said. 'We've got a basement but it's horrible. It doesn't have windows, not proper ones. You should have seen it when we moved in.'

Josh pulled an album out of the box and held it between his hands. 'This room's perfect. I can always hear Dad a mile off when he's coming down the stairs. And it holds the sound really well. Half of these records used to be Mum's.'

Freya wanted to ask where his mum was, but she didn't.

'You listen to music?' he asked.

'Yeah.'

'What then?'

'Whatever's on the radio.'

'Pink Floyd?'

'They did "Brick in the Wall", didn't they?'

He made a face. 'Three minutes out of a double album. Any

good album, you have to listen from the beginning to the end. Especially Pink Floyd.'

'Why especially Pink Floyd?'

'Because of this.' He opened the chest between the chairs and pulled out a bottle and a bowl. The bottle was plastic and half full of murky water. A piece of hose had been inserted through the side. 'You have to have a bit of this to really get where they're coming from.'

He offered her the bottle. She looked at it.

'It's a bong,' he said.

'I know what it is.'

'You ever smoked before?'

She shook her head. 'Not that.'

'It's a great way to deal with life in this town. Takes the edge off. Better than getting drunk. You want to try it?'

He put the bong in her hands.

'Let's start with *Dark Side of the Moon*,' he said.

He slid the album out of its sleeve, put it on the turntable, placed the needle in the groove. First there was only the crackling of the record, then came a beating heart. Josh sat down and began cutting threads of pot with a pair of scissors. A ringing cash register cut through the beating heart, and someone spoke— about always having been mad and knowing it—and then came laughter repeating in loops, and she felt an odd panic stir inside her though she hadn't even smoked anything yet, but maybe it was the thought of doing it or perhaps it was the day, the week, the last two months—God, had it really been that long since they'd arrived in this city?—and that tightness was there in her lungs the way it so often was. From outside, the bell on the nearby clock tower rang once and then faded. Didn't they say that some people got schizophrenia when they smoked pot? Smoked it once and never came back, if you had it in you, that madness, and maybe that was what she was feeling, and Mum would kill her if she could see her right now. Then came the warm strum of a guitar and Josh was passing her the plastic bottle. He showed her how to put her lips to its mouth and pull the air into her lungs while he held the lighter to the tangle of dark green.

His hands. They rested on hers just a moment. Josh was very careful, the way he did things. She inhaled, felt the burning fill the back of her throat. A hot numbness crept up from the bottom of her lungs. The bud caught fire and shrivelled into a black seed. Her chest felt small and frail. The music was all around her. He kept the flame going and she sucked the last burning fragment through the small brass bowl and at the same time felt a rush into her head, and it was like shutting a door on everything, and there was suddenly all the space in the world inside her, but if you looked closely, it wasn't space at all, just thoughts so crowded together you couldn't tell where one ended and the other began.

Josh didn't touch her again, although his hands were near hers. They were nice hands, with slender fingers. He refilled the bong, pulled it clear in one go—the soft pop as the last fragment succumbed to the flame—and then squinted, holding his breath, the fleeting ghost of an old man in his drawn expression, before he released the smoke and sank back into his chair.

They sat side by side in silence while the music shook around them.

'You're right,' she said.

'What?'

'You have to listen from the beginning.' She giggled. 'You have to sit in front of these big speakers and just let your ears get ripped off.'

They both began laughing. Then they fell silent again.

'You got a hi-fi system at home?'

'We used to,' she said. 'Right now we just have a radio.'

'I got this one from my dad,' he murmured. 'He used to put on these albums all the time. Now it's all classical music he buys on CD.'

'Why doesn't he listen to them anymore?' she asked.

'Listen—I love this part.'

A woman on the record was wailing out notes. It sounded chaotic, random at first, but then it started to find some kind of shape, to make sense.

Freya liked sitting there with Josh and the swallowing feel of the chair, and being underground in a basement listening to music she'd never heard with someone she didn't know but felt as if she did. She even liked the smell of his room. No one at home knew where she was. She could get on a train and leave this city and go all the way back to Nan's before anyone knew any better. It would only be for a while, before it all came crashing down, but still, wasn't that how everyone lived? Then she glanced across at Josh, sitting there nodding to the music, drawing notes out of an acoustic guitar on his lap, and it was enough just to watch him.

He put the guitar down suddenly, stood up.

'I've got something else for you,' he said.

'What?'

He picked up a pen, kneeled beside her chair and took her by the wrist, his fingers firm and warm against her pulse. 'My number.' He wrote it on the inside of her forearm, without looking up at her. 'Call me whenever you want. I'm always around.'

~

Walking home, she felt strange, the way her feet hit the ground subtly distorted, the world's timing somehow out of sync. As she opened the front door, she heard a noise, a plaintive wail, followed by a squeak. Daniel and his clarinet.

Dad was in the kitchen, naked from the waist up, lying on his side and shaking a can of spray. The muscles in his hairy shoulders rippled as he sprayed up under the sink. There was sweat on the folds of his soft belly. The radio was on. Bon Jovi— 'Dead or Alive', the guitar solo. Dad looked up at her as she stood in the doorway. Above them, another squeak from the clarinet cut through the sound of the radio.

'He's been doing that for hours,' he said. 'You think he's going to get any better?'

'Yeah,' she said.

He smiled. 'You've always been the optimist in the family, Freya. You get that from me, I reckon.'

Freya didn't say anything.

He shook his head. 'These bloody ants. They're everywhere.' He cursed under his breath and kept spraying.

Freya looked at Josh's phone number on the inside of her arm, and thought of Nan. She went upstairs, unzipped her suitcase, and pulled out the book of Greek mythology. She stood there holding it, listening to her brother, and the silence between his notes. The house creaked and groaned around her, and the roof keened against the wind, like it might at any moment peel away.

~

There was a phone booth overlooking the sea. Freya looked up at the hospital through the hazy glass, pitted by the sand and the salt, with the receiver to her ear.

'If anything ever happens,' Nan said at the other end of the line, 'I can always come and get you. Or you could always hop on a train.'

'I know, Nan.'

A boy on a skateboard rattled past. He wove across the footpath, launched onto the road, and hopped the board smoothly up onto the next kerb. Two kicks and he kept flying along. Freya put her extra coins in front of her and pressed the phone more firmly against her ear.

'Nan, I don't know how long I've got before I run out of money.'

'It's just lovely to hear your voice. I was wondering how you were, if you were okay. How's it going with your father then?'

'Good. I don't know.' She looked down at her bare feet, studied their unevenness.

'Is that why you called? Is he behaving himself?'

'Yes.'

'Has he done anything?'

'No.'

Nan cleared her throat on the other end of the line. 'Well, we can only live in hope. Just like your mother. It's certainly an adventure.'

Freya could picture Nan standing there in her living room, her fierce grey eyes, her tight-lipped smile.

Nan chuckled darkly. 'Sometimes you just want boring, don't you?'

They both laughed, the way they so easily could. It had driven Mum mad back in Sydney, and Freya had enjoyed it, but she felt a flush of guilt now as she stood there in the phone booth, in the shadow of the hospital, as if every window looking down on her were an eye. Perhaps Mum would see her from wherever she was

89

in the hospital and ask why she'd been talking on a public phone when they had one in the house.

'—anytime, you know that, right?'

'Yes, Nan, I know.'

'Are you holding anything back?'

'No. I mean…'

'What?'

'It's nothing.'

'What?'

'No, nothing,' she lied. 'I just have to go. I've run out of money.'

'Call me if you need to. Or even if you don't. Doesn't matter if you've got no money. Reverse charges. Just make sure your mother doesn't find out. She'll hate it if she thinks we're talking.'

'Okay,' Freya said, desperate now to hang up the phone.

A couple of nurses walked past. One of them glanced at her.

'You know how to do reverse charges, don't you?' Nan asked.

'Yes,' she said, not even understanding the question until after she'd answered. She didn't know how, but she could figure it out some other time. She hung up the phone, then took it off the hook, put in a few more coins and dialled the number on her wrist. It rang half a dozen times before a sleepy voice answered.

'Hello?'

'Josh,' she said.

'Freya? I didn't expect you to call that soon.'

'Sorry.'

'No. Don't be dumb. I'm glad you called. Are you okay?'

'Does it make you feel weird when you start to sober up, the pot?'

'Sometimes, I guess. Depends what I'm thinking about.'

'Right.'

'You okay?' he said again.

'I'm okay.'

Josh was quiet for a moment. 'I guess you just have to go with it, you know. Don't panic. Settle into it. Want to come back here? Want me to walk up and meet you?'

Freya wanted him to. 'I'll see you at school tomorrow.'

She hung up and started walking home.

8

The basement. Maryanne stood in the middle of it, with a bottle of wine in one hand and a glass in the other. Of all the places she could sit and drink, why here? Because when she drank alone, she never drank to enjoy it. Then why drink at all, Roy had asked her once. She hadn't answered. But why did people do half the things they did if enjoying it was the point? It was more a reflex action, the drinking, a way to let things out when there was no one around to see it.

The concrete floor beneath her feet was uneven, rough, and still ingrained with dirt. It was cool down here, despite the afternoon warmth that filled the rest of the house, but it still smelled faintly of bleach and rising damp. It was really Roy's domain, and that was fine by her. His workbench was set up there, and he'd put up some metal shelving on which his various tools were arranged. They'd cleared out all the rubbish, but there were a few random milk crates lying around. She sat down on one of the crates, poured herself a glass, and took a mouthful. It wasn't a terrible wine, but it wasn't great.

She looked at the tools in front of her and thought of Roy, how he was always working on something, pacing around, restless, until the moment he collapsed onto the couch or into bed at the end of the day. At night, when she was often struggling to sleep herself, he ground his teeth. She'd lie beside him, just listening. It sounded like he was breaking rocks in his mouth. Sometimes he'd moan and grunt and whimper, or even start crying, almost awake, but not quite, and his face would look like nothing so much as Daniel's, full of vulnerability and fear, though his eyes remained shut. She'd gather herself around his naked body, holding him until he fell into a deeper sleep. He had always done it, as long as she'd known him.

He never remembered it in the morning, though, and there was no hint of that vulnerability during the day. Sometimes, when he was working on the house, she'd get her cup of tea and watch him, how he moved, the easy way he had of picking things up and putting them in their place without seeming to pay any attention at all. There was an expression on his face when he worked that she'd never really been able to read, like he was on autopilot, like he wasn't there behind his eyes.

It was the same thing that happened when they fought, that sudden absence, that sense of a part of him just going missing. The first time they'd ever had a fight, a real one, anyway, was when they moved in together, into their first flat, on the very first night, when they'd both been exhausted, strung out, fed up with all the packing and unpacking, the endless minutiae that came with uprooting yourself and planting your life anew. What had it been again? What had they been fighting about? Something about her parents. She'd wanted to ring her mother, once they were in the flat, just a quick call to say they'd got there, and Roy had told her not to.

It wasn't so much what he'd said about them—she agreed with half of it—but how he'd put it, the way he'd told her that she wouldn't be calling her mother. They argued then about how they spoke to one another, and he threw her own words back at her, things she'd said to him months before, things she couldn't remember saying. When she'd told him that, he'd asked if she was calling him a liar, and after an hour of words and accusations and justifications thrown back and forth, she wasn't even sure what he'd said to start all this, and what she was trying to say in return.

They'd been arguing from one room to the next, and ended up in the kitchen screaming at one another. What a lovely introduction that must have been for the neighbours. She called him an arsehole, told him he was stupid, and she did it deliberately, because he hated being called stupid. He picked up a cup and threw it against the wall, near where she was standing. Something small hit her below the eye, a sharp razor point of pain. It had been a sliver of the cup—the rest lay in pieces on the floor—and he'd stood breathing hard, surprised, shocked even, as if she'd been the one to throw the cup.

'Fuck,' he said. 'Why'd I do that?'

Maryanne reached up to touch the spot below her eye, and came away with just enough blood to cover her fingertip. He stepped towards her tentatively, as if he expected her to shrink back. They both looked at the blood on her hand. He examined her cheek carefully and shook his head.

'Why'd I do that?' he said again. 'I could have really hurt you.'

'It's okay,' she said.

'It's not. I wasn't thinking.'

He was crying, she realised—suddenly childlike, like when he dreamed.

'It's okay,' she told him again, and she hugged his head to her chest, running her hand through his thick, dark curls.

When he finally straightened and stepped away from her, he picked up a sliver of broken cup still lying on the floor and pressed it deep into his finger until a large, bright drop of blood sprang up around it. He gently touched her face with his other hand, dabbed the fresh drop of blood there, mixed it with the blood on his own finger, then stuck it in his mouth.

'Now we're the same,' he said.

They cleaned up together, and then finished unpacking. For the rest of the night, Roy did exactly what she asked, deferring to her suggestions about what went where in the apartment with quiet affirmations of her expertise. They made love that night, in a fierce, tender, complete way that was nothing like they ever had before, as if they'd each revealed parts of themselves that they'd been holding back, as if now there was nothing left for them to hold back. She didn't call her parents, though.

Later, while she lay with one leg slung across him, her face nuzzled into his neck, he told her about things he'd only hinted at before, the death of his mother when he was so young he could barely remember her, and the barren pathways that led from one part of his childhood to the next. He talked of the bitter, determined way his father had used words and his hands to hack at everyone he should have cared for, and that Roy had learned to forgive him for it, because there'd only been the two of them. These were things he'd never told another human being. She'd walked around with the glow of that night for days afterwards.

Maryanne found herself searching for the scar under her eye now, but her fingertips felt dull and clumsy, and the scar was hard to pinpoint at the best of times. The bottle, sitting there beside her on the concrete floor, was half empty. She hadn't even noticed herself drinking so much. She felt heavy and she closed her eyes. It was very quiet in the basement, but when she had her eyes closed, when she just sat there, swaying a little, she could hear a soft rushing noise, and she wasn't sure if it was inside her head— the sound of her own blood being pushed through her body—or whether it was coming from around her, coming into the room from the walls, or the floor perhaps, which felt cool and damp when she touched it with her hand, even though it was dry.

'How do you know,' one of her friends had asked her once, in an argument about him, 'that anything he says to you is true? Maybe that's why he never trusts you. Untrustworthy people are always the ones who trust others the least.'

They weren't friends anymore.

That noise, that soft, full rushing of life, seemed to grow in her ears, and she imagined herself trapped in this basement, and it was filling, filling with water seeping up through the fine cracks in the concrete, rising around her, full of salt and carrying up all the stains that had accumulated over the years, rising around her so that she would take her next breath and draw it in, make it hers.

The glass slipped from her limp hand and shattered, and as she kicked out her leg to right her balance, she hit the bottle and knocked it over. It rolled away on its side, the remaining wine glugging out of it in red gulps.

9

'What's this?' Dad asked. He'd spent the afternoon smashing out the wall between the kitchen and the dining room with a sledgehammer, and he'd gone upstairs to wash the dust off his face.

'What?' Freya said.

'Look up.'

Freya looked up. On the ceiling of the bathroom, white clumps, twenty or thirty of them. She knew what it was—toilet paper soaked in water, squeezed into shapeless masses that stuck to anything. The boys were always doing it at school.

'It wasn't me,' she said.

Dad's voice was soft. 'There's only one person in this house who would do something like that to a freshly painted ceiling.

But why, Freya? Why, when there is so much to do, why does he make more work?'

A kind of resonant sigh came from deep in his throat. He walked out.

Freya stared up at the ceiling. Dad's feet creaked down the stairs. His voice drifted up, the thrust and jab of his words. She heard her brother reply.

A moment later, Daniel came upstairs. She was still standing there, but he went into his room without looking at her and shut the door. He stayed in there and did not make a sound. She felt angry at him for a moment, her brother. Couldn't he see even ten minutes in front of him? He was like a kid with a box of matches, dry leaves everywhere around him, and all he had to do was sit still, not do anything. How hard was that?

She went to his door and opened it. He was sitting on his bed, one leg crossed over the other, his chin in the splay of one thin hand.

'What did he do?' she asked.

He wiped his eyes. 'Not much.'

'What, though?'

'Nothing,' Daniel said. 'He didn't do anything.'

'What did he say?'

His mouth tugged down at the corners. 'Not to do it again.'

'Then why are you crying?'

Daniel shook his head, looked away. 'I don't know.'

Dad came back up the stairs. She waited for him to come into the room, but his footsteps did not slow as he walked past. She turned to leave.

'Maybe,' Daniel said softly behind her.

'What?'

'He wanted to. He lifted his hand and he looked at me, but then he didn't.'

'Better not do it again,' she said.

Dad was in the bathroom, with a broom, gently knocking each clump of toilet paper from the ceiling. He glanced sideways at Freya as she walked past, his face blank, then he turned his attention back to the ceiling.

~

After school the next day, Freya walked home with Josh. They shared a joint in his room and listened to the whole of *Dark Side of the Moon* again. They lounged sideways on his red chairs, with their feet pointing away from one another, addressing their comments to the ceiling.

'You hear the girl that's singing now?' Josh said. He reached behind his head to offer Freya the joint.

The girl on the record wasn't using words but singing with her whole voice, like it did not need words, like she was shaping something out of her own soul and throwing it into the air. Freya couldn't describe it any other way.

'Yes,' she said, taking the joint from his hand. 'What about her?'

'They brought her into the studio and didn't tell her what to do. They just told her to come up with something, and then they didn't even say if it was good or anything. She only found out she was on the album when she bought a copy.'

'That's crazy.'

'Yeah.'

'I know how she feels, though,' Freya said.

'What do you mean?'

'That middle bit, where she just lets it all out. I want to do that.'

'When?'

'All the time. Or a lot, anyway.'

'Now?'

She pulled back on the joint, slowly exhaled. 'Maybe not now.'

'Why?' he said.

'Just listen to her. That's why.'

'Yeah,' he said.

Their fingers brushed together as she passed him the joint.

'Time drags on here,' she said after a while. 'Not here, but this city. Or maybe it's just in our house. We're all stuck there together, like all we're doing is waiting for something. Sometimes I don't think I can last here.'

'Yeah, right. But what choice do you have?'

Freya didn't have an answer for that.

'Where's your mum live?' she asked, to change the subject.

'Overseas. I don't really know. She left a few years back.'

'Why?'

'She never said. Don't ever mention her around my dad. He's not over it yet.'

'I won't. I'm sorry.'

He laughed softly. 'Don't be sorry. Maybe it's better this way. Who knows.'

'It must suck, though, not having her around.'

'It's fine. Dad felt so guilty about it—when she was gone. He just gave me money, whatever I wanted. He still does. Want to stay for dinner? Dad won't mind.'

She pushed herself to her feet, drew her hair back into a ponytail with an elastic she'd had around her wrist, and gave him a half-smile. 'I'd better get back home, otherwise they'll have a fit.'

'Fair enough,' he said.

Freya walked past the beach before she went home, to clear her head a bit before she had to face Mum, her schoolbag slung over one shoulder. Several men leaned on the balustrades of the concrete promenade with their backs to the sea, bare-chested, tanned. They turned to watch her, one after the other, and she felt suddenly aware of the lightness of her school uniform, how her whole body felt like a stranger's under their gaze, how they weren't worried about being caught looking at her, not like boys close to her age were. She walked past them a little more quickly, hating that she felt like she had to.

She'd be out of this town as soon as she finished high school. Out, out, out. She'd go back to Sydney, stay with Nan. She wanted to squeeze all that time together, shove it into some dark hole, get it over with. She passed the corner store up the road from the beach, and there was a sign on the inside of the window, written in a scrawling, uneven hand. *Help wanted, apply within*. She stood in front of it, regarded her own reflection in the glass, hovering over the sign, then walked in. The old man behind the counter had a walrus moustache wider than his face and cheeks that sagged across his jaw. He was reading a tattered book with a three-headed dog on the cover. A radio crackled behind him, and a song she liked was playing, the one about how good it would be to be in someone else's shoes and wish yourself away.

He looked at her with rheumy eyes. 'What are you after, love?'

'The job. Is it still available?'

He brushed a stray lock of long thin white hair across his skull and put the book down on the counter so that the three-headed dog faced her.

'What job?'

'The one in the window.'

'How old are you?'

'Fourteen.'

'Really? You look about twelve.'

She pointed at the cover of the book. 'That's Cerberus. The guardian of the underworld.'

He nodded. 'Well spotted. It's science fiction. But go far enough into the future, and I guess you'll end up in the past again. Ever worked in a shop?'

'No.'

'It's easy. Even I can do it. Six dollars an hour. Eight on the weekend. Be about two shifts a week. I suppose they're yours if you want them.'

'Okay.'

'What's your name?'

'Freya.'

He extended one hand across the counter. She'd never really shaken a man's hand before. She liked it—as if she were agreeing to something as an adult, rather than just nodding her head in deference to one.

His grip was dry and loose and cool. 'Patrick's my name. Come by tomorrow after school. We'll get you started then.'

~

Mum was home. Freya could always tell as soon as she came in the front door—it was like a presence you stepped into. She went through to the dining room, startlingly bigger now that the back wall was gone. There was a vase full of flowers on the table, their smell filling the room. The petals were fat and fleshy white, stained with red on the inner surfaces.

'Aren't the flowers beautiful?' Mum said, coming out of the kitchen with a stack of plates and cutlery.

'They're beautiful,' Freya told her.

'Smell them.'

Freya leaned down. 'Where'd you get them?'

'Oh, a friend,' Mum said, as she set down the plates and started laying out the cutlery. 'Don't they just brighten the room?'

'They do,' Freya said. 'I've got a job.'

Mum turned, a look of surprise on her face. 'When did you manage that? Where?'

'The corner shop.'

'Are they paying you?'

'That's what a job is, isn't it?'

Before Freya knew what was happening, Mum had drawn her into a hug and was holding her tight, pressing one hand against her hair so that their heads were close together.

'Well, that's good, Freya. That's very good. Your first job. Like that, it just happens. You grow up.'

Mum was still holding her, her breath hot against Freya's ear. She smelled of wine. An empty bottle sat on the windowsill of the kitchen. Freya waited.

Mum let go and walked into the kitchen. 'I'm making spaghetti Bolognese. That's your favourite, isn't it?'

It hadn't been for a long time, but Freya nodded and followed her. 'I can help, if you like.'

'Well, start chopping. Tell me about your day while you're at it.'

Mum handed her a knife. In the quiet, a sound drifted down to them from all the way upstairs—a slow, steady fall of notes from Daniel on his clarinet.

'He loves his new room, doesn't he,' Mum said.

'Yeah,' Freya answered.

'Getting him out—now there's the challenge.'

Freya got the chopping board out and carefully began to chop up the onion.

'Doesn't it make you cry?' Mum asked.

'What?'

'Chopping onions.'

'No.'

'Amazing.'

'Yep.' Freya dropped the onion into the pan. 'I love that smell,' she said, as they began to sizzle. She poured in a bit more olive oil and stirred.

Mum picked up her wineglass from the benchtop, took a good mouthful and stared outside at the dulling sky. Suddenly she lifted a finger to her lips. '"Greensleeves!"' she said. 'That's what he's playing. You just have to speed it up in your head. I love this song. Do you know it was written by Henry the Eighth?'

'Isn't he the guy that cut off all his wives' heads?'

'That's him. I don't think he cut off all of his wives' heads. Just some.' Mum pushed the hair from her face with the back of her hand and grinned sideways at Freya, a sparkle in her eyes. 'Probably the troublemakers, right?'

'I guess this was him in one of his lighter moments.'

'He did keep managing to get married. Must have had something going for him. Those sorts of men always do.'

They both smiled.

'Make sure the onions are browned before you put in the meat,' Mum said, picking up the knife.

Freya kept stirring. Overhead, 'Greensleeves' had started up again, the long, hesitant notes struggling to find one another.

'He's getting better, isn't he,' Mum said.

'Yeah.' She hesitated. 'Mum?'

'What?'

'Do you miss Nan?'

Mum glanced at her. 'Why do you want to know?'

'No reason,' she said.

Mum studied her face, then nodded and began chopping the garlic with short, even strokes, the grip of her hand assured, methodical, staying clear of the blade. 'Of course I do. Maybe I should call her. Maybe it's time for that.' She caught herself with a laugh. 'No. It's not.'

'Why not?'

'It's hard enough as it is keeping things together. The moment you take your eyes off what's happening in front of you'—she slid all the finely chopped garlic onto the side of the knife and dropped it into the pan—'things fall apart.'

'Like what?'

Mum looked at her again. 'Why are we even talking about this?'

'I just wondered, that's all.'

'Keep stirring.' Mum tipped the mincemeat into the pan. 'Freya, we can't rely on Nan to make things better. You understand that, don't you?'

Freya nodded. She looked down, unable to meet Mum's gaze, and couldn't look up again, not for ages.

~

When Dad came home later, he was in a good mood. Freya could tell because he was whistling when he walked in the door.

'I was expecting you home earlier,' Mum said. 'Where have you been?'

Dad was looking at the table. 'Where'd the flowers come from?'

'A girlfriend,' Mum said. 'Aren't they pretty?'

Dad didn't answer at once.

'I've got a surprise,' he said finally. 'Don't come into the living room until I say, okay?'

He glanced at them all, winked, turned and went outside again.

'What do you think it is?' Freya asked.

They heard him come back into the house, his breath labouring as he carried something into the other room.

'It could be anything,' Mum said. Her arms were crossed, slender and pale against the dark fabric of her dress, and she was smiling. 'He gets an idea into his head, doesn't matter what it is, and he just goes with it—you can't stop him.'

'Can I go and look?' Daniel asked.

'No, let him have his fun,' Mum said.

Freya and Daniel sat at the dining table. The smell of the tomato sauce and the dried herbs and garlic made Freya's stomach ache. Daniel said he was hungry. Mum went into the kitchen and came back with garlic bread. She put it on the table, broke it open and they each took a piece.

'This'll bring him out,' she said.

Dad went on shuffling around in the other room.

'I remember this one time,' Mum said, 'when we were just going out. I was still in high school. He'd been working a few years. He said he had a surprise for me. Said he'd only give it to me if I could guess what it was. I didn't guess. He got me a car. He'd restored it at a friend's place. He taught me how to drive, and you wouldn't believe it, but I don't think I've ever seen him that patient, not before and not after—God, he was good.'

Freya tried to imagine that, Dad being patient, him and Mum in a car together with her behind the wheel. She could only imagine them as they were now.

'I was a slow learner,' Mum went on, 'but your dad was a great teacher. My father was furious. I think he was just jealous. They were down on him right from the start. Tried to tell me not to see him, all of that sort of thing—but that just made me want to see him more. Anyway, it was a good car, for as long as it lasted.'

'Okay,' Dad called from the living room. 'Are you ready? Don't come in yet. You still have to guess. Are you listening?'

After a pause, they heard the hissing warmth of a record player, and a female voice began singing in what sounded like French.

Mum put a hand to her chest. 'Oh my goodness. Edith Piaf!'

She went into the living room, and they followed. In a corner, Dad had set up a record player with a large cloth-covered speaker either side. Next to it was a wooden cabinet, full of records.

'My record player.' Mum walked over, began thumbing through the cabinet. 'They're all here. All of my records. I thought you gave them away!'

He was grinning. 'I've been keeping them at an old mate's, waiting for my chance. He brought them down for me today.'

She threw her arms around him, and they kissed.

'I can't believe you managed to keep that to yourself for so long—or that you held on to them in the first place.'

'Come on,' he said. 'I wouldn't throw something away that you cared about.'

'You must have been confident we'd get back together,' she said.

'Confident,' he said after a pause. 'Confident isn't how I'd put it.' He took her face in his hands and kissed her again, on the lips. They began dancing, close together, small, shuffling steps in the space between the couch and the window. Her head rested briefly against his shoulder.

'No regrets,' he said against her neck. 'Isn't that what she's singing?'

They kept dancing until Mum pushed him away with a laugh. 'Let's eat.'

~

They spent that weekend and the next scraping wallpaper off the downstairs walls, and then the layers of old paint underneath. A record was always playing from the other room and Freya had to admit that it did make it feel more like home.

'God,' Mum said. 'I can't wait to start painting.'

'Well, you're going to have to.' Dad was scowling as he ran the heat gun over the walls. The old paint and paper came off in big, curling flakes. Freya swept up the mess and Daniel held the garbage bag, dragging it along until it was so full it bulged.

'That paint's probably been there a hundred years,' Dad said.

Mum flashed Freya a smile. 'Hope it doesn't take us that long to get it off.'

'One day,' Dad said, 'someone will probably be saying the same about our work.'

'I hope that's not for a long time.' Mum leaned across suddenly and kissed Dad.

'What was that for?' Dad said.

'I'm starting to see it.'

'What?'

'The house. It's starting to grow on me.'

'You weren't sure before?'

'I had my doubts.'

He laughed and slapped her on the bottom. 'You certainly kept that to yourself, you deceitful woman.'

'Watch out,' she said, kissing him again.

After dinner, they went to the beach for a swim. Even Mum jumped in. She was a great swimmer. She had an effortless stroke, like she belonged in the water. Only Daniel did not swim. He stayed on the edge of the water near Mum, making shapes in the sand with a piece of driftwood. They were halfway into autumn now, and the days were growing shorter, but the weather was still perfect and the water warmer than the air. Freya noticed the waning of the season more at the end of the day, the sudden coolness as soon as the sun dropped out of the sky. It was already getting dark. They walked home, Daniel and Freya lagging behind, while their parents walked ahead.

10

Maths, a double period jammed into the heart of the day, and the thought of all that time with a textbook in front of her was unbearable. Freya felt nauseous, disoriented, oppressed by the heat, the unseasonable burst of it, how it beat down on the school, filling every corridor and room, weighing down every step. Her armpits were wet with sweat, chafing where she'd shaved and nicked herself with a blunt blade.

Everything seemed especially raw today, grating against her, laughter and shrill voices rising and falling in exchanges that echoed along the corridor, a dying fluorescent light flickering overhead, the jostle of arms and shoulders as she climbed the stairs, someone tugging at her bag, gone when she glanced back, wads of gum fossilised into the weave of the blue carpet under her feet.

Mr Hind had a nose like a triangular sail. Every time he turned, a shadow fell across her book, or that's what she said to Ally to make her laugh. She looked down at the numbers, the formulas, the symbols, and dug her pen into the page of her exercise book. Sine and cos and tan. Made-up words that belonged here and nowhere else. The seamed creases of her blouse rubbed under her armpits. She was aware of the boys behind her, smelled the sweaty sour smell of them, the room dank with it after sport, along with the chemical flower scent of girls' deodorant.

The noise never stopped in Mr Hind's classroom. Some teachers knew how to stop it, had an authority you could respect, give in to, even if you didn't think much of them, but not Mr Hind. After twelve weeks in his class, she liked that Mr Hind didn't do much about the noise, but she despised him for it too. He had a voice that barely carried across a room and didn't pack enough of a punch to make people want to listen.

He was scraping notes on the blackboard. 'Now, write this down,' he murmured. 'And work your way through the questions. You'll need to know them for the upcoming test.' He sat back at his desk and let his gaze drift to the window while the noise rose and fell around him.

'So anyway,' Ally said, 'what do you think of him?'

'Mr Hind?'

Ally made a face. 'Josh, stupid. Are you two going out?'

'We're just friends.'

'Like friends or like *friends*?'

'Friends. We just hang out. I don't really know what I think about him.'

'With all that stuff in his face? Come on. Tell me you're not interested in him.'

'I don't know.'

Ally laughed. 'You know, Freya. You know. Tell me.'

Mr Hind's voice lifted again over the noise. 'Ally, Freya, bring your work up here.'

'But sir, we weren't doing anything. Look at everyone else!'

'Now, Ally.'

They took their books to the front. Someone wolf-whistled behind them. Ally had somehow managed to do some work, and Mr Hind sent her back to her desk with a nod. Then he glanced up at Freya. He took off his glasses. Without them, his eyes looked startlingly naked.

'Well, show us what you've got,' he said.

'Yeah, show him what you've got, Freya,' someone called out.

Half the class burst into laughter.

'Who said that?' Mr Hind put his glasses back on, scanned the room and then glanced up at Freya again.

'Not much to see, sir,' she said.

'Show me the book.'

She put her book down in front of him. The top button of his shirt was undone. She caught sight of the skin between his shoulder and pectoral muscle as he leaned forward. He opened the book and flicked through it until he came to the last page, where she'd drawn a picture of a girl's head with cracks in it. There was a hole in the side of the head, and a bird was visible inside, a piece of eggshell skull falling away from its beak.

'Artistic,' Mr Hind murmured. 'I like the shading. Where's the maths?'

She was aware of everyone looking at her, waiting.

'You tell me,' she said.

Laughter erupted behind her.

Mr Hind's expression didn't change. 'Lunchtime, then.'

When the other students had all gone, Mr Hind sat down

next to her. He smelled of soap and aftershave. He took her calculator, began punching in numbers with quick stabs of his finger. He wrote down SOH-CAH-TOA in her book, and then drew diagrams, small carefully labelled triangles, to explain what SOH meant, and CAH, and TOA, and the whole time he spoke in that gentle, vaguely amused voice. Then he made her do a few examples while he looked on.

'You're getting it,' he said.

'I just don't know what good it'll do me,' she answered.

'It'll make you smarter. You could do this in your sleep if you tried.'

'That wouldn't make me smart. It'd make me good at things.'

Those words were classic Mum, and it was weird to hear them coming out of her own mouth. But she did what Mr Hind asked her to, because it was easier than explaining to him why there was no point to it, and when she did it, and he put his hand on her shoulder for a brief moment, and told her, 'See, you are clever,' she felt good.

He let her out for the second half of lunch. Two boys were walking in front of her, collars up, shirts loose over their surf shorts.

'Hey, Ange,' one of them called to a younger girl coming the other way. 'Where's your sister?'

The girl made a face. 'None of your business.'

'Fucken baldy,' he called back at her. 'Your sister's an ugly stuck-up slut anyway.'

The other boy shoved him. 'Don't pretend you wouldn't fuck her, mate.'

'I'd only finger her. Let her suck my cock, tops, if she begged.'

'As if she'd let you finger her!'

'Who says I haven't already? Smell it?' He waggled his finger under his friend's nose, grinned, glanced back over his shoulder, and caught sight of Freya for the first time, walking behind them. He looked uncertain, then he grinned, elbowed his friend in the ribs, and muttered something under his breath that ended in laughter.

Freya felt herself flush. She wanted to swear at them, tell them they were nothing, tell them they didn't even know what they were, but they were already gone by the time her mind kicked into gear.

~

After school, she had a two-hour shift at the corner store. Patrick was sitting in the back room reading a book. She wasn't really sure why he'd even given her the job. The place wasn't that busy—there didn't seem that much to do—and if he wasn't going anywhere, what was the point? She supposed that maybe he just liked having the company, and the four shifts she'd worked so far meant she had a bit of money, even if she hadn't started saving up yet.

He came out wearing a jacket that hung down halfway to his knees.

'I'm going for a walk,' he told her.

He came back fifteen minutes later, and stood at the counter with his coat on, as if he weren't sure if he had just returned or was about to head out, his hair a white scrawl blown across his shiny scalp.

'The beach looks nice,' he said at last. 'Still good for swimming, but it won't be for long.'

'Yeah.'

'So your mum's a nurse, is she?'

'Yeah.'

'And she works over in the hospital?'

'Yeah.'

'It's a good place.' He sighed. 'I was born in that hospital. I've been there a bit. Had a couple of operations. My tonsils, a kidney. My mum was born there too, and died there. Lung cancer. Not long before she died, she said she could still remember me being born there, and how she held me up to the window to show me the sea. That view was one of the first things I saw, and the last thing she saw.' He shook his head, ran one hand through the wispy lengths of his white hair. 'I reckon all hospitals should be beside the sea. Does your mum like it there?'

'I think so,' Freya said.

'What does your father do again?'

'He builds stuff.'

'Good for him,' Patrick said. 'He's come to the right town. This place always needs builders.'

~

When Freya got home, there was no one else around. She went through her schoolbag and found the latest bundle of tobacco and filters she'd stolen from Dad. She rolled a neat, thin cylinder and went out through Daniel's room to the small balcony that offered a view over the alley behind their house. She leaned gingerly on the railing, put the cigarette to her mouth and brought the lighter to it.

'Hey,' a man's voice called.

The unlit cigarette dropped from her hand to the courtyard below. She was confused for a moment, until their neighbour, Richard, the one Mum was always chatting to, leaned out over the railing of the balcony next door. Richard had a mug in his hand, took a sip, swallowed, looking at her the whole time, a slight smile on his face, like he was happy not to mention the cigarette if she didn't.

'What are you up to?' he said.

'Nothing.'

He gave the beginning of a laugh. 'Kids are always doing nothing these days. I guess that's mainly what I used to do.'

Freya smiled back at him. She was thinking of a way to retreat from the balcony without being rude.

'How's your mother?'

Something in his tone prickled her. 'Still breathing.'

He laughed fully now. 'That's a start. How you liking this place?'

She shrugged.

'That's Newcastle,' he said. 'Ships from all over the world coming and going, and there have been people living here for thousands of years, but it still has a certain smallness to it, don't you think?'

'I guess.'

'It can be a very lonely place if you're different.'

'I'm not different,' she said.

He smiled. 'I am. It only seems like a bad thing when you're a kid. When you grow up, you can turn around and say, *Who gives a shit? I'm different*. At least I know that about myself. You'd be surprised how many people go through their lives not knowing a thing about themselves.'

Someone called to him from inside. A man's voice, intimate and soft. Richard looked over his shoulder into the house, and smiled like he was sharing a joke.

'I'd better go,' he said.

'Maybe I am too,' she said. 'Different. Just a bit, though. Not

116

as much as you, maybe.'

'That's the spirit.' He turned to go back inside, gave her a final glance. 'Say hello to your mum for me.'

'Okay,' she said.

~

The next day she didn't go to school. Instead, she and Josh retreated as the bus approached. They watched the other kids climb aboard and then walked away.

'Let's go shopping,' he said as they cut through the park.

'I don't have any money,' she said. 'I get paid on the weekend.'

He grinned at her. 'Who needs money?'

They wandered around the lower part of the mall, right away from the hospital, near David Jones. The sky was clean and blue and full of light, and the tall buildings protected them from a cold offshore wind. They went into the packed-out pharmacy opposite the department store and Josh, walking ahead of her, showed her how easy it was to pick up a stick of deodorant and drop it into his bag.

'It's all about confidence,' he told her. 'That's the secret to shoplifting. Soon as you make up your mind to do it, you check once, and then you put it in your pocket like you own it. If you believe it, you really believe it, everyone else does too.'

11

There was a knock on the door, a light, playful tap. Maryanne was expecting it to be Freya, home from school, but she opened the door to Richard.

'You got any garlic?' he said.

'I think so,' she said. 'I was about to have a coffee. You want one?'

'Well,' he said, following her inside, 'if you're making it anyway.'

A door slammed above them. Daniel came down the stairs. He reached the bottom step and, with one hand on the balustrade and the other holding a comic, swung out into the hall and landed at the same time on both feet.

'Hey, kiddo,' Richard said. 'That was a pretty good superhero move. How was school?'

'Horrible.'

'Really? Why?'

'Because it's always horrible.'

'That sounds exactly like school to me,' Richard said. 'What comic are you reading?'

'Conan the Barbarian.'

Richard squinted at the cover of the comic—a muscle-bound Conan, seated on a horse half his size, skidding down the face of a mountain with his sword raised above him. 'He looks pretty strong. I bet he's smart too, just like you. I bet he got that strong and smart because he went to school and hated it. What do you think?'

Daniel smiled a little. 'Maybe.'

'He's got holidays now, though,' Maryanne said, 'so it's not all bad.'

'What?' Richard sounded amazed. 'They give you holidays? That's insane. For how long?'

'Two weeks.'

'Lucky you!'

'But then it's thirteen weeks of school again.'

'Is that so? Well, you've made it this far.'

Richard was standing there in front of her son with his hands in his pockets, elbows sticking out, like they were two kids in the playground together. Totally comfortable. Some men were just like that. It made Maryanne think about Roy, and the ease with which he did everything he put his mind to—everything except interacting with his own son.

'Are you all right, Maryanne?' Richard said.

'What? Yes.'

She made the coffees, and they sat out the back at a table Roy had built, beside a pile of wood and other debris from the renovation, while Daniel sat on the ground nearby with his comic open in his lap. She'd been about to bring in the washing. The basket sat beside the table and clothes still hung from the lines that Roy had stretched from one wall to another, but they could wait for now.

'It's true,' Richard said. He'd been telling her about a vast network of mining tunnels that ran under the entire neighbourhood, and under half the city.

'Really?' she said. 'Even under our house?'

'Everywhere,' Richard said. 'This town is built on them. Weird, isn't it—all that coal's gone now, puffed up into smoke and heat and dust more than a hundred years ago, and all that's left is that empty darkness under our feet. There's probably people buried down there too, convict miners buried in collapses. They didn't really know what they were doing, and their lives weren't worth much to the people in charge.'

The front door opened and slammed shut. Maryanne turned as Freya walked outside. 'How was your last day of term?' she asked.

'Just fantastic,' Freya said.

'She's really being a fourteen-year-old at the moment,' Maryanne said to Richard. 'I hope it changes when she hits fifteen.'

Freya dropped her bag on the ground. 'Yeah, she's standing right in front of you, Mum.'

Maryanne turned back to her daughter. 'Do you have to use that tone?'

'I don't know,' her daughter shot back. 'Do I?'

Maryanne looked at Freya, the defiant expression on her face. She wasn't a child anymore, but that didn't necessarily make her anything else, and Maryanne wanted to hug her and slap her and shake her until she understood how difficult it all was, how

120

difficult it would be for her one day. Freya would have her own time to figure that one out, though.

Maryanne forced a smile. 'Richard was telling me that there's tunnels under our house. I think he's making it up.'

'It would have been in the contract,' Richard said. 'Mining subsidence. Every now and again a hole opens up somewhere under someone's house. The thing is, with lots of those tunnels, they've forgotten where they are. There could be one right under here.' He tapped the ground with one foot.

Freya went inside and came back out with a glass of cordial and a biscuit. She pulled a chair out from the table and sat angled slightly away from them, as if she weren't interested in what they had to say. Daniel had rolled up his comic and was using it as a pretend telescope to observe Maryanne and Richard.

'It's hard to imagine,' Maryanne said, flicking her cigarette ash into her empty cup. 'Tunnels under all of these houses.'

'Yeah,' Richard said, 'you just take it for granted that the ground is solid. I'll tell you what, though.' He gave a quick wink in Daniel's direction. 'If you go down to your basement and put your ear against the ground, you might hear the sea.'

Maryanne felt a shudder run through her. She drew back deep on her cigarette and let the smoke soothe her from the inside. 'Now I know you're making things up.'

'Seriously,' he said. 'There are tunnels running under these houses that go out to the ocean. Some of them have been sealed off with concrete, and some have been flooded.'

Daniel lowered his comic telescope. 'How'd the water get into them?'

'That's the sea for you.' Richard tapped the side of his nose. 'In the end, when you're this close to it, the sea gets into everything.'

'Why?'

Richard laughed. 'Because that's what the sea wants.'

From within the house came the sound of the front door opening and closing again.

'That must be Roy,' Maryanne said after a pause. 'He's home early.'

She smiled at Richard. He smiled back. Neither of them spoke. Part of her wanted to tell him to leave, just disappear out the back, but she didn't. Roy's footsteps rolled towards them. Her husband appeared in the doorway and stood there like he had come to the wrong house, or had discovered strangers inside it.

'Richard,' he said.

Richard got to his feet. He almost knocked over his coffee mug but steadied it just in time. 'How are you, Roy?'

'Good.'

Richard put his hands in his pockets and took them out again. 'I was just admiring all the work you've done. The house is really coming along.'

Roy nodded. 'It is.'

He walked over to Maryanne. She stayed in her seat and tilted her face up to him. He rested his hand on her throat, looked into her eyes and kissed her. As he straightened again, he kept his hand at her throat for a second longer, and a flush of heat filled her face. She could see Richard trying to look in any other direction but at the two of them. She resisted the urge to wipe her mouth.

'I love the floors,' Richard said. 'What kind of wood did you use?'

Roy rested his hand on the back of her neck. 'Blue gum. Like the dining table. Want a beer?'

'I'm fine. I'd better be off anyway.'

'I'll walk you to the door.'

'No, no. I'll let myself out.'

They remained in the courtyard, the four of them, listening to the passage of his feet down the corridor and then the door gently closing.

Daniel picked up his comic and began reading again.

Roy had a tight smile on his face. 'How long's he been here?'

'Half an hour. Why?'

Roy lifted the hand from the back of her neck and scratched the dark stubble on his own. 'Just wondering. You didn't say he'd be coming around.'

'He came to borrow something.'

'What?'

'Sugar.'

'He didn't leave with sugar.'

The heat rose again to her cheeks. 'Actually, now I think of it, it was garlic.'

Roy showed his teeth. 'He didn't leave with that either.'

'Well,' she said carefully, 'he must have forgotten. We had a coffee and he forgot.'

Roy rolled himself a cigarette, put it in the corner of his mouth without lighting it and eyed her speculatively. 'Would you have told me he was here if I hadn't come home early?'

'Do I have to tell you everything now?'

'That's not an answer.'

'I probably would have mentioned it, yes. Why not?'

He disappeared into the kitchen and came back out with a beer. He lit the cigarette, pulled back on it and let the smoke spill out through his nostrils, then drank half of the beer in one go, studying her the whole time.

Freya got up and went inside.

'Does he come by often?'

'Roy, he's a neighbour. That's what neighbours do.'

'That's right. They come by to borrow things. What was it, sugar? Or garlic?'

She stood up, began pulling the washing from the line and dropping it into the basket. 'I don't know what you're getting at.'

'I'm just having a bit of fun.'

'You know Richard's not into women, don't you?'

'That's what you told me. I don't remember you ever telling me that he's been dropping by when I'm not around, though.'

'I don't know what to say to that, Roy. Maybe it's just the timing of it.'

'Maybe,' he said.

Daniel, she realised, was gone now too.

'Well,' she said. 'I still have things to do. I've got a pile of things to do before dinner.'

'It's not any different for me,' Roy said. 'Maybe you've noticed that.'

She couldn't keep the edge out of her own voice. 'Yes, Roy, everyone knows how hard you work.'

He was blocking half the doorway, and she brushed past him as she carried the basket inside. Roy remained out in the courtyard, drinking his beer, cigarette in hand, as she folded the laundry on the dining room table. She could see the back of his head.

When Maryanne had finished, she went upstairs to Freya's room. She knocked and then opened the door. She put the washing on Freya's desk and peered out through the window.

'What a view,' she said. 'Have you got used to it yet?'

'It's fine,' Freya answered. She lay on her bed, on her belly, her feet up in the air behind her, hair hanging around her face. She had a book in front of her, but Maryanne could tell she was only pretending to read it.

'That's not what I asked.' Maryanne waited for her daughter

to look up, but Freya kept pretending to read. Maryanne sat down on the bed, stroked her daughter's hair with one hand. 'I want us to be happy.'

Freya finally glanced at her. 'I know that, Mum.'

'If there's something, anything at all, that troubles you, you do know you can talk to me. I never could talk with my mother, but you can with me.'

'I know.'

'Well?'

Her daughter offered a quick smile. 'Thanks, Mum.'

'Okay, then.' She smoothed the front of her dress down with her palms. 'I love you. Have you got any plans for the holidays?'

Freya shrugged. 'You know—friends, stuff. Not really.'

'We'll do some things together too. Go for some walks. We always used to go for walks, you and I—do you remember that?' Maryanne looked down at her daughter, who showed no signs that she'd heard, and then rose to her feet.

'Mum,' Freya said suddenly.

'What?'

Freya turned on one side, looked up at her. 'Are you okay?'

The question was so simple, so quietly put, so unaffected, that Maryanne felt almost unable to answer it. She blinked, smiled against the stiffness in her face. 'Of course I am.'

She closed the door behind her. As she went down the stairs and into the room below Freya's—the one she shared with Roy—the image of Roy's face as he'd stepped out into the courtyard sprang into her thoughts. She pushed it away.

She opened the windows, let the air pour around her, cool on her skin, then turned back to the room. Their bed occupied the largest part of it, the legs of the frame broad and sturdy and dark with varnish. Roy had built it himself. The doona made a high crumpled heap on one side—Roy's side, as if he might still be under there—while the queen-size mattress they'd recently bought was exposed on her side. She could see whitish stains on the fitted sheet. The bedding was well due for a wash. For years Maryanne had made the bed every morning, painstakingly smoothing the sheets and tucking in the corners, but now she was always forgetting.

She wanted a drink, a glass or two of white wine with a few ice cubes in it—that was what she wanted. She reached for the doona and began to pull off the sheets. Most of the best times she'd had with Roy were in bed. Not only because of the sex. The simple need as well, the need to find one another, to know that the other was still there. No relationship looked much different from the next, she supposed, not from the outside. You had to be inside to know it. In the dark of their first room together, when the quiet between them had been uncomplicated, there'd been playfulness, light, and they hadn't had to work for it.

Maryanne had always enjoyed having her feet snug inside the tucked edge of the bed. Roy had liked his feet to be free—he still did. The first thing he would do when he crawled into bed beside her, back when they'd first started living together, was kick out the tucked-in corner of the sheets with a fierce, muscular motion of his body. His feet, he'd tell her grinning, needed air. It didn't matter how cold it was. If her feet brushed his in the middle of the night, he'd complain that they felt like ice, but it wasn't a complaint really, more an affirmation of their difference—the sort of difference that made you happy to have the other person around.

She marvelled sometimes to think of him back then, not that he'd been all that different, but she'd seen him differently, as you did when you were young, when everything was mixed together in a way that thrilled you, and the things that worried you were caught up in everything else, and difficult to recognise or untangle.

Apart from that one fight when they'd moved in, they hadn't fought all that often when it was just the two of them, not at first. Had she gone along with him more, given in when it counted? They'd had more sex—that had probably helped. What she remembered, though, was that they'd play at fighting. He'd kick at the sheets and tell her that he was making a break for it, that a part of him at least would get out of her grip. She'd laugh and poke him between the ribs to make him flinch and tell him that he was never, ever going to get away—they both knew the joke in that. They'd tease each other in the way that you could when the space between you wasn't riddled with wounds.

And he'd been charming—God, he'd been charming. Something boyish about him, something that came out even now, though in rarer moments. A smile, a warmth that made you think of nothing more than perfect sunlight and dazzling potential. It had pushed her on for years, that smile, the promise in it, even as it became more memory than fact.

His hand on her throat, his mouth against her lips, his eyes.

Maryanne paused, the sheets stripped, bundled in her hands. She blinked against the sight of the bed, the naked doona gathered like a wave at one end. Her eyes were wet, and the floor felt as if it were swaying beneath her. At least she still loved him, after all this time. That was more than a lot of people had. If nothing else, there was that—wasn't there?

She lifted the sheets against her face, breathing in their familiar smell to calm herself, to ease the dangerous dizziness in her head. Letting herself think too much when she was in a low mood was dangerous. It was better to let the thought pass without examination. She would feel that intense love for him again—she was sure of it. There'd been glimpses of it already, hadn't there? No matter what happened between them, that love always returned. So come on then, she told the silence, come back.

'What are you doing?' Roy had come into the room behind her.

'Nothing,' she said.

He put his arms around her, pulled her in. 'Well, don't relax too much.'

There was beer on his breath, and underneath that a smell that was distinctly his, wild, musky. The scent of his body, it seemed to her, changed subtly with his moods. She often loved it, but sometimes it repulsed her. She'd never say that to him. Sometimes you lied for the sake of intimacy. Sometimes the intimacy itself was a lie. It had to be, so that you could get to the parts that were real again.

'I won't,' she said.

12

Freya woke up with a dull ache in her belly. She'd been dreaming about Nan again. Don't forget, Nan had been saying. Don't forget. The numbers on the clock did not make sense at first, then she realised it was six in the morning. The holidays were gone, the first week of school was nearly finished too, and it was almost winter, cold enough already to be *called* winter, and she had her period. It was too early to get up, but the pain made her restless, and she didn't want to stay in bed.

Her brother was on the landing outside the bathroom, squatting over Dad's tool bag. Dad was in the shower, getting ready for work. She could hear him whistling.

'What are you doing, Daniel?'

He smiled at her brightly. 'Just looking.'

'You know what'll happen if he finds you looking through his stuff.'

He kept rummaging through the bag. 'You steal cigarettes from him.'

'Just be careful.' She gave him a gentle push. 'Don't do things he tells you not to. It's worse for you when he catches you.'

They went downstairs and sat next to one another at the dining table eating cereal while they watched *Battle of the Planets* and he explained the latest gigantic monster to her even as it exploded and collapsed into the sea. The villain escaped in the middle of the explosion, like he always did, in some hidden spacecraft.

The shower turned off, and Dad's bare, heavy feet padded down the stairs. She glanced up from the television in time to see him walk past the doorway in nothing but a towel. His muscular body was flushed and shiny from the heat of the shower. Only his belly stuck out a little, a grotesque, hairy barrel. Mum was in the kitchen and gave a squeal when Dad hugged her from behind. He said something in a low tone, and she laughed and said, 'Not now.'

After a while, Dad was gone again.

Daniel went upstairs and began playing his clarinet. The doleful tones drifted down the stairs. Freya went to the living room and sat on the couch, legs stretched out on the coffee table in front of her, and watched the television over her own bare, uneven feet.

Mum came into the living room. 'Shouldn't you be getting ready for school?'

'Yeah,' she said, but she didn't get up.

Mum walked out of the room and came back with two Panadol and a glass of water. Freya took the Panadol and drank the water. Mum smiled at her sympathetically, and Freya waited for her to say something comforting, but she didn't.

'Can you pick up Daniel from the bus stop today?' Mum asked.

'Yeah,' Freya said.

Mum rested a hand on her shoulder, then took the glass and walked out of the room.

~

Then it was school, and she had science first, in a stifling lab that stank of gas fumes from the heaters. The gleaming grey paint of the bench she sat at was scored with names and dates scratched into misshapen hearts, the dates long since come and gone, the students too, as old now as Mum, or even older, some of them, and as she sat there listening to Mr Hunter drone on about catalysts, she thought she might well die of old age herself before the lesson was over.

As the day dragged on she wandered from one class to the next, that dull pain in her belly, filling her books with new assignments, more homework.

In maths, Mr Hind wrote his lesson up on the board and then stood at the window for nearly the whole period, staring outside.

In cooking class, they wrote about the theory of proper hygiene in the kitchen.

In history, they talked about a place called Tiananmen Square, how protestors had been on hunger strike there for nearly two weeks, three hundred thousand of them. Troops and tanks were gathering around the city, but the people were refusing to go, and no one seemed to know what do next.

'It'll be like *Les Misérables*,' Josh said to their history teacher, 'only with a happy ending.'

Miss Grey gave him a level stare. 'What do you know about *Les Misérables*?'

'It's a good play, miss. My dad took me to see it in Sydney.'

Miss Grey almost seemed to smile. With her short, finely sculpted hair that closely followed the line of her skull, she was one of those teachers who looked young and old at the same time, like she had never been either. There was often a dry, vaguely contemptuous edge to her voice, but never when she spoke to Josh.

'Can you imagine *Les Misérables* with a happy ending?' she said.

In English, they discussed a novel they were supposed to have read in the holidays, about a young Native American girl who'd been abandoned on an island. The girl had to use all of these skills she already knew to learn how to survive. That was the whole story—her just learning to use what she already knew.

'This is boring,' one of the boys said.

Mrs O'Neill frowned at him. 'That's because you think you know everything already. But that's not the same as knowing it.'

The boy didn't back down. 'Maybe I do, miss. How would you know?'

'You don't know anything, Bill, because you never pay attention.'

He leaned back on his chair. 'Isn't that your fault if I don't, miss?'

Mrs O'Neill nodded. 'Maybe it is, maybe it is. The question is what *you* can do about it, my boy. Will blaming me be enough for you, five years down the track, or ten, when you are nowhere, when you've done things you regret?'

'You'll probably have died of old age by then, won't you, miss?'

Mrs O'Neill was not just their English teacher but also the deputy principal, and she was only good-natured for as long as you didn't cross her.

'Probably,' she said, and jerked her chin towards the open door. 'Now get out.'

~

After school, Freya got off the bus and waited for Daniel. He was the last to emerge from his bus, and barely acknowledged her as they fell into step.

She poked him in the shoulder. 'How was your day?'

'Not good.' Her brother trudged on without looking up, hands jammed under the straps of his bag, pulling it forward, as if he were making his way up a steep incline.

'Why?'

'I lost it.'

'What did you lose?'

He gave her an anguished stare. 'The clarinet. I was supposed to have it for band today. I took it with me, and then I didn't have it.'

'You're joking,' she said. 'How could you lose it?'

'I don't know.'

'Are you sure you took it?'

He bit his lip. 'No,' he said. 'I mean yes. I don't know.'

'You're hopeless, Daniel.' Freya stopped and eyed her brother critically. He stopped too, his head bowed. 'You'd better not have lost it,' she said, 'or Mum's the one who's going to lose it.'

He began crying. 'I don't want to tell Mum.'

She started walking again. 'We won't, if we can get away with it. She's got enough on her plate.'

'Mr Smith told me to bring it tomorrow or not to bother coming at all.'

'Who's that?'

His eyes were large and drowning. 'He's the boss of the band.'

'Who cares about a school band, anyway? You probably just forgot to take it.'

Daniel shook his head. 'But what if I lost it?'

The ache in Freya's belly was wearing at her patience. She just wanted to get home and curl up in bed.

'I'll think of something,' she said.

'Like what?' he said softly.

'I don't know, but I will.'

Daniel hunched deeper into himself. 'I want to stay in the band.'

She hugged him and stroked his head like she'd seen Mum do. 'When you're in high school, you'll look back at primary school and think how small everyone really was. Even the teachers.'

They looked when they got home but couldn't find the clarinet anywhere. Maybe Mum or Dad had moved it without thinking, she said, to calm him down. She promised him she'd look again later, made him some toast with butter and honey mixed together into a paste, the way he liked it, then she parked him on the couch in front of the television and slumped down beside him. *Monkey Magic* was on. Monkey was, as usual, irrepressible.

~

After dinner, they were all in the living room, watching *Sale of the Century*. Mum and Dad were on the couch, Mum in her nurse's uniform, ready to go to work, because she'd been called in early. Dad had a beer in his hand and took swigs of it in between questions. He never really drank that much, just a beer or two at the end of the day.

Tony Barber read out the next question. 'To anticipate what someone else is going to say is—'

'Is to be an impatient prick,' Dad interjected.

'To take the words out of their mouth,' Mum said.

'Ah,' Dad said.

He offered the beer to Mum.

'Not before work,' she said. 'You know that.'

He dropped his hand to her thigh. Mum moved her hand on top of his.

Mum got the next three questions right. Dad didn't come close.

'What specific time of day is sun-up?' Tony Barber asked.

'Dawn,' Dad said quickly. 'I'm a genius too.'

'What kind of creature is an oxpecker?'

'Ask the ox,' Dad said. 'Or maybe the ox's wife.'

'A bird,' Mum said.

Dad laughed. 'Yeah, right.'

But it was.

'It *is* a bird,' Daniel said, smiling at Mum.

Dad scratched his chin. 'Seriously, how'd you know that?'

'My father,' she said.

'He knew a lot of unimportant things, didn't he. Is that a genetic thing?'

'A trait.' She lifted her hand away from his and ran her fingers through her hair. 'A genetic trait. And no. My father was just a smart man.'

The phone began ringing. Dad got up and went into the hall to answer it. He came back in and stood inside the doorway, watching the television.

'Who was it?' Mum asked.

'Hung up,' he said. 'That's the seventh time.'

'Oh. Since when?'

'Since we moved in. Has it happened to you?'

'I can't believe you keep count,' Mum said.

'Seven isn't hard to count to. Has it happened to you?'

'Maybe you answer the phone more than me.'

'Maybe I do.' He showed his teeth, large and white against his stubble-darkened face. 'You don't think it was your boyfriend, do you?'

'Who?'

'You know who.' Dad was leaning against the inside of the doorway, his arms crossed. Even though it was cold, even though it was nearly winter, he was only wearing a T-shirt. 'Next door. Richard. The one you're always talking to. The one who comes over to borrow things and then doesn't borrow them.'

'Why would he call,' Mum said, 'if he can just knock on the door?'

'Because I'm here right now. I don't think he wants to see *me*.'

She shrugged. 'He talks to you too.'

'Not that way.'

'Well—' Mum looked as if she were about to go on, but then she shut her mouth.

'What?' he said.

'Nothing,' she answered.

He looked down at her with an unwavering stare. 'Go on. Say it.'

'You know,' Mum said, 'you can make people uncomfortable, Roy.'

Daniel was fidgeting, looking absently around the room. Freya caught his eye. He gave her a strange smile.

Dad was still glaring at Mum. 'Did *Richard* say that?'

'Of course he didn't. I'm just speaking generally.'

The way Dad stood there, he filled up the whole doorway. 'Now why would I make a man who's talking to my wife uncomfortable?'

Mum gave a short laugh. 'Roy, is that all you do inside your head? Make up these stories? A gay man talking to your wife? What are you so afraid of?' She laughed again.

Dad bristled at that. 'I'm not afraid.'

'Right,' Mum said.

'Don't,' he said.

'What?'

'Use that tone.' His gaze found Daniel. 'What's so funny?'

'I don't know,' Daniel said.

'What's he supposed to have done now then?' Mum asked.

Dad's expression was hard and flat, his eyes narrow, chin jutting. 'He's sitting there with a smirk on his face.'

'He gets nervous and he smiles. You know that.'

'What reason,' Dad said slowly, staring at Daniel, 'would he have to be nervous?'

'Leave him alone,' Mum said. 'You're making *everyone* nervous, just standing there. Can't you see that?'

'Why do I sometimes feel,' Dad said, 'like this whole family is against me?'

'Only you can answer that,' Mum answered. The next round of *Sale of the Century* started. She patted the couch next to her and smiled, but the smile didn't reach her eyes. 'Sit down and relax, for God's sake. I have to go to work soon.'

Dad looked from Mum to the television and back again, then came into the room and sank back down beside her. They all watched the next round together in silence. In the ad break, Daniel disappeared up into his room.

When *Sale of the Century* had finished, Dad got to his feet, surveyed the living room as if he were alone in it, then went without a word down into the basement, and the sound of hammering and sawing came up through the floorboards.

Mum went upstairs and put Daniel to bed.

When she returned, she poked her head into the living room, where Freya was still sitting, watching television. 'Do you want to walk me to work?'

'Yeah,' Freya said.

It was dark outside, and cold. They passed the brothel and Mum shook her head. 'Your father told me all about the hospital, but not the brothel around the corner. That's men for you. They know how to tell a story.' She gave a short, tight laugh. They walked on for a while in silence, only their footsteps sounding between them.

Freya was tempted to tell her about the missing clarinet, but it was Mum who spoke first.

'Do you think he goes there? The brothel?'

The question caught Freya off guard. 'What?'

'Never mind,' Mum said. 'How's school going?'

Freya stared back behind them and then looked at Mum. 'Fine.'

'We've stopped talking, you and I,' Mum said. 'Don't think I haven't noticed. Ever since we came back to your dad.'

'We? Since *we* came back to him?'

Mum looked at her sharply. 'Since I *brought* you back to him. Is that better?'

'What do you think?' Freya said.

'I have no idea.' Mum faltered but then kept walking. 'I really don't. Certainty is something you lose as you get older.'

The hospital came into view across the park. The path was well lit and busy. A couple of nurses huddled on one of the benches near the fountain, talking and laughing in the shadows. The fountain lifted its five pillars of water one after the other to the sky, and one by one they dropped into nothing before it all started again. Spray drifted across the dark sky. Ahead, the North Wing with its turrets loomed over the Norfolk pines, the other sections of the hospital towering around it. Freya could see a few people on the balconies of the Nickson Wing, where Mum worked, looking out to sea, their faces small and blank. An ambulance crawled past up Ocean Road.

'You know,' Mum said, 'if you really understood…'

'What?'

'Forget it. I don't know why I'm always trying to explain things to people.' Mum stared back the way they'd come, back towards the brothel, maybe, the muscles of her neck taut beneath her skin. Every line in her face was subtly altered, as if she were immersed in some silent argument with herself.

Freya had a startling thought. It wasn't Mum she was looking at, not the Mum she knew or had known. But before she could pin the thought down, Mum was moving again, and soon they had reached the end of the park, across the road from the hospital, where the noise from the city and the harbour and the ocean washed together against the brick surfaces.

'Go straight home,' Mum said.

Freya nodded.

'Make sure Daniel's okay tonight,' Mum added. 'Listen out for him. He knows I'm on night shift, but you know how he is— he forgets sometimes. So listen out for him.'

'You've told me that a hundred times, Mum.'

'Yes, I know. I worry, that's all.' Mum took hold of her hand. Freya could feel the bones in her fingers. 'I'm always worrying, about everything. All the time. I wish I didn't. But whatever I do, in the end, it's about you and Daniel. You realise that, don't you?'

Freya nodded again. She felt sorry for Mum all of a sudden, having to deal with Dad, the thought she put into everything, the weight of that thought, all of it written in her face.

Mum crossed the road. Freya turned and began walking home.

'Freya!'

She looked back. Standing at the entrance to the hospital, Mum waved at her and smiled—in encouragement, in consolation, or to apologise for something, she wasn't sure. It took Freya too long to react. An ambulance passed between them, and then Mum was gone.

13

The next day, Mrs O'Neill was sitting at the front of her desk, talking, just talking, about her cigarettes, how she knew they were killing her. She'd just caught a couple of girls smoking in the toilet, the *staff* toilet no less, during class.

'I have to say that I am utterly disgusted,' she said. 'I know, I know. I smoke too. I'm so upset about this that I could use one right now. But I just can't help it. It's how I was brought up, the only example I ever had. God, people thought it was *healthy* when I was young. There's no question of choice for me, but for you girls, if I catch any of you smoking in the toilets, a good smack on the behind will be the least of your worries, believe me.'

'I don't think you're allowed to hit students anymore, miss,' one of the boys behind Freya said.

Mrs O'Neill fixed him with a glare, equal parts mocking and serious. 'Oh, shut up. If I ever hit you, it'll be for a reason. And it'll be good for you.'

There was sniggering somewhere in the back of the classroom, but Mrs O'Neill either ignored it or did not hear, and then it was quiet for a moment, but not really. When the background muffle of noise died down in the room, you just heard it from somewhere else, further away. Mrs O'Neill began writing on the blackboard. A note was being passed across the room from one hand to another, turning over and over in the light. A girl unfolded it, read it carefully, cupped beneath her desk, and then looked over her shoulder at a boy at the back of the room and smiled. He winked at her and tilted on the rear two legs of his chair, hands behind his head, the buttons straining on the front of his blue shirt. When Freya glanced in Josh's direction, he was looking at her. He offered a lopsided grin. She smiled back, and it felt good to do that, like she had a secret from the rest of the world—a good one.

~

And then it was the first day of winter. Instead of going to school, she went with Josh to the pharmacy at the mall. While she approached the front counter and bought a packet of throat lozenges and some batteries and asked a question about a sore throat she didn't have, he found a glass cabinet with a key still in the lock, leaned across the counter, quietly slid aside the door and pulled out a bright red display Walkman that they'd been eyeing off for the last couple of weeks.

He was already gone by the time she walked out. The girl at the front counter gave her a look, but no one stopped her. At the edge of the mall, Josh slid a tape into the Walkman, pressed *play*, gave it to her and gently put the headphones over her ears. She listened to 'Over the Hills and Far Away', by Led Zeppelin.

They took turns listening to songs, walking together in a kind of comfortable silence. The beach was flat and clear, the waves large and perfect. There wasn't a wisp of cloud in the clean winter sky. A westerly wind poured a near-constant sheet of icy air over the buildings at their back. They turned, followed the concrete promenade, so close together that their hands brushed by accident every now and again. It was pleasant, the unexpectedness of it. They ended up on a bench overlooking the sand, the Walkman stowed away in Freya's bag.

A surfer came dripping out of the water, his wetsuit glistening, hair slicked back from his face, and walked up the sand past them with squelching steps. It was only after he'd passed that Freya realised it was Mr Hind. She stared over her shoulder at him as he climbed up the stairs and walked over to the shower.

'Isn't he meant to be at school?' she said.

'Freya, so are we.'

'But he's supposed to set an example.'

'He is. Look at the surf.'

'Do you think he saw us?'

'Trust me,' Josh said, 'he's not going to want the hassle.'

'It's weird, isn't it. Seeing teachers outside of school.'

'Yeah.'

Mr Hind was under the shower now, his wetsuit stripped down to the waist, angling his head against the water.

'Anyway,' Josh murmured. 'Mr Hind is all right. Half the time he's wandering around the school, he's totally stoned.'

'How do you know?'

'Look at his eyes next time you see him.'

'Maybe he's just thinking.'

'You reckon he'd be at school if he was actually *thinking*? No, if a teacher looks like they're thinking, they're probably just stoned.'

She laughed. 'Maybe.'

They watched Mr Hind walk off to the car park, board under his arm.

'You know,' she said, 'I'm glad it's you and me here together.'

'Yeah?' He leaned slightly towards her, made a silly face, puckered his lips.

She pushed him away with a laugh, jumped to her feet and got down onto the sand. That wasn't what she'd meant to say at all. What she'd really wanted was to talk about Mum, the walk with her to the hospital. The dreadful feeling she'd had of not knowing her, of not knowing what lay ahead of them. She laughed again, broke into a run, and waited for him to catch up.

They left the beach and went to a shop on Hunter Street that had a wall full of Doc Martens, and bongs under a counter, and silver jewellery, and she bought a small ring to put through her lower lip.

Later on, back at Josh's place, she sat on his bed while he prepared everything.

'Hold still,' he said.

'Now?'

He drew close to her, pinched her lower lip between his fingers, held it out. She tried not to wince as he pushed the needle in, and then as he threaded the ring through her lip.

'There,' he said.

She looked at herself in the mirror, wiped a spot of blood from her chin. 'That wasn't too bad at all.'

'Nah,' he said. 'Easy. You've got good lips for piercing. Full.'

'Liar.'

'They are. What do you think?'

She studied her face in the mirror. 'I like it. It's like damage or something, but good, like I get to choose it. Mum's going to go psycho about it.'

'Do you want to take it out?'

'No. I hope she does say something. I dare her to. She's already mental anyway.'

'So's my dad,' he said. 'In his own way. It's not his fault.' He leaned in again and carefully dabbed away a drop of blood.

Afterwards, they went up to the cathedral that sat above the city. They wandered among decaying headstones on the side of the hill, the mall and the harbour beneath them, the afternoon winter sunlight beating down.

'What are the things you'll remember,' he asked her, 'when you look back on all of this?'

'What do you mean?'

'When you're old, do you think you'll suddenly just go, yeah, that's what I remember?'

Freya thought about it. 'My dad says he remembers things now that he didn't before. Like bits of being a kid and stuff.'

Something came into Josh's expression. 'I hope I remember more of my mother.'

'Maybe you'll see her again when you least expect it.'

'Maybe.'

They fell silent. Freya traced a mossy outline on a stone with a date beginning 1862. The sound of the mall, and of traffic crawling along below, seemed distant here. Birds were calling to each other, flitting through the foliage of the trees that pressed close together along the slope that ran down from the cathedral.

'Do you think they're still buried under us?' she asked.

'Yeah. That's probably why it's so green up here.' He hesitated. 'If I kissed you right now, we'd totally remember today, no matter what else happened.'

He grabbed for her hand.

She pushed him away with a laugh, pointed at the ring through her lip. 'You stuck a needle through my lip today—that should be enough for now.'

~

They went back to his place again, smoked pot, listened to music and lay on his bed staring up at the ceiling without really seeing it. Then they played Turbo OutRun on the Commodore 64, with its looping soundtrack and its broad road with palm trees and blue water and beach and clear sky and the girl with dark hair sitting in the open car next to the boy as they drove forever across the wide, bright landscape. There was something dreamy and sad about that soundtrack, especially when you were stoned. Their hands touched as they passed the joystick between them.

Next they watched *Pretty in Pink* on the video player upstairs.

'I like it until the end,' Josh said. 'It's always the jerk who gets the girl. All he has to do is *change*. What kind of a name is Blane, anyway? He'll be a jerk again.'

She giggled. 'I know. But then he'll change again, and it'll be awesome.'

There was disappointment in his pot-glazed eyes.

'I'm joking,' she said. 'He's not even real.'

He smiled. 'It's true, though. I see that happen at school all the time. Natural selection. The girls nearly always go for jerks, talk about the jerks, think about the jerks. And then they wonder why boys are such jerks.'

'The nice boys'll have their chance,' she said.

He laughed. 'Only the ones that survive. When they're not being crushed by girls who want to go out with a jerk, they're getting beaten up by the jerks.'

'Well, if that's all it takes to crush them, they're not very strong, are they.'

He looked at her for a moment in silence. 'Maybe.'

'My dad should have been called Blane,' Freya said.

'Really?'

'Nah. He's more of a jerk than Blane—and he doesn't have a decent car.'

'Shame.'

'He changes, though. He changes all the time.' She laughed.

'I should change too,' Josh said.

'Trust me,' she said, pointing at him. 'You're perfect.'

When she got home, Mum was in the hallway, checking herself in the mirror, about to leave for work. She asked Freya about school, and Freya, still mellow, looking at everything from a pleasant distance, said it was fine.

'I've been called in early again,' Mum said, 'so I didn't have time to cook anything for tonight. I've left money on the bench in the kitchen. Go to Hamburger Haven and buy everyone a burger and chips. Don't leave it too late.' She paused. 'What have you done to your face?'

Freya felt herself tense, but she tried to be offhand about it. 'You can see for yourself, can't you? I just got my lip pierced, that's all.'

'Right.' Mum finished buttoning up her shirt and frowned again into the mirror at her own face. 'Well, I look a wreck.'

'You're not going to tell me to get rid of it?'

Mum glanced back at her. 'Do you want me to?'

The front door opened and Dad came into the hallway, several bulging plastic bags full of groceries in his hands. The hall seemed very small all of a sudden with the three of them standing there.

'I'm going to cook,' he announced, then took in Mum, there in her uniform. 'I thought you didn't start until ten tonight.'

'They asked me to come in early.'

He frowned. 'Again? You didn't think you'd check in with me first?'

'We need the money,' she said. 'And they needed someone.'

The plastic bags crinkled in his grip. 'I called. You didn't pick up the phone. Didn't you hear it?'

'Maybe I was in the shower.'

'You should wait. It won't take me that long. Got all the ingredients here.'

'I'm sorry—I have to go.'

'Right,' he said.

Mum hesitated. 'Maybe you can put some aside for me?'

Dad nodded, but his expression didn't change.

'Your daughter's pierced her lip, by the way,' Mum said.

Dad looked at Freya for the first time. 'What, are you turning into some sort of punk now?'

'No,' Freya said.

'It's that kid you're hanging out with, what's his name.'

She stared at him blankly.

'Josh,' Mum said. 'His name is Josh.'

'Well,' Dad glanced at Mum, then back at her. 'I'll leave that one for your mum to sort out. It's not like she was a princess when she was your age.'

He walked off towards the kitchen. Mum stared after him, then opened the front door and looked at Freya. 'I'm not saying I like it, what you've done to your mouth.' She smiled, a teasing

148

glint in her eye that carried also a hint of sadness. 'I'm not saying I *don't* like it either.'

And then she was gone.

~

They ate, Freya and Daniel and Dad, with the television on. Dad had cooked pasta, and a rich tomato sauce with fresh tomatoes and dried basil—he'd even bought cheese.

'Good?' he asked.

Daniel made a noise through his full mouth.

'It's good,' Freya said.

Dad nodded. 'I used to cook this all the time when I was your age, Freya, for my old man. He never appreciated it. Some people are just hardwired not to appreciate things. Doesn't matter what you do.'

For a while they watched the seven o'clock news. The protests were still going on in China. The television cut to images of tanks and soldiers.

'Idiots,' Dad said.

'My teacher thinks there might be another revolution,' Freya said.

Dad snorted.

'What's a revolution?' Daniel asked. He had pasta sauce all down his chin.

'It's when shit falls apart,' Dad said, 'and someone takes advantage. The same people end up in charge—they just have different faces. That's probably all you need to know. See, who needs to go to school?'

'Does that mean I don't have to?' Freya said.

Daniel laughed with his mouth full again, then wiped his face with the back of his arm.

'Of course you do,' Dad said, 'because your mother wants you to. And we always do what your mother wants.'

Apart from that, they ate mostly in silence.

'Right.' Dad stood up and pushed back his chair. 'I'm going out for a while. The two of you can clean up.'

He left the room and went out into the hallway. Daniel and Freya went into the kitchen together and started doing the dishes. Freya washed and Daniel dried. Then the front door slammed shut and Dad was gone.

'The school called about the clarinet,' she said.

Daniel nearly dropped the plate he was drying. 'What did you tell them?'

'I pretended I was Mum, but I'm not sure they believed me. I told them I'd call back. We might have to tell her.'

'We can't.'

'You want Mum finding out before Dad does, don't you? Imagine if he'd picked up the phone instead of me. It'll be okay. She'll sort it.'

'But she'll be mad.'

'She'll find out anyway. And maybe if she does, Dad won't.'

They stared out at the courtyard, lit only by the light spilling out from the kitchen, and finished the dishes. Then they watched television, and Freya made sure that Daniel had a shower. By the time he was lying in bed, and she was lying next to him with a book in her hands, Dad had not yet come home.

~

There was a noise inside the house. It brought her out of a restless sleep. Someone was in her room. No. *Something*. And not in her room—it just sounded like it, because of the shape of the house or something. She guessed that it was a rat. Its claws were scraping along the inside of the walls or the floor or the ceiling in furtive bursts of activity. She stood up and went to the window. The street below was deserted, mournful under the sparse streetlights.

Dad's station wagon stood out the front. He hadn't gone off in it. He was out there, wandering through the neighbourhood. She thought of the brothel, the expression on Mum's face when they'd been walking past. The sky was very clear tonight, the houses sharply outlined. She went back to bed.

She might have been asleep again and dreaming, or lifted briefly towards a waking moment, when she heard the front door open and shut and Dad's footsteps climbing the stairs. He went into his room, just below hers, the room he shared with Mum, and he did not stop pacing up and down for a long time.

14

'I'm beginning to think you enjoy doing this,' Mr Hind said. The noise from the quadrangle carried through the closed windows. It was bright outside, the sun shining over the rooftops, but she could hear the wind and knew it was cold. At least it was warm in the classroom.

'Can I listen to some music?'

'I just want you to get your homework done. Doesn't matter how you do it.'

Freya took out her Walkman and put it on the desk.

Mr Hind looked at it like he knew it had been stolen. 'I'm going to the maths staffroom,' he said. 'I'll be back in twenty minutes. If you've got the first five problems done by the time I'm back, you can go.'

She pressed *play*. The tape kicked in with a soft hiss. 'Mother' by Pink Floyd filled her head.

The bombs were beginning to fall in 'Goodbye Blue Sky' by the time she realised Mr Hind was in the room again. He was standing at the window, staring outside, but when she pressed *stop* and took her headphones off, he turned around.

'What are you listening to?' he asked.

'Pink Floyd.'

'That's a bit old for you, isn't it?'

Freya looked at him with interest. 'Do you know them?'

'Shouldn't you be listening to one of those boy bands? What are they, Milli Willi? The New Boys on the Block?'

'Nineteen eighty-nine,' she said, 'is not a good year for music.'

'I saw them once,' he said. 'Pink Floyd, I mean.'

'You did?'

'What's so strange about that?'

'I didn't think they ever came here.'

'I saw them in England. You think I've been stuck *here* all my life?' He grinned at her and walked to the door. 'Any time you need any help, just let me know. I'll see you later.'

She grabbed her books and shoved them into her bag.

'Will do, sir,' she said.

She stepped out of the maths block, pulled the sleeves of her jumper down over her wrists. To her left, in the shadows thrown by the Moreton Bay figs beneath the science block, she saw a crowd of boys. They were standing in a circle, like a football team in a huddle before a game, so close together that they were shouldering each other for room.

'Cunt, cunt, cunt,' they were chanting.

From the other end of the quadrangle, Mrs Vaughan, the careers teacher, was sauntering in their direction. The circle of boys broke apart. A girl emerged from their midst, her hair and face covered in gobs of spit. The girl walked towards the toilets without looking back, sobbing, wiping her face with the backs of her hands. Mrs Vaughan was walking away again, as if she'd seen too much already.

'Think she broke up with one of them,' Ally said as Freya sat down beside her at their usual bench.

'Should we go in and see if she's all right?'

Ally shrugged. 'Stay out of it, let her get over it by herself. They're animals, those guys from Stockton. They're king shit over there. If you piss off one of them, they all get in on it.'

'Jesus.'

Stockton. Freya could see it from her bedroom, across the broad grey swathe of the harbour. She couldn't see much of it—just a few outlying houses among the Norfolk pines that hid away the rest.

'What's a baldy?' she asked.

'What?'

'I hear the boys say it sometimes.'

'You don't know?' Ally shook her head. 'It means girls that don't have any hair down there. Because they're too young, right? Year 7 girls. Some of the boys like them because you can get them drunk easier, and make them do things they don't want to.'

'That's gross,' Freya said.

Ally shrugged. 'That's how they think.'

~

There was finally something happening in China—they were watching it on the television while they ate dinner. Tear gas rising in plumes. A grainy image of tanks rolling down a main street.

A man carrying a shopping bag standing on a crossing, waving the bags, refusing to move while a column of tanks banked up in front of him.

'Look at that dickhead,' Dad said. 'You don't think they'll put a bullet through his head when this is all done?'

'That's one way of looking at it,' Mum said.

'What other way is there?'

'He believes in something. Isn't it good to believe in something?'

'Right. That'd be something you'd do. You'd be right there, *believing* in something, standing in front of a tank, daring them to roll on over you.'

Mum gave a short shake of her head. 'Can we change the channel?'

'You like to be informed, don't you?'

'I just don't want to hear the news today while we're having dinner.'

'Freya wants to watch it, don't you?' Dad looked at her. 'She's learning about it at school.'

'Well,' Mum said, 'she can watch it later.'

Dad got up and switched off the television.

'So,' he said, as he sat down again, 'Daniel. How's the clarinet going?'

A sensation of dread washed through her. She kept eating, but she didn't taste what she was chewing. Daniel didn't say anything. He gave an anxious smile and nodded his head, as if he didn't trust himself to speak.

'Been practising?'

'Yes.'

'Haven't heard you playing for a while. Seeing as your mother doesn't want to watch television, why don't you give us a concert? Show us what you've learned?'

Daniel picked up his glass of milk, drank long and slow. He put down the glass. 'I don't want to. I feel sick.'

'Leave him alone,' Mum interjected.

'You don't *look* sick,' Dad said, ignoring her.

'What are you doing, Roy?' Mum said.

'I'd like to see what we're getting for our money.'

'Roy.'

'Guess what.' He leaned forward, planting his elbows on the table, and looked only at Daniel. 'I got a call from school today. I just happened to be here to pick up the phone.'

'So?' Mum said.

His eyes cut towards her. 'They said that they spoke to you. Did they speak to you?'

'About what?'

'About him. The clarinet. Do you want to guess what they said?'

'No,' she said. 'I don't know what you're talking about.'

'You're lying.'

Mum shook her head. 'Why would I lie?'

Dad looked at her steadily, and then at Freya, who kept her face still and didn't look away. Eventually he nodded and looked back at Mum. 'They spoke to *someone*, apparently. He's missed his lesson and turned up at band practice without his clarinet, and now he's been kicked out of the band.'

'Why?'

'You going to tell her, Dan?'

Daniel's mouth was quivering.

'He lost the clarinet,' Dad said. 'So much for being musical.'

A look of disappointment crossed Mum's face. 'Oh, Daniel. You didn't. When?'

Daniel shrugged and stared at the table.

Dad snorted. 'He hasn't even been at school for the last few days.'

Mum stared at Dad. 'That's ridiculous. If I don't drop him at the bus stop, Freya does.'

'Tell me, do either of you wait to *see* him get on the bus?' He stared at Freya until she shook her head.

Mum looked confused. 'But I've been picking him up the last few days too,' she said.

'Do you see him actually walking *out* of the school? Have you actually been paying attention at all?'

Mum looked at Daniel. 'Is this true?'

Daniel began crying.

'Do you even know where you lost it?' Dad said.

Daniel swallowed and wiped his face. 'I didn't lose it,' he muttered thickly.

'What then? Where is it?'

Daniel looked down at the table.

'What?' Dad put his hand to his ear. 'Go on, Daniel. Tell us what you did. Show a bit of spine.'

'Roy,' Mum said. 'He's only eight.'

'Old enough to join a band, you seemed to think.'

'That doesn't mean he won't make mistakes,' Mum snapped back.

Dad pointed his fork at Daniel's face. 'I'll tell you what you did, Daniel. You left the clarinet at the bus stop. You got on the bus and you left it there. I know because I saw it when I drove past on my way to work. I should have left it there to really teach you a lesson.'

Mum's voice was quiet. 'When did that happen?'

'More than a week ago. I was waiting for him to mention it, but he didn't. He didn't have the guts to come clean.'

Mum was staring at Dad. 'You just let him stew?'

'He needed to be taught a lesson.'

'Roy, what a horrible thing to do.' Mum's neck was flushed.

'What?' Dad exclaimed. 'I'm the one who's done something wrong now?'

It took Mum a moment to speak. 'Imagine,' she said in a soft, clear voice, 'if I'd let you stew.'

There was a long pause.

'Jesus,' Dad said, 'that again?'

Freya didn't know what they were talking about anymore.

Mum didn't answer, just glared back at him.

'So,' he said. 'When I make a mistake I have to carry it around for the rest of my life and you get to treat me like dirt. But him—that's different.'

'You didn't just *make a mistake*, Roy.'

'The thing is,' Dad went on, 'if you were a bit harder on him, he'd be normal.'

'Stop being such an arsehole, Roy.'

Dad's knife and fork clattered onto his plate. He got to his feet. 'Or what?'

~

Freya woke because she needed to go to the toilet. She felt her way down the stairs, paused at the threshold to the bathroom, and fumbled for the switch. She found it, blinked against the dazzling revelation of light—the smooth white tiles, the restored claw-foot bath, everything polished and clean. There was a smell of paint, of newness, of possibility. But the showerhead, a gleaming new chrome one, was still leaking.

As she left the bathroom, she heard her parents. At first she thought they were still arguing. Their door was closed. She stood near it, listened. Dad said something, then made a low, repetitive series of grunts that sounded frustrated, pained.

'Come on, then,' Mum said suddenly. 'Come on.'

She backed away. For a second, she thought Mum was calling to her. But no. The bed was jolting against the wall.

Later, as she lay in her room, not even feeling drowsy anymore, she thought she heard Mum crying. But then perhaps she wasn't sure, because when she really listened, she heard only the distant hum of night-time work across the harbour and the thump, thump, thump of a helicopter over the city.

When at last she fell asleep, she dreamed that she was with Mum, who was wearing a white dress, her hair pulled back tight from her face. Red lipstick, like she sometimes wore. The two of them were standing on the street, out the front of the brothel.

'I'm waiting for him to come out,' Mum said to her. 'So we can all go home as a family.'

'Where's Daniel?'

Mum turned. Only her eyes held any life, a dark gleam of panic. 'Who?'

~

Mum went with Daniel to school the next day, and by the time she'd come home, everything was sorted. When Mum dug in, nothing could stop her.

'So then,' Dad said over dinner that night. 'Did you use your feminine charms?'

'The man who runs the band is obviously a bully,' she said. 'So I treated him like one.'

'How's that?'

'I told him I wasn't leaving until he apologised. He should have spoken to us directly before kicking Daniel out of the band. Telling an eight-year-old not to bother coming back unless he can find his instrument! He's dealing with children, not army conscripts. I told him to let Daniel back in and to treat him kindly.'

'And did that work, then?'

'Not exactly. I had to keep talking.'

'So what'd you say?'

'I told him you'd come in next.'

He laughed. 'I'm glad I'm useful for something.'

'So am I,' she said.

Their eyes met, and there was a pause, as if each didn't know what the other was going to do. Then they smiled at one another and kept eating.

After dinner, Freya helped Mum clean up, and then Mum lay on the couch for a while, listening to music, while Dad worked upstairs, and Freya sat at the dining room table, doing homework. The television was on. The protests in China had been crushed. No one knew how many people had been killed.

It was bitterly cold, the small bar heaters barely making a difference in the old house with its draughts and high ceilings. Freya was in bed, under the covers, long before Mum went off to work her night shift.

15

The wind was coming straight off the ocean again. Maryanne had never noticed wind as much as she did in this city. Perhaps because she'd never lived so close to the coast, or maybe it was the broader streets, and how quickly the traffic died off once people had gone back to the suburbs at the end of the day. Perhaps—even with the noise of the harbour and the nearness of the hospital—there was just more stillness for the wind to fill, so that you knew it constantly, even in its absence.

She glanced past her own reflection out to the lights of container ships suspended over the cold darkness of the sea, and then back at the ward, one long, open corridor from one end to the other. Her eyes came to rest on the girl in bed number 15.

The girl was seven years old, and came from a family of three children, but Kate, the other nurse on duty, had told Maryanne that the youngest had drowned a year ago, in a backyard pool. Perhaps it was this—the thought of that family, with one loss already, the slightly distant look in the girl's eyes—that had filled Maryanne with an undercurrent of disquiet ever since she'd started her shift.

The girl had had a tonsillectomy, three hours ago now. Her observations were normal, there was nothing Maryanne could point to, nothing at all—and yet.

She returned to the girl, took her wrist in her own hand. 'How are you feeling, Sally?'

'Good.'

'Can you open your mouth for me?'

Sally opened her mouth, showing her small, white teeth. The front two were missing. Maryanne shone her torch across the girl's small pink tongue, checking the cauterised stumps of her tonsils at the back of her throat. They looked purple, a little more inflamed than usual, but there was no blood. Nothing obvious she needed to worry about.

But still—

She had learned, in her time as a nurse, to rely on instinct, always knowing that anything might happen, working away in every direction while drawing on a sort of subconscious perception developed through years of experience. A part of you was honed to know more than the rest of you did, attuned on some subliminal level to trouble and ready to respond.

Trusting it, and trusting yourself, that was the key.

That was what she'd failed to do on the day she'd left for work—a year and a half ago now—when she'd said goodbye to Roy, when they'd lived that other life together in Sydney, on the day he'd made his *mistake*.

He had kissed her goodbye, his lips hard and dry, his eyes unmoving. They'd been fighting the night before. She couldn't even remember why, did not know so much the substance of the exchange that had led into their fight, only its shape, the sudden twist of words that had opened something beneath them, and there they'd been, sliding into it. He hadn't hit her that time, but he'd come close, and maybe it would have been better if he had. Her arm had been bruised where he'd held it. He'd *wanted* to hit her and had somehow pulled back from the edge. They'd gone to sleep without talking and woken up in silence, exchanging only a few scraps of talk in the morning before she had to go. There'd been that look in his eyes as they kissed, empty and dangerous and difficult to pin down all at once.

Daniel had already been awake. He'd been playing with his Lego in the living room. She'd kissed him goodbye while Roy looked on.

At the door, she'd hesitated before leaving. 'Why don't you drop them off at my mother's?'

He shook his head. 'They're my children. I can look after them.'

Maryanne had gone to work, and then the day had taken over. That early morning unease had almost left her until the moment, that terrible moment in the afternoon, when they had phoned her.

~

She was leaning over the bed, holding her breath as she checked Sally's pulse.

'When can I go home?' Sally asked.

'Probably tomorrow.'

'In the morning?'

'Maybe later.'

The girl's face fell a little at that news.

'You know,' Maryanne said, 'I have a son your age. I hope he's asleep right now.'

'I'm not sleepy,' Sally answered, lifting her chin.

'That's okay.' Maryanne winked. 'You're in hospital. You don't have to go to sleep if you don't want to. I won't tell anyone. Let me know if you want something.'

'Ice-cream.' A bargaining look came into the girl's eye. 'And some jelly?'

'I'll see if I can find some.'

She smiled at the girl again and went to the main desk.

'I'm worried about the girl in bed 15,' she said to Kate, who was sitting there doing paperwork. 'Who's covering the ward?'

Kate rolled her eyes. 'Dr Davis.'

'Really?'

'I'm afraid so,' Kate said.

'Right.' Maryanne picked up the phone. 'Best call him then.'

Ten minutes later the resident came shambling in. Dr Davis was a cumbersome, untidy-looking man who couldn't have been much older than she was, with a broad face, ruddy features and small, cold eyes behind thick-rimmed glasses, and a shape to his body that constantly made his shirt pull out of his trousers. There was an ironic edge to his voice whenever he spoke to the nurses, as if he knew something they didn't.

'So who is it then?' he said, as he walked with her to the girl's bed.

'This is Sally,' Maryanne said. 'She had a tonsillectomy today.'

'Hello, Sally,' he said, giving a perfunctory smile and checking the girl's chart. He looked into her mouth with his torch and then nodded.

Maryanne followed him back to the nurses' station.

'She's perfectly okay,' he said.

Maryanne shook her head. 'There's something not right about her.'

Davis looked Maryanne up and down. 'What isn't right about her?'

'It's just…well, something intangible.' She felt stupid trying to explain it, not because she thought it was stupid, but because of the way he was looking at her.

'Intangible,' Dr Davis said.

'Yes. The obs are fine, but there's something not right about her.'

'The obs *are* fine,' he said.

'I know, but I have feeling—'

'You have a *feeling*.'

She held her ground. 'I've been doing this a long time.'

His lips pulled back slightly from his teeth. 'I'm covering three wards tonight, so maybe you should give me a call if the obs change. What's that song? *More* than a feeling? You know that song, don't you?'

Maryanne stared after him as he walked off. Kate was sitting at the station, watching him walk off too.

'What's black,' Kate said, 'and hangs off an arsehole?'

Maryanne looked at her. 'You want me to answer that?'

'A stethoscope,' Kate said. 'It's always a stethoscope.'

~

Maryanne kept taking the obs. In between other patients, in between checking the lines and changing drips, in between administering medication and receiving more patients from the theatre with more badly written instructions from doctors, and comforting the family who sat in the dim light around the grandmother in bed 7 who had died two hours ago. In between keeping an eye on the man recovering from a bowel resection in bed 8 and making sure his saline irrigation wasn't leaking. In between small conversations with the young man in bed 11 who was only now starting to understand that his leg was gone for good. She was always careful with the young men who had lost a limb. They were always the most likely to do something stupid—never let them tell you that women were less rational or more emotional. She would never forget once, back in Sydney, the one who went out to the balcony on his crutches, hobbling on his one leg, and—before anyone one could come close—swung over and vanished to the footpath four storeys below.

But whatever she was doing around the ward, she did not long take her eyes off the girl. She brought her jelly and ice-cream and sponged her upper body, taking in every small detail as she did—its lightness, its fragility, so reminiscent of Daniel, the way her fingers seemed to sink into the meagre flesh of the girl's arms to rest on the thin bones. There was nothing much to point at, but still she found herself waiting, watching.

Maryanne called the resident back in again on the hour.

'Her condition's changed then?' Dr Davis said as he joined her by Sally's bed.

'There's something going on,' she told him.

'She's just had an operation.'

'Look, I'm not an idiot.'

He put his hands up. 'There's no need to get defensive.'

She took a breath, kept her voice level. 'It's not like I'm calling you back because I miss your company.'

Something deflated in him, if only slightly. 'I'll look again.

Because I'm here.' He peered into the little girl's mouth. 'No blood. The ligatures are holding. It's all good. Nothing to worry about.'

She walked after him as he headed towards the exit. 'There's also the colour of her skin. Can't you see that?'

He turned on his heel beside the nurses' station. Kate was pretending to focus on her paperwork, but not putting too much effort into the pretence. Air puffed out of the corners of his mouth. 'There's nothing here that can't wait until morning. I mean, it's getting *late*.'

'I think you need to call the specialist.'

He laughed incredulously. 'Do you ever stop? Even if you think you're not joking, you are.'

He walked off stiffly.

'He's angry now,' Maryanne said. 'But so am I.'

Kate looked at her and smiled. 'He's a real ladies' man.'

'I'm sure he makes someone very happy.' Maryanne picked up the phone and dialled the specialist.

It rang a long time, and then a voice answered, tight, alert. 'Yes?'

She cleared her throat. 'Dr Godfrey? Sorry to call you. This is Maryanne, at surgical. I have a seven-year-old girl here.'

'The girl with the tonsillectomy. What about her?'

'Something's not right with her.'

'Has the resident seen her?'

'Yes.'

'What does he think?'

'He's not sure either.'

'Then why isn't *he* calling me?'

'Okay, he doesn't think you need to come in. But I do.'

'And why do *you* think I need to come in then?'

She told him what she'd told the resident. She waited. It was silent at the other end of the phone. She realised that she was expecting him to laugh or come out with some cutting comment, and she was ready for it, ready to fight, to threaten, to see what she could force through.

'Is there anything else?' he said. 'Anything at all?'

'If it was my child—' She paused. 'You know the history of the family, right?'

'Of course.'

'If it was my child, I'd want the specialist to be here.'

'Let me know if anything changes. I'm only half an hour away.'

'If something happens, I think it'll happen quickly. That's what I think.'

'Okay then,' he said. 'Thanks for calling.'

'I'll document that I called you.'

If he considered that a threat, he didn't let on. 'That's good. You should.'

And then he too was gone. As she jotted down details of the call, a cold, frustrated fury boiled inside her. If she was right, what good would it do, what would it matter to the girl if she *wrote it down*?

Sally was lying on her side. There was a laboured sound to her breath now: a ragged quality to each exhalation. The tub of jelly was untouched on her bedside table, the ice-cream melted beside it. Maryanne sat her upright, leaned her over a pillow to help her breathing, ran a hand along her back. Her skin was clammy. Maryanne could feel her ribs, and the rasping meagreness of each breath.

'I'm going to stay with her,' she told Kate.

It meant Kate would have to take over the rest of the ward,

would have to work twice as hard, but she just nodded. She at least didn't need convincing. They'd worked together enough times now to trust each other.

'Tell the resident to come back up too,' Maryanne said.

'He's not going to like it.'

'Tell him I've talked to the specialist.'

Kate laughed. 'Got it.'

Maryanne sat down, enclosed the girl's small hand in her own, and waited.

~

A brain injury. Her son had suffered a brain injury. That was what they'd told her over the phone that day. There'd been an accident. After the call she'd gone straight from the hospital she worked at to another one nearer to home. They'd been operating on him when she'd arrived, and been in there for an hour already. They'd had to drain away blood from inside Daniel's skull. Roy had been sitting in the waiting area, his face ashen. When he saw her, he began crying.

'The police,' he said. 'They want to talk to you.'

'Why?'

'They think—'

'What?'

He shook his head. His eyes cut up towards her. 'I don't know.'

She was standing over him, staring down. 'Did you do something?'

'God, Maryanne,' he'd said. 'He's my son. *My son.*'

'What happened?'

'Nothing. It was stupid.' He lowered his voice. 'I pushed him. He hit the table.'

'You *pushed* him?'

'I didn't mean to, not that hard, but yeah. It's not what I told the police, though.'

'What? What did you tell them?'

'I said he tripped. You know what the cops are like. You think they'd let it go, if I said I was involved? It was an accident.' He lifted his hands to his face.

'Roy—'

'I just wanted to get his attention. For God's sake, Maryanne, don't look at me like that.' Roy was crying again. 'I know I fucked up. There's nothing you can say to me that I haven't already thought. I fucking *hate* myself.'

She didn't say anything.

'They'll want to talk to you,' he said, wiping his nose with the back of his arm.

'I know.'

'What are you going to tell them?'

Maryanne shook her head. 'I just want Daniel to be okay.'

She sat down beside him, because the seat was there, because she could barely support her own weight. He put his hand on hers, and kept it there, hot and heavy and slack, until she moved it back onto his lap. He reached for it again seconds later.

'Don't,' she told him, in a tone that made a few others in the waiting room look across at them.

'I'm sorry,' he murmured. 'Tell them whatever you want. I deserve it.'

The police didn't talk to her after all, for whatever reason— some other disturbance they'd been called to—but then a doctor asked to speak to her alone.

Roy was waiting near the entrance of the hospital, pacing back and forth, smoking a cigarette.

'What did you tell them?' he asked.

She could have tortured him then, let him sweat on it for a while, let him stew.

'Nothing,' she said. 'I told them nothing.'

His relief hadn't lasted long. She had left him that day for her mother's. Looking back on it now, as she stood in a different hospital, beside another child, there was so much she couldn't understand. Why hadn't she told that doctor everything? It might have ruined Roy's life—that was one thing. And that was something you didn't do lightly to another person. *She* couldn't, anyway. And she had loved him—God, she'd loved him so much. Even when she was angry or scared, some fundamental belief in his potential beat inside her like a second heart, kept hope moving through her, so that everything needing to be nourished somehow received just enough. She had wanted, no, *needed*, to believe that it was an accident, that it would never happen again, that it was an aberration. And, until then, his lapses in judgement had only ever truly hurt *her*.

~

Maryanne looked at her watch. Fifteen minutes had passed and Davis was nowhere in sight. Sally was deteriorating, she was sure of it now—some subtle but essential part of her draining away. The wind outside lifted into sudden gusts, rattling the windows. Maryanne took the obs again. She thought about that boy, the one who had lost a leg and taken a dive off the balcony. The horror of seeing him vanish. The way it had become an image in her mind with no sound.

The girl's pulse rate was increasing. Maryanne lifted her shirt, saw the rapid flutter of her abdomen, the drawing in of the muscles around her ribs and shoulders with each breath.

'Sally?'

The girl swallowed as if she were forcing something down. Maryanne hit the emergency buzzer. She looked into the girl's mouth, saw nothing, was doubting herself, wondering if everything, absolutely everything in the last few months—God, nearly the last year and a half—had been too much for her, had taken hold somehow, distorted her instinct. Was everything these days in her head? Could she not trust her own instincts at all anymore? And then, between the girl's teeth and her inner cheeks and under her tongue, she saw it.

Dr Davis had come up behind her. 'What now?'

'She's started to bleed.'

'Let's have a look.' He tilted back Sally's head and opened her mouth.

Then it came, a kind of gagging moan from deep inside the girl's throat, and the jet of blood, spraying across the doctor's face, his eyes blinking pointlessly behind his glasses, and there was so little time in which something might be done, in which that sudden outflow of life from the fragile body might be stopped.

'Jesus!' he said, and it was clear that he had no idea what to do.

~

In the morning, Sally was gone. The blood was cleaned up. The bed sat empty, stripped of sheets. Maryanne started to walk home, but she stopped in the park. She sank down on the grass by the fountain and lit a cigarette.

The water rose and fell in front of her, spray drifting on the light breeze that feathered across her skin. The sun was rising. She drew the smoke in, felt its pleasant, numbing effect on her lungs, let her eyes close just a little and concentrated on the sunlight against the side of her face. It was all before her—those terrifying seconds as the blood had poured from the girl's mouth in that torrent, Dr Davis's stupefied, helpless expression, and the footsteps behind her.

Dr Godfrey, the specialist, was in his fifties, but he had moved like a much younger man. He'd shouldered the resident aside, picked up the girl, and gone running down the ward, shouting orders as he went.

Later, he had found Maryanne. He'd left for the hospital straight after her phone call.

'It was something in your voice,' he said. 'I've been around long enough to take notice of it.'

She'd laughed. 'I can be pushy, I know.'

Adrian Godfrey was a handsome man, fine-featured, unassuming, a melancholy look to his grey eyes that she found attractive. 'Thank God you are,' he said. 'You're the reason she's still alive.'

When she'd finished her cigarette, Maryanne got up and walked the rest of the way home. She opened the door to the house and stepped inside. It was Saturday morning. Everyone was home. Roy was home. She could hear him clomping around upstairs. There was a song playing softly, the Beatles—'Lucy in the Sky with Diamonds'—and she guessed that he had put the album on knowing she would be home soon. He was like that sometimes. In the hallway, with the door still open, the light outside, the shadow of the house around her, she considered him for a moment longer. The house seemed so peaceful now, most of the work already done. It was home.

But still—

She closed the door and took off her shoes, the floorboards

cool and solid beneath her bare feet. Her son was in the living room, on the couch, reading a comic. He glanced up at her with a quick smile and kept reading. Sitting on the armrest of the couch beside him, she kissed the top of his head, ran her hand through his soft, light brown hair, and felt the scar there. It had healed well, but it would always be there. She watched the slow rise and fall of his chest and let herself feel the joy of seeing it, the joy and only that.

'What?' he said.

'I'm just looking at you,' she answered.

16

The Walkman, four bottles of perfume, some deodorant, five packs of razors, a bunch of magazines and a belt—that was the tally so far in the month or so since Freya had started shoplifting with Josh. Every couple of weeks they took a day off, wandering the mall to steal things for the thrill of it, and then to the beach, the hills and cliffs that climbed over the inner city and the windswept winter coast, just the two of them.

'My report's going to be a shocker,' she told Josh.

He laughed. 'Yours and mine both.'

They always gave it a few weeks before they returned to a particular shop, always acted like the things they were taking belonged to them, like they had nothing to hide. That was what you did, what everyone did—you hid things by showing you had nothing to hide. Sometimes they went in together, and sometimes they took turns, waiting outside the shop for the other to emerge.

Her knees would tremble beforehand, anxiety building to a thrum of doubt in her gut, but once they got away with it, she'd feel a rush of elation, of release, of power, of confidence. They'd end up at Josh's house with whatever they'd stolen, reading magazines they'd shoved under their shirts at the newsagent, getting stoned, playing his Commodore 64, listening to music, feeling like they had something over the world.

She always checked the mail when she came home, caught the absentee letters from school before anyone else did, faked Mum's signature and took them back. She supposed that they would catch on eventually, but she didn't care.

~

Dad was around more than usual, filling the house with his work and his mess and his moods, and his sudden bouts of swearing.

'Seventeen percent,' he was saying from the kitchen. He was standing in his singlet and shorts in front of the open fridge. 'They reckon interest rates can't go up again, but that's what they said when they hit sixteen percent too. We're not paying anything off at this rate. Just getting deeper into debt.'

Freya and Daniel sat at the table in the dining room, eating their cereal, with the cartoons on in the background—Astro Boy, a robot with big doughy eyes, blowing up other robots with a machine gun in his arse.

Dad poured some milk into his coffee, then took a swig out of the bottle. 'Of course it has to happen when the work dries up.'

Mum was standing near him, buttoning up her work uniform. 'I thought they promised you a full year. Wasn't that the whole reason we came here, because you had that sorted?'

'They did,' he answered. He rubbed his temple, leaving a grimy smudge on his face. 'I *did* have it sorted.'

Daniel was knocking his feet lightly against the rung of his chair, a muffled, agitated noise that carried over the sound of the television. Roy glanced in his direction, a vague irritation in his expression.

'Did you misunderstand them?' Mum said.

'What, am I an idiot?' There was a sneer in his voice. 'Of course I didn't *misunderstand* them. Something's fallen through. They explained it to me, but it didn't make any sense. It's changed, that's all. Some weeks it'll still be every day. Some weeks it'll be nothing.'

Mum shrugged. 'Well, we just have to do what we can. We can't throw our hands up in despair every time something goes wrong. Hopefully you'll find more work soon.'

He closed the fridge and scowled at her, arms folded across his chest.

'What?' Mum said.

Freya walked between them. She rinsed her bowl, put it on the rack and passed between them again on her way out of the room.

'You know what,' Dad said.

He shook his head, finished rolling a cigarette, brought it to his mouth and pulled a lighter from his pocket.

'What are you doing?' Mum said as he brought the lighter to the cigarette.

Dad looked at her over the flame.

'Right,' he said. 'I'll go outside. Because that's what *I'm* doing for *you*.'

Freya picked up her bag and left the room. 'I'm going to school,' she shouted down the hallway.

Mum walked out after her. 'Here—your lunch.'

Freya took it, but Mum didn't let go.

'Do I get a kiss?'

She kissed Mum on the cheek.

'That's better. Can you pick up your brother from the bus stop today?'

'Sure,' she said.

Mum put a hand against her cheek. 'I love you,' she said softly.

'I know.' Freya went outside.

She didn't look back as she walked off, didn't hear Mum close the front door, and she didn't go to school.

~

Instead, Freya wandered around Newcastle East with Josh and up to Fort Scratchley. It wasn't much of a fort, just a series of abandoned bunkers on a grassy bluff that looked towards the mouth of the harbour on one side and the ocean baths on the other. Two cannons in concrete gun emplacements pointed straight out over the ocean—for what?

'It was the Japanese,' Josh said. 'Back in World War II.'

'They attacked here?'

'Yeah, and the cannons fired back at them.'

'At what?'

Josh peered out over the ocean as if he might see it. 'I think it was a submarine. No one hit anything.'

They followed the road that ran down the coast alongside the beach and past the hospital, then made their way up through the park that rose in terraced layers above the sea and into the high, saltbush-covered cliffs beyond. There was a complex of tunnels beneath the cliffs, Josh said, some of them to do with coal mining, some with the war. He led her down a narrow, dipping path that skirted a sheer drop to the ocean below and ended at an opening carved straight into the cliff face. The concrete facade around the entrance was scrawled with graffiti, the mouth of the tunnel strewn with rubbish. They stood among the beer bottles, the shattered glass and food wrappers, the black maw of the tunnel to one side and the ocean filling the horizon on the other.

'I always used to be afraid of the dark,' Josh said. 'One day I just got sick of it, got sick of being scared, and I made myself go down this tunnel. I went to the end of it with a torch, and then I turned the torch off and just stood there.'

'What's it lead to?'

'I'll show you.' He took her hand and pulled her with him, so that they stepped across the threshold together.

'Are you scared of the dark now?' she asked.

'Now I like it,' he said. 'You?'

'No,' she said. 'Maybe sometimes. But...'

'What?'

'It's not the dark we're scared of, right? It's not knowing what's in it.'

'I guess so.' He lit a match. Broken glass crunched under their feet. The smell of piss mixed with the odour of the saltbush and wet earth. They walked down a long, straight length of concrete tunnel, then turned a sharp corner into a closer darkness.

The tunnel ended after another twenty metres or so in rubble, as if there'd been a collapse. The light of the match in Josh's hand spilled across the jagged edges of bricks and broken stonework.

'Blocked off,' he said.

He dropped the match as the flame approached his fingers, and they stood in blackness until he lit another. There was a joint in his mouth, his lips tight around it, arches of shadow dancing over his eyes.

'If you had to die,' he said, handing it to her, 'what'd be the way you'd choose?'

She pulled the smoke deep into her lungs, held it there until it hurt, let it drift out around her. 'I don't know. What about you?'

'Buried alive,' he said.

'Really?'

He smiled. 'Nah. Jumping, maybe. A joy flight before the end. Don't you reckon?'

'Maybe,' she said. 'I wonder what they're doing at school right now.'

'Nothing that matters,' Josh said.

'I know,' she said. 'They could fit it all into a year or two if they wanted to. Most of it's just wasting time.'

'Think of all the dickheads who'd be out of jobs then.'

They laughed together and the joint went out and they were in the darkness and then they fell silent. She wanted to see his face, but all she had of him was the sound of his breath, the warmth of his nearness. They walked back outside and stood blinking on the concrete bulwark of the bunker, foamy white breakers washing against the glistening rocks a long drop past their feet, the ponderous shadows of clouds darkening patches of the sea. She lifted her gaze towards the horizon. There was a part of her that wanted to keep walking straight out, if only for an instant, until gravity caught up.

~

On her way home, she waited for Daniel at the bus stop. She didn't let on that she hadn't gone to school herself. When they got home, the phone was ringing. She stared at the receiver, rattling in its cradle, and let it ring a while longer, but it didn't stop.

She picked it up. 'Hello?'

There was no reply.

'Hello?'

The line crackled and hissed, and a woman at the other end cleared her throat.

'Maryanne?'

'No, I'm her daughter.'

'I'm after your mother, dear.'

'She's not here.'

'Do you know where she is?'

'She's at work.'

'Can you get a message to her?'

'Yes.'

'I'm calling about your grandmother, dear. She's in hospital. She's had a heart attack.'

Freya wrote the details on a scrap of paper with a shaky hand and put the phone down. Daniel was looking at her.

'Come on,' she said. 'We have to go.'

'Why?'

'It's Nan. She's sick. We have to tell Mum.'

~

They stood in the shadow of the hospital, the afternoon sun lost somewhere behind it. The hospital was huge when you were up close, and there were so many different parts to it, balconies and windows and doors and stairways from every angle, like a bunch of mazes thrown into a pile. Somewhere inside all of that, Mum worked.

'This is the right part,' Freya said. 'I think.'

Daniel tilted his head, looked up at her. 'Don't you know?'

She gave her brother an irritated look. 'I haven't been here any more than you.'

'But you're older than me,' he said. 'You should notice more.'

'You're going to have to start noticing things too, you know,' she told him.

He stared up at her blankly.

'Okay,' he said.

They went inside.

'Can I help you?' one of the receptionists asked.

'I'm looking for my mum.'

'Is she a patient?'

'She works here.'

'Which ward, dear?'

'She looks after people who've had operations.'

'That'll be surgical. That way, two floors up.'

They walked together down the corridor and into a lift with metal doors. They got out on the second floor and turned a corner. Freya saw Mum down the corridor. She stopped and made Daniel stop too. Mum, her light brown hair pulled back into a tight ponytail, was talking to a man with tanned skin and short white hair, all neatly dressed in pants and a shirt and a tie. He said something, and Mum threw back her head and laughed. The light from a window gleamed on her neck.

Freya hesitated.

'What?' Daniel said.

Freya didn't look at her brother but kept her hand on his shoulder. There was something about Mum, her posture, her voice, that same strangeness from before, when they'd walked together to her work. Like she was wearing a disguise—not now, but when she was home. Mum looked unburdened, younger, stronger. She laughed again, gave a quick nod of her head, touched the man's arm. Then she glanced down the corridor towards them and froze.

Freya started walking.

17

The dog was barking again. Its noise was more agitated than ever, as if it knew Maryanne was sitting in her courtyard and wanted to get at her. That mad, stupid, tireless dog. Did the owners not hear it too? Did they not wonder why the hell they were keeping it?

'So—' Richard shifted in his seat, crossed one leg over the other. 'Is your mother okay then?'

Maryanne shrugged. 'Pretty much. I called the hospital, and they said it was relatively minor. She was very lucky that they got to her as quickly as they did. It sounds like she'll make a full recovery.'

'I didn't think heart attacks were ever minor.'

'Well, some are more minor than others, I guess. She'll live.'

'Did you talk to her?'

'Why?'

'To see how she was.'

'What'd be the point?' She smiled. 'My mother could be at death's door and she'd say she was doing okay.'

'Pretty much like you then?'

Maryanne lit a new cigarette, took a drag and narrowed her eyes. 'Don't tell me that I'm like my mother, Richard. It's too early in the morning.'

'It's two in the afternoon, Maryanne.'

'Still too early, Richard.'

They drank their coffees and smoked in silence.

'So are you going to talk to her?' Richard asked at last.

'I don't know.'

'She'll always be your mother.'

Maryanne made a face. 'Now *you're* starting to sound like her.'

'From everything you tell me about her, I like her. It sounds like she loves you. That's more than I can say for my mother.'

'I know, I know. But...'

'You love her, don't you?'

'Richard, you don't know what she's like. She never admits a single mistake, and she's always there, judging me.'

'But she'd drop everything if you asked her to.'

Maryanne shook her head. 'Whenever I ask my mother for help, she makes me pay for it.'

Richard studied her with an air of bemusement. 'In what way?'

She tried to think of how she might sum it up for him, the subtle and not so subtle things her mother said, the pressure she exerted, the way every conversation was loaded with allusions to Maryanne's past failures—the drip, drip, drip of her commentary. 'It's hard to explain,' she said.

'You need friends, more than just me, and you need your mother. You need to know you can pick up the phone. You've got an excuse to contact her now. Just don't tell Roy.'

'Oh, but you know…'

'What?'

'Roy thinks that we should always be completely honest with one another.'

'Like he was about Daniel's clarinet?'

'He was making a point.'

'He was being a psychopath. I think that's what you call it.'

She flicked the ash off her cigarette and sighed. 'I guess he was a bit.'

'Maryanne, are you actually honest with Roy all the time?'

'I try to be honest where I can. It sounds stupid when I explain it.'

'Maybe because it *is* stupid.'

'You must be sick of hearing all of this.'

He winked at her. 'This is the best entertainment I get all week.'

'Well, at least there's that,' she said dryly.

'Just call your mother, Maryanne.'

'If I'm going to call my mother when I promised Roy I wouldn't, I might as well go off and sleep with another man. He'd probably prefer that, actually, if he could choose.'

He grinned. 'Why not do both? And when you're finished with the man, send him my way.'

'Right.' She laughed again. 'Roy's due home soon. You'd better be out of here. Maybe out the back way is better.'

He stood up. 'Yes, we really need a secret passageway between our houses.'

'I'll ask Roy to put one in.'

'It's always worth asking,' Richard said.

They went to the gate, and she unlocked it, setting off another angry round of barking down the lane.

'Do you think you could kill that dog for me?' she said.

'Have you asked Roy?'

'Oh, he'd do it in a heartbeat,' she said.

Richard watched her.

'That was a joke,' she said.

He hesitated. 'I worry about you.'

'Well, you don't have to.'

As she faced him, her hand on the gate, she suddenly remembered Roy, the day he'd come to her at her mother's house almost a year ago now, the way he had been there at the threshold, all of him bunched together, as if he were waiting to be invited in, not into the house, but into her whole life. What would he have done, if she'd refused him?

Richard tried again. 'Are you sure you're okay?'

She hadn't even told him what had really happened to Daniel back in Sydney. She'd never admitted that to anyone, not even her mother, though she was fairly sure her mother had guessed. As for Daniel, he acted as if it had never happened, as if he couldn't remember it at all.

'I probably make it sound worse than it is,' she said. 'I know how to handle Roy. We wouldn't have made it all this time without me knowing how to handle him. And not just that—I love him.'

'Do you really?'

'Get out of here, Richard.'

'Call your mother,' he said, and then he was gone.

Maryanne stood alone in the courtyard and smoked another cigarette. The dog, the dog, oh that bloody fucking dog. She took their coffee cups back inside, washed them, dried them and carefully put them in the cupboard, side by side. Then she looked at them again, took one out and put it in the sink. She went through the bottom of the house after that, dusting the furniture, and she came to a halt at the phone, sitting on its small, wooden table in the filtered light of the hallway. She walked away from it, and then turned and walked back.

The receiver was in her hand. She dialled.

Her mother answered almost immediately. 'Alice speaking.'

Maryanne thought about hanging up. Her fingers tightened around the receiver and she took a sudden, deep breath. 'Are you okay, Mum?' she said, and just saying those words set something in motion—or perhaps the motion had long since begun.

'Maryanne,' her mother said. 'I've been better. And you?'

18

Freya was sitting at the dining table, books spread out in front of her, staring at them without seeing them, when she heard Dad's footsteps. He went into the kitchen and poured himself a glass of water. He gulped it down and then turned, leaning back against the sink to watch her.

'What are you doing?' he asked.

'Homework,' she said.

He gave her a teasing look. 'You do homework now?'

Freya smiled back. 'Sometimes.'

'What is it?'

She frowned. 'Maths.'

She hadn't started yet, the pen loose in her hand. She'd been thinking of Nan, wondering about her, hoping she was okay.

She'd tried calling her last week, from the phone booth near the beach, but she'd only reached the answering machine.

Dad walked across and peered over her shoulder. 'Ah!' he said. He sat down beside her, slid the book away from her so that he could look at it. 'Algebra. It's not that hard. I'll show you.'

He took her biro and began writing. He smelled of sweat and tobacco and cut wood. He'd been working down in the basement, the dull whine of an electric saw alternating with hammering. Now he began explaining the first problem to her. His thick fingers, ingrained with paint and dirt, seemed too large for a pen, and he held it at an awkward angle, but he wrote neat, square numbers and did not slow down, explaining what he was doing all the while, his words rising barely above his own breath, as if he were telling only himself.

'Do you get it?' he said at the end.

'Not really.'

The phone began ringing. They both turned towards the sound. Dad got to his feet and pointed one finger down at the open book.

'That's how you do it. Look carefully. You just have to be methodical.' He went into the hallway and picked up the phone.

'Hello?' A floorboard creaked as Dad shifted his weight. Somewhere over the harbour, a ship's horn lifted and fell five times.

'Who is this?' Dad said into the phone. All the volume of his voice compressed into something heavy and low and dense. 'Just fucking *talk*, whoever you are, or I will fucking—'

There was silence. The receiver clattered back into the cradle.

Freya closed her book just as Dad returned. He cast a lingering glance back into the hallway, as if there were someone waiting for him there. Something twisted across his face, a kind of shuddering glimpse of emotion that he quickly pushed away.

'They hung up,' he said.

She didn't say anything.

'Do you know where your mother is?' he asked.

'Isn't she at work?'

Dad took a deep breath without opening his mouth. 'She should be home.' He thrust his hands into the pockets of his shorts, took another breath, then curled his lip up into a smile. 'I'll run you through it again. If there's one thing I can help you with, it's maths.'

Freya was on her feet already, her books gathered in her arms, and stepped past him to the stairs. 'It's fine, Dad. That's why they have teachers at school, right?'

She went up to her room, put the books on her desk and closed the door. She sat on her bed and painted her nails. When she came down to phone Ally half an hour later, Dad was sitting at the table, his large hands resting flat on the surface, eyes fixed on some point beyond the wall, like he was awake but dreaming.

~

And then holidays, two weeks that would take them from the dregs of winter into spring and the last thirteen weeks of school before the yawning expanse of summer. Freya worked a bit more at the corner store, enjoyed sitting there at the counter watching the sun move in and out of the front window while Patrick pottered around somewhere else or sat in the back reading a book. It wasn't that busy.

During a particularly quiet spell one afternoon, he asked her to make him a coffee, and she accidentally dropped a cup. Shards of cup and instant coffee exploded across the floor. She found herself on the verge of crying as she swept it up.

Patrick watched her from behind the counter. 'You all right?'

She didn't meet his eyes. 'Yeah. Just stuff. Life, you know.'

'Don't worry about it,' he said. 'Whatever it is, it hasn't happened yet or it's already gone. Like that cup.'

She paused, glanced at him. 'Do you ever worry about *anything*?'

Patrick shrugged. 'There's no point. You know that thing where some old fellas tell you they still feel the same on the inside as they did when they were young? Not me.' He patted his belly with both hands. 'This is me now.'

'What—old?'

'Not old. No, love, that's not what I mean.' He chuckled. 'I'm worn, maybe. My mind's fraying a bit at the edges, but that's to be expected. It's more that I don't get so worked up over things. I don't have the same passions I used to. Or they don't hit me so hard. I remember being a kid and hearing a song for the first time—and you usually *heard* them first back then, you didn't have all these televisions—and feeling like I was the only one hearing it. The song was coming straight down the line only to *me*. Now I just listen and I know everyone else is listening too, and that it's just a song and it's different and the same for everyone.'

He watched as she tipped the broken pieces and coffee into the bin. He boiled the kettle, poured two new cups, put in a couple of sugars and half milk in one, and handed it to her. They both stood behind the counter, drinking their coffees, their attention fixed on the street outside with its blue edge of water.

'It's not bad, you know,' he said.

'The coffee?'

'No, not the coffee—I mean getting used to how life works. Realising that a lot of the feelings you have aren't as big as they seem. They matter, but they're not important in the way you think they are. You can't get the exact same ones back and you can't hold on to them. You can really only tell what matters when you look back.'

She regarded him dubiously. 'So I won't be able to tell which of my feelings are important until I'm old?'

'Sort of.' He shrugged. 'It's like driving down some winding country road at night and all you can see is what's in your own headlights, right up close. And because that's all you can see, you focus on it like it's the only thing in the world. But it isn't. Do you follow me?'

Freya shrugged. 'Maybe.'

'Enjoy what's in front of you, Freya, but try not to get too caught up in it.' He leaned forward on the counter, rested his elbows on the glass. 'I wish someone had told me that when I was your age.' He sighed. 'The coffee's not bad, though. Enjoy the little things. Enjoy everything.'

'I'll try,' she said.

~

School started again, and the days were getting longer, especially at school. They were into the second month of spring, and they were studying *Julius Caesar* now in English. Freya had missed a few of the classes, but she'd skim-read the play at home. Mrs O'Neill was talking about Caesar's death, the mystery of it. 'Now, I've had a thought—Caesar, he gets all of these warnings, but he still goes down to the forum alone. Why? Write this down. Caesar dies because he can't stop being Caesar. Discuss.'

At lunchtime Freya snuck out of school with Josh. They headed for the mall. They didn't know what to steal, so they settled on some magazines from the newsagent and a couple of bags of lollies.

~

And then it was the first Friday night of October, and she was standing on a stranger's balcony, and the harbour glittered under distant, illuminated columns of industrial smoke, and she was thinking, yes, she would enjoy all of this, why not? Even if none of it would last. A tug slid past the gap between two buildings down on the mall. And up above it all, on the other side of this insanely tilted street, other houses faced this one—this house abandoned by its owners and left to a bunch of teenagers—with blank stares.

Only a dense green garden overgrown with vines separated the house from the next one down on the hill. There was a boy under the balcony on all fours, his moaning rising above the sound of 'Sweet Child o' Mine' as he vomited into the vines. Another boy was talking to him in reassuring tones over one shoulder while he pissed against a tree.

'Look at him,' Ally said, disgusted. 'It's only a matter of time before someone calls the cops now. Or maybe they already have.'

They went back inside. Someone had thrown up in the bathroom too—there was vomit on the wall over the toilet. They descended a steep wooden staircase. Freya pushed past people in the darkness, shared the last of a bottle of Passion Pop with Ally, took a swig from someone's vodka, and then a police car did pull up on the street outside the open front door, its blue and red lights flashing silently along the hallway.

Josh appeared in front of her. 'I'll walk you home,' he said.

'She's fine,' Ally told him. "She can get a lift home with my dad.'

'No,' Freya said. 'I want to walk.'

She said goodbye before Ally could say anything else, and then she was walking with Josh through the backyard. They climbed over the neighbours' fence and followed the street up into the quiet of the rich neighbourhood around the cathedral.

She felt like she could breathe again. It was a windless night, warm for spring. The noise of the mall and the city below them grew fainter, their footsteps suddenly loud. They talked in fits and starts until they reached a sandstone bluff crowned with grass and palm trees, and—higher than anything else and with spotlights trained along its length—the huge white obelisk she had seen for the first time, months ago now, from Ally's house. They sat at its foot and shared a joint.

'Look at it all,' he said. 'You can see everything from here, without being part of it.'

'Best way to see it,' she said.

He laughed.

'At night,' she said, 'even the factories look good.'

'There's enough of them, all right.' He handed her the joint. 'Lie on your back, put your feet against the obelisk.'

She lay back, faced the sky with the thick grass damp against her neck, and placed her feet on the stone. He lay beside her.

'Now,' he said, 'imagine the obelisk is like a stone path. Can you imagine walking straight down it into the stars?'

'Don't you mean *up*?'

'In space, up or down is whatever you want it to be. Just look.'

She stared up at the tip of the obelisk. It pointed into a clear sky so layered with stars that she could see the arm of the Milky Way curving away on the other side like the tail of a monstrous fish in deep water.

'You can almost feel the earth spin,' she murmured.

'That's just your head.' Josh's hand brushed hers. His fingers pulled back, then returned, resting just against the tips of hers. She kept her own hand where it was.

'What is this thing, anyway?' she asked.

'What?'

'The obelisk.'

Josh's voice was dreamy. 'Dad told me they used to have them in Egypt thousands of years ago. But this one got built like a hundred years ago for the ships coming into the harbour. There used to be an old windmill here for grinding the city's grain or something, back when they first built this place, and when that came down, they put this here instead.'

'I would have liked the windmill better,' she said.

'Me too,' he said. 'Imagine that, if they'd kept a windmill as the highest thing in the city. Do you ever wonder what it was like before that, before any of this stuff, before white people came here?'

'Beautiful, I'll bet.'

'Better than all this.' He rose to his feet, held out his hand. 'Come on.'

Freya took it and let him pull her up. They left the bluff, wandering further away from home, along the cliffs, following the narrow ridge that went on past the lookout at Strzelecki Point.

He stopped suddenly, held up his hand to her, and then leaned a little towards the edge, towards the sea. 'Do you know how many people jump off these cliffs?'

'How many?'

'Heaps. They just don't tell anyone.'

'Why?'

'They reckon once you know someone who's done it, it's like you can't stop thinking about it.' He picked up a rock, dropped it over the edge, peered down after it. 'Like it's a disease you can catch.'

'How'd you know that, about the people jumping?'

He didn't say anything. The crunch of the waves against rock and sand below them seemed to grow louder.

'A few of my dad's patients are cops,' he said finally. 'Whenever they get a call to come up here, they know what to expect. And they get lots of calls. Not just for people who kill themselves, though. They're always out our way too, the cops. They tell my dad all the time that we should move, that he should set up his practice somewhere else. They say the east end of Newcastle is one of the most dangerous places in Australia, at night. There's an abandoned house up the road from yours, like about five minutes from your place. A few years back they found a woman in there impaled on a stake. Someone put a stake straight through her, from the top to the bottom. Must have been more than one person that did it—they never found out who, though.'

'Fuck.'

He looked at her. She couldn't quite see his eyes.

'I don't think I've ever heard you swear before,' he said.

'I do, though. All the time. Do you think your dad will ever leave?'

'Nah.'

'Why not?'

'He just won't.' Josh cleared his throat. 'He'll be here forever.'

They stood there a while longer, staring out at the darkness.

'What about your parents?' he said.

'The only thing I know for sure is that I'm leaving. As soon as I can.'

He didn't say anything.

'It was my birthday,' she said.

'When?'

'Last week. I'm fifteen now.'

'Why didn't you tell me?'

'I don't like to make a big deal of things like that. It's not like I *did* anything, just something stupid with my family.'

'Well, now I'm going to have to get you a present.'

'You don't have to.'

'Do you feel any different?'

'More tired, maybe. Not now, though. Only when I'm supposed to be awake.'

'Yeah,' he said, 'who wants to be awake when you're actually supposed to be?'

She laughed.

'You want to go for a swim?' he said. 'We can go home past the Bogey Hole. You game?'

'Not after that story you just told me.'

'It's like any place, Freya—you just have to know where to go and not to go.'

They followed a path through the saltbush to the sea below and then walked along the road that climbed up the coast until they reached a place where the cliffs rose over their heads. A concrete staircase led down from the road to the dark swimming spot that the locals called the Bogey Hole. As they descended the narrow concrete steps to the water, with the slap of the waves echoing around them, Josh told her how, back when the whole of Newcastle had been a prison outpost, convicts had gouged away the rock to make a pool for the governor. The place felt as if it had been abandoned to the elements ever since. An iron chain, dark with rust and algae, was draped from a few heavy spikes driven at intervals into the stone shelf that separated the pool from the ocean. She'd seen boys clinging to that chain in big seas, screaming with reckless laughter and holding on while the foamy breakers crashed and swirled around them.

'Turn around,' she told Josh. 'Don't look until I'm in the water.'

It was cold, and only waist deep, the uneven bottom all slick, rocky crevices, covered with sand and shells and sea anemones, and there was a constant noise of water trickling into the sea from channels in the rocks. They swam in nothing but their underwear, and she was shivering, but she felt good, wonderfully awake— loved the idea that most of the city was sleeping, but here she was, with Josh, beneath the sheer, glistening face of the cliff, his shoulders gleaming white in the moonlight.

Afterwards, they climbed back up the stairs, and walked together in their damp clothes up along the coast, following the road as it rose and fell, past the police station and finally the hospital. They'd just reached the esplanade overlooking the beach and were nearly home when the clock tower rang out from the distance—two in the morning. The floodlights on the promenade carved a swathe of sand out of the darkness below.

'I'm so sick of waiting,' she said.

'What do you mean?'

'I don't know,' she said. 'For something to happen.'

'What?'

'I'll know it when I see it.'

She could have said that sometimes that sense of waiting made her feel good, like the world was awash with potential, with possibilities, and sometimes it filled her with an anxious dread that was unbearable, but she kept silent.

An ambulance came past on its way to the hospital. There were a few lights on in the three towering spokes of the Nickson Wing. As they turned up the street away from the beach, they heard a car horn blaring somewhere near the mall and, a little closer, someone shouting *fuck* over and over again, his voice, raw with anger, muffled by the wind.

They turned into the alley that ran behind her house.

'I think I can make it from here on my own,' she said.

Josh shook his head. 'You don't want to be walking around here alone. Not at this hour.'

'Right, the woman impaled in the abandoned house.'

'It's not funny. You know, druggies used to shoot up in your house. They'd break in and hang out there. I think they were the ones who set it on fire, with candles or something. Fuck knows what else happened in there.'

They'd reached the back of the house. She turned to face him. He was right beside her, so close it surprised her.

'Watch out,' she said with a laugh.

He tried to move closer, or maybe he was off balance, reaching out for her hip, and she put her hands on his chest, not sure if she was pushing him away or drawing him in, and then his mouth was on hers and their tongues met and his lips were softer than she'd imagined, despite the braces, and warm, and she liked it—then she pushed him away.

'See you tomorrow at school,' she said.

He looked a little dazed, but then grinned at her. 'It's Saturday tomorrow, you dork. But you can come over to my place if you want.'

She climbed up on the back wall and looked down into the courtyard, swaying there against a breeze that had suddenly come up. There was a light on inside the house, not in the kitchen but beyond it, probably in the hallway. She could smell cigarette smoke.

'Shit,' she said. 'Dad's still awake.'

'Will he be mad?'

'Don't know. Are you staring up my skirt?'

'Of course not.'

Freya laughed. 'Yes you were. See you.'

She dropped into the courtyard and listened to Josh's footsteps recede. She thought of his mouth again, the carefulness of him, how he tasted, something she couldn't describe, just different. His hand on her hip, not pushy and not searching, just there. A low cough drifted through the house towards her. With her shoes in her hands, she went inside. Dad was sitting out on the front doorstep in his singlet, his back to her, looking out at the street. She might have tried going up the stairs, but they always creaked, so there wasn't really any point.

'Hey,' she said.

He looked at her for a moment without seeming to recognise her. 'It's late,' he finally said. 'Didn't your mum say eleven?'

'You going to tell her?'

He turned back to the street, took a drag of his cigarette. 'What she doesn't know can't hurt her. Come here.'

He patted the steps and shifted to give her room. She dropped her shoes in the hall and went to sit beside him.

'I couldn't sleep myself,' he said, rasping one hand across his stubbled chin. 'When your mother's at work, when she's not in the bed, I struggle. Always do.'

She didn't know what to say to that.

He cleared his throat. 'So, were you out with some boyfriend?'

'Just a party.'

'You drink these days?'

'No.'

He grinned. 'Really?'

'A bit,' she admitted.

'Of course you do. You're fifteen now. I was out of home by then.' He drew back on his cigarette. 'Is that all it is, drinking?'

It took her a moment to figure out what he was saying.

'Oh, no,' she said. 'No. I mean, yes, that's all it is.'

He looked at her directly. 'Good,' he said. 'I was your age once. I know what teenage boys are like. You can't trust them. There's only one way they look at girls. One thing they're after. Whatever they pretend. Doesn't matter if they're smart or dumb or weak or strong or what they say. You're the one that has to be careful. You understand?'

'Yeah, Dad.' She thought of him as a teenage boy, and in spite of herself, maybe because she was still drunk, she laughed.

'What?' he said.

'Just trying to imagine you at fifteen.'

'Is it that hard?'

'You just seem so old now.'

He raised his eyebrows, looked down at the slight bulge of his belly and then back at her. 'Come on. I'm thirty-nine. That's not old, is it?'

She laughed again. 'I don't know.'

'Your mother wasn't that much older than *you* when I met her.'

'What was she like, when you met her?'

He exhaled smoke from the corners of his mouth. 'Soft. Couldn't imagine her pissed off or anything like that. Now look at us.' He leaned forward over his knees. The muscles in his arms rippled across one another as he held his hands in front of him and flexed. He shook his head. 'I'm sure you can handle yourself. Better than your mother could. Better than me.'

She didn't say anything and got up.

'Hey,' he said. 'Don't I get a kiss?'

Freya kissed him on the cheek and put her arms around his neck. He smelled of all the familiar smells she'd known forever. But the comfort that came with those smells did not come by itself.

19

'So, your son…' Mrs Morrison said and smiled, as if Maryanne wouldn't need to hear anything else, as if she'd be able to fill in the rest.

The woman was one of those weathered veteran-teacher types, with the close-cropped curly hair, reddish spots in her upper cheeks, a wrinkled triangle of skin between her shawl and blouse. There was a knowing quality in her eyes, a kindness that made Maryanne wary.

'Daniel is no problem at all. He just needs to focus more. We all need a little help sometimes, though, don't we?'

Maryanne nodded. She had no reason to be wary, not really. Maybe she was just having a bad day, misreading the woman's tone, her air of concern—looking for trouble where there was none, expecting to feel judged and found wanting. Maybe that's what some part of her wanted from other people. Her mouth felt dry. There was something going around and around in her head, some loose thought she couldn't quite grasp. Her dress was damp with sweat, the empty classroom yawning behind her, the teacher on the other side of a neat desk on which everything was in order, everything perfectly arranged.

Mrs Morrison waited a beat and then went on. 'He doesn't cause trouble, but he keeps to himself perhaps too much. He doesn't really seem to *be* there. I'm just not sure why.' She smiled at Maryanne. 'Are things at home okay?'

Maryanne gave a quick nod.

'Are *you* okay?'

Maryanne suppressed a flash of irritation, made herself smile. 'Yes. Of course.'

She felt the weight of her hands folded in her lap, beneath the table, as if she were in trouble.

'The thing is,' Mrs Morrison went on, 'he can be very focused. He'll notice the most extraordinary details in something I read to the children when they're doing comprehension, for example, but then he can't answer the questions afterwards. It's like he switches off. He probably just needs to learn the strategies.'

Strategies? He was eight. What did an eight-year-old need to know about strategies, for God's sake? Maryanne didn't say anything—she just nodded, to get out of there as quickly as possible. She had enough to worry about.

Then the interview was finished, and she left the school grounds clutching her handbag as if it were the only thing stopping her from being swallowed by the footpath.

~

'His problem,' Roy said to her that night in their room, as they rested together against the bedhead, shoulders touching, 'is partly you. You have to see that, now it's not just me noticing.'

'Noticing what, Roy?'

'You go too easy on him. He thinks that's how the whole world works.'

'You really think that's what Daniel's learned over these last few years?' Maryanne nearly burst out laughing. 'I'm sorry I said anything.'

It was quiet outside. The street lamp filled the curtains hanging limp over their window with a dull yellow glow.

'A bit of discipline, Maryanne.' He looked at her. 'Boys need that. Maybe if you were a bit firmer with him, it would be easier for everyone.'

A cold thrill rippled through her chest. 'Do you remember where that attitude took you last time?'

'Last time?' He stared straight ahead. 'That's a long while ago now. I don't know why we're still talking about it, why you keep feeling the need to bring it up. And it wasn't all my fault.'

'You didn't say that at the time.'

'What did I say at the time? That I was sorry.' His eyes met hers. He tapped his temple with one finger. '*You* need to listen, Maryanne.' He looked straight ahead again, away from her. 'I'm sorry. Of course I'm sorry. My point is that maybe you should have been sorry too.'

'For what?'

'You indulge him. He doesn't learn. Does the same things over and over again. That's not safe. That time, he pushed me to the point where I couldn't—'

'Couldn't what?' She was eager for him to say it.

'I don't know,' he said in a more subdued tone. 'Think straight.'

205

'And that's it? That's why you put your son in hospital?'

'I didn't *put* him in hospital. You make it sound like that's what I set out to do. He ended up in hospital. One thing led to another. Accidents happen, Maryanne.'

'You told me you'd never forgive yourself.'

'People say that with accidents. It was no one's fault.'

'No one's fault? Do you think I would have come back to you if you'd said that?'

He laughed harshly. 'Would you really have come back to me if I'd done something to him on purpose? What sort of mother would come back if that's what she really thought?'

'You bastard.'

Neither of them spoke then. The curtains slid and billowed against one another in the breeze. Freya was walking around in her room above them. Neither of them spoke until it was quiet again upstairs.

'Maybe I *am* a bastard,' Roy said then. 'The fact is, you're a good enough mother—I'm not saying you're not—but I'm good for him too. He needs some survival skills.'

'Survival skills? You're fucking kidding me, aren't you?' Her voice came out louder than she'd expected it to. Before she could go on, the door to Daniel's bedroom creaked open.

'Mum?' he called out.

Roy sighed beside her. 'Speak of the devil.'

She swung her legs out of the bed. 'Yes, darling?'

'Are you okay?'

'Yes, darling. Are you?'

'I woke up.'

'This again,' Roy muttered. 'You really think he needs to do this?'

'What do *you* know?'

His eyes narrowed at her. 'You're not as clever as you think you are, Maryanne. He's controlling you.'

She ignored him.

'Survival skills,' he said. 'That's what you can't give him. What's he going to do when you're not around?'

He had his hand on her wrist, heavy, hot, unmoving. It reminded her of being in the hospital with him while the doctors had been draining Daniel's skull, everything in the balance, Roy sobbing, needing reassurance. An accident, he'd called it at first, there at the hospital, then a mistake, and now it was no one's fault.

She leaned back into bed, put her other hand on top of his. 'Listen to me,' she said. 'Forget everything else, change your story however you want to, but don't forget this. I don't care about survival skills. If you touch him again, I'll—'

'What?' he said through his teeth. 'What will you do?'

'Whatever I have to.'

'Like what? Call the police, is that what you're saying?'

'If I have to, Roy, yes, I will. They're my children.'

His grip slackened, and before it could tighten again, she was out of bed and out the door.

Daniel's sheets were sodden.

'You wet the bed?'

'I was having a dream.'

'That's okay,' she said.

There was a spare set of sheets for him in his room. She changed them—it was a relief to do something—and put him in new pyjamas. His body felt warm, full of childish heat. As she was putting him back to bed, she stopped and straightened. The smell of cigarette smoke wafted around her. It was coming from nearby, from inside the house.

From their bedroom.

Roy gave a soft cough. Her heart began to beat more heavily. What would happen if she told her husband to go outside with the cigarette? Where would they go from there? Nowhere good. She wondered if Freya were asleep yet. She thought back to all the fights she'd ever had with Roy, the serious ones, how she'd always told herself that her children were asleep. She couldn't bear to imagine it any other way. What a way to live, though, telling yourself these sorts of things.

'Mum?' Daniel said.

It was a warm night, one of those early harbingers of the approaching summer. She sighed and wedged open the door onto the balcony just a little to let in the fresh sea air. An oceanic moan filled the room.

'Everything's okay,' she said, and it occurred to her that she was trying to convince herself as much as Daniel. She sat beside him, rested her hand on his head. 'Was it a bad dream?'

'I can't remember,' he said. 'Can you wait with me?'

Maryanne thought of Roy waiting there in their bed, smoking his cigarette. She stroked Daniel's head as if she were stroking her own heart, trying to ease it back into a steadier rhythm. 'Of course,' she murmured. 'Of course I'll wait.'

20

Josh shifted beside her. They were sitting together on the edge of her desk, which they'd pushed up against the open window, their legs dangling in the air, all that space underneath their feet. They'd just finished putting up half a dozen posters on the freshly painted walls of her room. They sat very close, so that she could feel his warmth. He had been looking at her quietly, from the corner of his eye, but pretending not to, which only made it more obvious. She'd liked that, the feeling of his attention on her, but it unsettled her too, to be near him, like she was waiting for him to act. Why wasn't he? She stole a glance at his pale, freckled face. Josh cleared his throat and ran his tongue across his braces with his mouth closed.

'I should probably do some stuff,' she murmured.

He nodded, pulled his legs back into the room and clambered off the desk.

They walked together down to the front door. 'Thanks for the posters,' she said.

Josh smiled at her as he stepped outside. 'No problem.'

She closed the door behind him and turned back down the hallway.

'Freya.' Mum was sitting at the table in the dining room. 'Is he gone?'

Freya stood at the foot of the stairs, with her hand on the bannister. 'Yeah.'

'He's really such a nice boy. Gentle and kind. Just what a girl needs.'

'He's a friend,' Freya said. 'That's all.'

'Of course.'

'What?'

Mum shrugged. 'Nothing. Sometimes I think you're a bit too much like me.'

'Don't worry,' Freya said, surprised at the sudden hardness, the anger in her own voice, the eagerness to provoke the same from Mum. 'I'm probably less like you than you think.'

Mum didn't bite back. 'Come, sit with me for a while.'

Freya hesitated. Mum looked so small and sad and fragile, like a piece of wire covered in cloth, bent in upon itself. Lonely, maybe, or lost, like she needed someone to talk to.

'No,' Freya answered. 'I have things to do.'

With that, she went back upstairs and into her room. She closed the door behind her, locked it, and took the bong from under her bed. Returning to her desk, she packed a cone and sparked the lighter into reassuring life. She sucked the cone down in one go, held the smoke deep in her lungs and then blew it out the window. She sank onto her bed and fumbled with her headphones as the rush of the pot filled her head. Before she could get them on, the phone rang. Mum came up and knocked, called her name.

'Why do you lock it?' she said when Freya opened the door.

Freya stared at her blankly.

'The phone's for you,' Mum said.

Freya went down and picked it up. 'Hello?'

It was Josh. 'You want to go to the beach?'

'Weren't you just over?'

He gave a short laugh. 'I got home and realised I didn't want to be here.'

She saw Mum's shadow across the doorway to the kitchen.

'All right,' she said. 'I'm sick of being here too.'

~

The beach was a mistake. It was much brighter in the sunlight than she'd expected. There was too much of everything—glare, searing wind, heat radiating from the sand, the incessant clamour of the ocean echoing against the concrete surfaces between the beach and the road.

As they made their way along the esplanade and down towards the Bogey Hole, they passed a knot of bare-chested boys sprawled over benches under the shadow of the cliff at the southern end of the beach.

One wolf-whistled as they went by. 'Come on, girls, slow down,' another yelled, and all of them started laughing.

Josh looked towards them over his shoulder.

One of the boys stood up. 'What?'

It was the boy from school, the one she hardly knew who'd

yelled at her once from a car and pretty much ignored her ever since. Beau. She'd since seen him beat up two different boys at school, both smaller than him. He had left the others and was walking towards them. Freya felt a sudden tingling awareness of the way this part of the shoreline was separate from the main stretch, tucked away behind a saltbush-covered outcrop.

'Keep walking,' she said to Josh.

But Josh slowed down and stopped. Beau was broad, with a good layer of fat over his muscle, his cheeks gravelly with acne. He stood half a head taller than Josh. As he approached, the boys behind him began laughing again, like they were listening to a joke they'd heard before.

His eyes were bloodshot. He was probably stoned or drunk or both. He looked at Josh. 'What'd you say to me, cunt?'

Josh looked back at him, his slim body tense. 'I didn't say anything. Maybe you've got something in your ear.'

'Say it again.'

'Say what? Just tell me what I said, and I'll be happy to tell you again.'

'Faggot.' The boy shoved Josh. He did it without effort, but Josh flew back a few steps.

'Leave him alone,' Freya said.

Beau drew back his lips. 'What, is he like the queer you hang out with because you don't want a boyfriend? You going to protect him now, are you?'

Josh jumped at him then. He swung a wild punch that glanced across Beau's chin, then swung another. There was a flash of surprise on Beau's face, and a stunned hush came over the boys behind him, then he dropped Josh to the ground with a single punch. Beau was about kick Josh in the ribs and Freya was already stepping forward, when a voice rang out behind him.

'Don't, mate. You won.'

From amid the boys sprawled over the benches, a man got to his feet. He was lean and corded with muscle. No shirt, bare feet, tanned skin, dark hair on his chest. A beer bottle dangled from one hand as he walked towards them.

'Just go and mellow out, mate,' he said.

Beau stood his ground. 'He started it.'

'Mate,' the man said again. His lips compressed into something near a smile, like he was speaking to a stupid child. 'Listen to me. Just walk away.' He wasn't that old after all, Freya decided. It was more his manner. His eyes were hidden behind a pair of wraparound sunglasses. Beau spat on the ground, and went back to the group. The man turned towards Freya and Josh, who was bent over on one knee on the ground, hands cupped over his face, blood spurting through his fingers.

The man crouched in front of him. 'Give me a look. Ah, that'll be fine. You want some of this?' He offered the beer. Josh shook his head. With a shrug, the man rose to his feet. His loosely tied board shorts dipped a little under a swirl of black hair that crept across a flat, muscular belly towards his navel.

'Come on, Tim,' one of the boys shouted. 'Go on and poke her, why don't you!'

'Don't be so fucking rude,' he called back towards them. 'Where's your fucking manners?' He turned back to face Freya. 'What's your name?'

'Freya.'

'Freya,' he said, as if he were testing the word on his tongue. 'I like it.'

He lifted his glasses, his bright blue eyes sweeping across her in a way that startled her. 'Seen you around, actually.' His face broadened into a grin. 'That dickhead over there, Beau, he's my little brother. If they hassle you—or he does—let me know. I'll kick his arse for you.'

'Okay.' Josh was on his feet, wiping blood off his arms. 'I'll do that. Have you got like a business card or something?'

Tim glanced at him, his face expressionless, then he looked back at Freya and gave a quick wink before lowering his glasses.

'Don't be a stranger,' he said.

'Fucking idiot,' Josh muttered under his breath as they watched him walk off.

'Don't be dumb,' she said.

They began walking back the way they'd come.

'You okay?' she asked.

He wiped his nose, his wrist bright with blood, and didn't answer. He was crying, she realised, his shoulders heaving with each breath. When they got back to the main beach she bought some tissues from the kiosk there and helped dab his face clean.

'You should have kept walking,' she told him.

He gave a snort and a bubble of blood popped out of his nose. 'Maybe if they were just talking about me. But they weren't.'

'You're lucky he stepped in when he did.'

'Tim?' Josh spat more blood onto the ground. 'Lucky *he* stepped in to save me from his deadshit brother? Why do you think Beau even had a go at me? Who do you think told him to? Are you that blind?'

Freya felt herself flush. 'Well, I'm not the one who got punched in the face.'

Josh shook his head. 'You know how many people Tim's beaten the shit out of? He dropped out of school in year 11. Now he just hangs around at the beach doing whatever the fuck he does. Selling drugs to people stupid enough not to realise he's ripping them off. Just because he stopped his brother kicking the shit out

214

of me, don't think he's a nice guy.'

'Josh.' She put a hand on his shoulder. 'Are you actually okay?'

He nodded, lips tight against his teeth. 'I saw how he was looking at you,' he said.

'I didn't notice anything,' she said. The lie came easily enough. It was something she'd heard Mum tell Dad more than once.

'Listen,' he said, but instead of going on, he leaned forward to kiss her.

Freya turned away, looked out to sea. 'You have to be careful. You're the best friend I have in this place.'

Something slackened in him. 'You're right—I was an idiot.'

'I didn't say that. You weren't.'

'Did I make a dick of myself?'

'Of course not.'

'I feel like I did. I should have stayed on my feet.'

'What are you, like a professional boxer now?'

'I've seen your old man. He looks tough as nails.'

'You wouldn't want to be like him. Trust me.'

Josh touched his nose and winced. 'Anyway, he's bad news, Tim. You don't want to know him. You just don't.'

On their way back home, a car slowed as it passed them. Beau was leaning out of the window with his usual empty expression, but he didn't say anything. She caught a glimpse of the driver, his brother, staring straight ahead, or perhaps his eyes briefly caught hers in the rear-view mirror—she wasn't sure.

'I'm pathetic,' Josh said suddenly.

'You're—' Freya began, but he cut her off.

'Don't try to make me feel better.' He studied his feet in silence. Then he shook his head and said under his breath, 'You have no idea what it's like to deal with fuckers like that every day.'

'How would you know' she said sharply. 'How would you

know what I have to deal with?'

He bared his teeth, wiped his mouth with the back of one hand. 'You're too busy feeling sorry for yourself to really have a clue what's going on.'

She crossed her arms. 'As if you know anything about me!'

Something nasty twisted through his face. 'Well, don't I? Tell me I'm wrong! You saw how he was looking at you. I bet you enjoyed it. You just don't want to admit it.'

'You don't know anything about me,' she said. 'You just think you do. You're the same as everyone else!'

She turned to go, but he grabbed her wrist.

'Wait,' he said. 'I'm sorry. Let's just hang out.'

She relented. They went back to Josh's basement, where they smoked some pot and slouched in his chairs listening to Neil Young's *Harvest*. Josh was in his own world, preoccupied. He picked up his guitar, began playing along to the start of 'Heart of Gold'. The space between them felt like a chasm.

'I have to go,' she told him.

He nodded.

'Don't be a stranger,' he said.

~

Later that night, in bed, she could hear Mum and Dad talking through the floor below her. There was a shape to their conversation—the long pauses, the shifts in tone—that made her think they were arguing, but she wasn't sure. It was late, too late to be awake waiting to fall asleep. The drone of cicadas had long since died away. She couldn't hear the sea. There was only the insomniac harbour and the murmur of traffic. She felt bad for Josh, wished they'd never fought, wished they'd never gone to the beach. She hadn't been angry with him. He hadn't been angry with her. Or at least that hadn't been the whole of it. She understood that, but she didn't know how to get past it. Maybe it hadn't even been anger.

Tim's flat, gleaming belly sprang into her mind, the dark wisps of hair, his loosely tied shorts. The confident way he'd stood with his legs planted solid into the ground, his shoulders, which reminded her of Dad's. She swallowed. Her mouth felt dry. What had Patrick said? Something about driving a car at night, and seeing only what was in front of you? She felt like that all right, but she knew enough about what was in the darkness, out of sight.

Dad was going to lose it soon. She knew this and she could tell that Mum knew it too. Everyone knew, and no one could do anything about it. Wasn't that what life was—knowing things and not admitting it until it was too late, looking the other way? Everyone was waiting. *What next?* Like it was all up to Dad. When she grew up, when she got clear of all of this, she would never let herself live like that again. It wasn't anger she felt at Josh, it was more like—what? Frustration? She wanted him to be surer of himself, not so full of doubt. She wanted to tell him that, but she knew she never would.

The town hall belltower sent its notes out into the darkness. The sound hung in the air for a long time, as if there were no room for it to fall away, as if the world were crowded already with sound that no one could hear anymore. She was in a car, and the darkness was around her and ahead, and she wanted to push her foot down, all the way down. Anything was better than waiting.

21

Towards the end of October the heat of the approaching summer fell on the city and clung to everything, distorting the black, broad streets, filling the mornings with promises as vague as they were intense, full of eucalyptus and disintegrating blossoms and distant burning. From the hills and higher places and sudden steep roads around the inner city, the murky brown palls of bushfire smoke could be seen unravelling across the horizon. At school, sunlight blazed against the windows and pooled in rooms and corridors, along with deodorant and perfume and body odour as students passed from one class to the next.

'Hormones,' Mrs O'Neill said in the swelter of the classroom. 'You girls are all wading through a soup of hormones. Don't take any risks. Don't trust your *instincts*, except when they tell you what

I tell you. If that voice in your head doesn't sound like me, it's not worth listening to. And you boys, God help you. Don't listen to anything that comes into your head. Not a thing, unless it's *stop, stop, stop*. You boys need stop signs tattooed on your foreheads. Not that you'd ever look at yourselves long enough to notice.' She gave a dismissive flick of her hand. 'Then again, there are always too many adolescent males in the species—stupidity is nature's way of weeding you out. The only thing I can say is try, just try, to be one of the clever ones.'

'Should we be taking notes, miss?'

'When's the last time you ever took notes, Ben? I'm just talking.'

She switched back to talking about *Julius Caesar*—again—about the scene in which he'd just been killed. The conspirators were standing around covered in blood. Cassius was telling them not to wash, because the blood was nothing to be ashamed of—it would show the world they were heroes.

'This,' Ally said softly, 'is what it'd be like if guys had periods.'

'I can just see them all,' Freya whispered back, 'waving their bloody tampons in the air, waiting to be told how great they were.'

Sitting where he usually sat, at the back of the room, Josh caught her eye, hands behind his head, leaning back on his chair, collar up, a button over his belly undone. His hair was wild, like he'd just rolled out of bed. She smiled at him and looked away. She pushed her knees together, thought of him on the ground, clutching his mouth, blood spilling through his fingers, his face a flushed collision of shame and fear.

~

Only Mr Hind, with his steady, implacable manner, seemed immune to the general air of exhaustion that hung over the school.

In maths, a double godforsaken period of it before lunch, he wrote on the blackboard, and as he wrote he spoke—about numbers and symbols, how they formed a language everyone could agree on, beautiful in its simplicity, a language that embraced everything.

'Now,' he said. 'I have your practice exams here, and a list of people I want to see after class.'

Freya was on the list. After the bell had rung for lunch, there were a few of them still sitting there, legs flung out beneath their desks. He went to them one by one and took them through their work, setting them problems they had to get right before they could leave. The noise of lunchtime came at them from outside. Mr Hind came to Freya's desk last.

'Your biggest issue,' he said, gliding one finger over her work, 'is just focusing on the problem. You know this stuff. I know you do. You were doing well for a while, but you're slipping now. Must be summer on the way.'

'What does summer have to do with anything, sir?' she retorted.

Her tone caught him off guard. His face fell and he gave a short nod. 'Maybe nothing, Freya. Maybe nothing. But the end-of-year exam is coming up, and I want you to do well. I want you to be *ready*.'

There was the usual smell about him of soap and the sea, like he'd come to school straight after a surf. Leather bracelets, all woven into one another, rested on the light brown hair of his wrist. The leather was faded, bleached by salt and sun. She thought of him rising from the water, dripping, surfboard under one arm, face calm, composed, as if his mind were still out there among the waves. He was so remote, like he floated above the regrets and sorrows of everyday life, like the world of numbers and symbols that he talked about really existed.

'There,' he said beside her, 'you just have to look at it. It's just problem-solving. You try.'

She could hardly breathe. There was a bird inside her head, hammering at the eggshell hollows of her temples.

'Here.' Mr Hind went through the problem with her. 'See?'

She nodded, the pen slippery between her fingers.

'Now,' he said, 'you try. Just talk yourself through it.'

She did not talk, but kept writing down numbers and symbols to satisfy him, patterns that shifted in and out of focus across paper already smudged with her efforts.

'Look more closely,' he said.

'I can't.'

She felt heavy, as if she might start crying. A ceiling fan was gyrating on its uneven axis. The air was turbulent, but it did not cool her down.

Mr Hind looked at the handful of students who remained and pursed his lips. 'You can eat while you work. I'll get my lunch, and then I'll come back. We'll sort this out before you go.'

Once he had left the room, she shoved her things in her bag and walked out.

~

And then came the weekend, and she stayed in her bedroom listening to music, except for when she went to work, and she was quiet at work too, but Patrick didn't mind. He gave her distance when she needed it, like some people knew how to do. Freya came home, ignored Mum's searching glances, ate dinner, watched television and went to bed early. She lay in bed forever without feeling sleepy, but when Mum came to the door she shut her eyes. The rest of the weekend passed just like that.

Halfway through the night before school, Freya suddenly sprang into wakefulness. She swung out of bed and went to her window. The moon threw a shimmering, unsteady band along the dark water of the harbour, but the air was hazy, Stockton on the other side of the water lost mainly in blackness, though a few far-off lights glittered back at her. The air smelled of distant fire. Someone was walking down below. She couldn't see them, but the skid and scrape of shoes carried to her. The footsteps trailed away, and she wondered if someone had been standing there, looking up at her window.

She crawled back into bed but didn't sleep for ages.

In the morning she overslept, and by the time she got to school it was after nine. There was a police car parked out the front. That burning smell still filled the air, and a hot, dry wind picked up leaves and sent them swirling across the ground. Everyone was in the assembly area near the main gates, on the grass field bordered by fig trees.

There was always an assembly on a Monday, but this was different—she knew as soon as she walked through the gate. Everywhere she looked she saw girls crying, huddled in agitated clusters. The boys were off-kilter too, but they showed it differently, carrying on muted, close-quarter versions of their usual playground games and fights while teachers roved between them with scowling faces. The principal was talking to someone near the foot of the podium.

Freya pushed her way through the crowd and found Ally. 'What's going on?'

Ally's eyes were red from crying. 'A girl's dead.'

'Who?'

Ally told her the girl's name, but she didn't recognise it.

'She was in the year below us, from Stockton. She was murdered.'

'Murdered? Like someone killed her?'

'Yeah.'

'Last night?'

'Yeah. They haven't caught who did it. She was raped, that's what I heard. And her head was smashed in with a rock. The sicko that did it is still out there. They reckon it might have been someone from school.'

An image sprang into Freya's mind of the girl they were talking about—dark, thick, curly hair down to her shoulders, and pale, freckled skin. Short. Always smiling, and there was a boy—not from Stockton, but from this side of the harbour—who she'd talk to. She'd stand there sometimes in front of the place where he sat with his friends, her arms folded or one hand on her hip, laughing as she talked.

The principal mounted the podium and tapped the microphone. 'All of you will know by now,' he began.

~

After school, she wandered down to the park with Josh, Daniel trailing behind them. Daniel was in his swimmers, his thin chest pale and fragile-looking in the afternoon light. The fountain in the park was pumping its five huge columns of water into the air. Daniel jumped from one to the next while they looked on. Whenever Daniel jumped into one of the columns of water, he disappeared completely from view.

'Is your brother always that happy?' Josh asked.

'He's never as happy as he looks.'

Freya's gaze wandered around the park. There were hospital workers sitting on the grass nearby. Two people, a man and a woman, backs turned, sat on a bench in the shadows of the trees closer to the hospital, leaning in towards one another. Mum. She was staring at Mum. She recognised the man, too, with his close-cropped white hair. He was the one she'd seen the day she'd gone to the hospital, after Nan's heart attack. Every now and again, Freya would see Mum's face almost in profile as she talked. Then the man reached across and touched her shoulder, and Mum stood up, and the man stood up too, and they embraced. Freya was waiting for them to kiss, but they didn't. They walked side by side, with very little space between them, back towards the hospital.

'What is it?' Josh said.

'Nothing,' Freya answered.

~

And then they were at his house, lying on his bed, staring up at the ceiling. They'd left Daniel back at home. When she'd told him to, he'd gone up into the house without arguing. He was probably sitting up there now in his room with the clarinet in his hands.

Josh was lying at the other end of the bed. She had waited for him to lie down first, made sure that there was enough distance between them so that there was no chance of them touching by accident. What had seemed like potential before was now a problem, something she had to focus on, and it occurred to her that she might not come here again after today. Josh passed her the joint, and she drew back hard, made the tip burn. A dreamy numbness washed through her thoughts.

'God, it makes you wonder, doesn't it,' he said.

'What does?'

He shrugged. 'Just life and shit.' He watched her draw back

on the joint again. 'We'll probably never know what happened,' he went on. 'They tell us we're too young for all sorts of shit, and then something like this happens. We know nothing, but then we know *this*, and have to pretend we don't, just to make adults feel better. That's the way it goes in this place. Adults act like we don't know half the shit we do.'

Their fingers brushed as she passed the joint to him. He sucked back deeply, suppressed a cough, hummed a fragment of song in the back of his throat.

'Hey, Freya. You know what I was telling you about my mum?'

'What are you talking about?'

'My mum, how she left.'

'Oh, yeah.'

'She didn't leave. She jumped.'

'What?'

'Off the cliffs. That's how she left.'

Freya sat up with a jolt. Her eyes felt dry, as if they were a thousand years old. 'Your mum killed herself?'

'Yeah.' He was looking at her, smiling strangely. He sat up too.

'That's…that's awful,' she said.

'My dad doesn't know that I know. He thinks I believed him when he said it was an accident. But I heard him talking once on the phone. I heard him say what happened when he was talking to my aunt.'

'Shit. Why didn't you tell me that before?'

His eyes were glassy. 'I don't know.'

'You should have told me sooner.'

'Yeah,' he said. 'I wanted you to know. No one else. Don't tell anyone else. It's only something I want you to know.'

225

He leaned in and, in one motion, his mouth found hers.

She pushed him away and stood up.

'What?' he said. 'Are you okay?'

'You shouldn't have—I'm fine.'

He stood up too. She stepped backwards.

'You sure?' he asked.

She swayed a little, wiped her mouth. 'I have to go.'

Before he could say anything else, she walked up the stairs and went for the front door. Josh's father was in the living room, but she didn't glance in as she walked past. She closed the front door behind her and walked towards the beach. Josh didn't follow her.

~

It was late afternoon. The cliffs went straight up and down, and as she walked along the rock shelves beside the sea, she moved through their shadows. The water was dotted with frenetic whitecaps, but clear underneath, because the wind was blowing offshore, straight off the cliffs. If you jumped now you'd fall outwards, towards the water, though not close enough to reach it. Everything was wild and harsh and pitiless. Coal ships lined up along the horizon, their red hulls and white towers like distant city blocks. She stared up at the cliffs and thought of the night, not much more than a month ago, when she had walked along them with Josh, somewhere up above where she stood now. She wondered if it was near here that his mother had fallen, if that was why Josh had stopped there with her that night. What would it be like, to fall, to know that those few seconds of falling were all that you had?

~

After dinner, Dad went out alone. Freya didn't know where or why, but she knew there was something happening again between him and Mum. There'd been tension between them over dinner, though nothing much had been said.

'It's terrible that girl was killed,' Mum said later as they washed the dishes together. 'Her whole life just gone, before it even really started. That's why I don't like you to drink. That's why girls should be careful at parties.'

'What, you think it's her fault?'

'Don't pick a fight with me, Freya. I'm just saying that the world isn't a safe place, especially for girls. That's just the way it is. You have to be careful.'

'Like you are?'

'What's that supposed to mean? Do you really have to get your hackles up like that just because I ask you to be careful?'

'I *am* careful, Mum.'

Mum plunged both hands into the foamy water, pulled out a pan and began scrubbing it. 'Are you, though? God, she was probably doing drugs or something too. Where were her *friends*?'

'I don't know, Mum,' Freya said. 'Probably doing drugs and getting drunk.'

Mum's hands became motionless in the water. 'Is that what *you* do when you go out?'

'Is that what *you* did, Mum?' Freya shot back. 'Is that how you ended up with Dad? What crazy drug were you on to end up with *him*?'

Mum lifted one hand out of the water with a jerk, and for an instant Freya thought she was going to get a slap, and she hoped she would, because then she could really go off, say whatever she liked, but Mum just pushed a strand of hair from her own face with the back of her wrist and went back to scrubbing the pan.

'We're not talking about me.' Mum said the words slowly and carefully.

'Of course not,' Freya said. 'You're always telling me to be honest, but you're not, Mum. You're not honest. You never are.'

Mum looked down at the dish in her hands, wiped away a layer of foam. 'Well, thank you for the insight,' she said, 'but maybe you need to take a good look at yourself first.'

As Mum's voice grew softer, Freya's grew louder. 'Right, Mum, pull that one out again. I'm a selfish teenager. Someone's just been murdered at my school, and you're giving me lectures because you feel guilty, because you know we shouldn't even be here in this shithole. Do the dishes by yourself.' She threw the tea towel on the floor and walked out.

'Freya, wait.' Mum followed her out to the stairs.

'What?'

'Don't be…' There was a pleading look on Mum's face. 'What's it like there, at school?'

'I hate it,' Freya said. 'I can't wait till the whole thing's over.'

'Till what's over? School?'

'I don't know. My life.'

Mum's face crumpled. 'Really? *You've* got the whole of it in front of you!'

'Mum, why are we even talking about this?'

'We could look at another school. Maybe.'

'Now you're giving me a choice? What, all it took was for a girl to get murdered and you're ready to let me *choose* something for a change. I never thought it would be that easy.'

'I let you choose things. All the time. More than a lot of girls your age.'

Freya laughed. 'I never had a choice in any of this. I was happy when we lived with Nan, when we finally just got away, but *you* weren't. For whatever stupid reason, you had to come back to him. But it's fine.'

Something cracked in Mum's voice. She was starting to cry. 'What do you want from me?'

Seeing her cry only made Freya angrier. 'I want you to tell the truth! I want you to at least have the guts to stop pretending that we're here because of Daniel and me. None of this is about us! You tell me I'm selfish, but *you're* the selfish one!'

She ran up the stairs. In her room, she locked her door, pulled her bong out from the box under her bed and opened the window. She pushed aside her desk, packed a cone with shaking hands and fumbled with her lighter until she had a flame, then breathed in the smoke, held it in her lungs as long as she could. When her head started to spin, she leaned out the window and blew the smoke out over the street, watched it drift away, as if it had never existed at all.

Mum must know that she was smoking pot. She just wouldn't admit to herself that she knew. It was what she did—ignoring things that stared her straight in the face, trying to pretend it was all okay. It made Freya think of Mr Hind, talking about those useless problems while everyone in the class did as they pleased. Just talking, on and on, like that was the only thing he needed to do to go home and feel good. And maybe for him it was. Was that all adults ever did, though—lie to themselves? About themselves, about their children? Was that all there was to look forward to?

She leaned out of the window, balanced there on the sill with her hands, her upper body in the open air, her toes barely touching the floor. She thought again of Josh's mother. When did you reach a point where doing that made sense? It was a very clear night, but really, what was there to see? Just stars. They weren't anything special. She swung forward a little more, felt

229

the weight of her body in her hands and wrists, the pressure of the windowsill against her palms and her belly, a different pressure in her head. The street looked hard. She leaned out a little more.

22

'Beautiful,' Dad said.

A cigarette was hanging out of his mouth, filling the air in the kitchen with a bitter haze. Freya looked in just as he began to lower a huge, dark slab of wood into place onto the cabinets under the kitchen windows, the full midday sun pouring in around him. One of his friends from work stood at the other end of the slab. He was a short, stocky man with eyes that made her uncomfortable, or maybe it was the sour smell of him, or his mouth or his posture, or all of it—it all felt directed at her, even when he wasn't looking her way.

The ruins of the old kitchen lay in a pile of debris out in the courtyard—she could see it through the open back door. Everything smelled of fresh wood and varnish. All the cabinet doors were shiny, with bright, silver handles. The wooden benchtop extended along the entire back wall of the kitchen, finished except for the hole where the sink should be.

'What do you think?' Dad turned to her. 'You reckon your mother'll be happy with this?'

'I don't know,' Freya said. 'I guess.'

Dad cast a sidelong glance at his friend and then laughed. 'You're right. It *is* hard to tell with your mother.'

'That's beautiful women for you,' his friend said. 'They're all the same.'

'Just be careful, mate,' Dad said. He winked at Freya, the skin on his face gleaming with sweat. 'The only one who gets to say that sort of thing in this house is me.'

~

Freya was in the kitchen sweeping up the lino floor when Mum came home from work. Dad's friend was gone by then, and the sink was in place. Dad was examining the inside of the cupboards.

'What do you think?' he said, when Mum walked in through the dining room.

Mum hesitated a moment. 'It's lovely,' she said.

'What?' Dad said.

'Nothing,' she said. 'The wood's very dark, isn't it?'

'What's that supposed to mean?'

'Nothing. It looks great.'

Dad nodded. 'It's an old piece of wood. Ironbark. It took me ages to sand it back. I could have gone a lighter varnish, I guess.' He looked at her. 'Is it too dark?'

'No, it's fine.'

He looked down at the benchtop, ran one thumb along the

hard, gleaming surface. 'You think I dragged this all the way here because it'd be *fine*?'

'It's beautiful,' Mum said. 'I've just come home from work. I'm tired. You haven't given me any time to adjust. It's lovely.'

'I didn't realise you needed time to adjust to a benchtop.'

'Roy, please.'

'I'm glad you like it.'

'I really do.'

He leaned against the counter and folded his arms, grinning at her without humour. 'By the way, Stan thinks you're beautiful. Isn't that what he said, Freya?'

Freya shrugged.

He turned back to Mum. 'You remember Stan, don't you?'

'Yeah. He's a bit off. I don't like him.'

Dad shifted, unfolded his muscular arms. 'You reckon he's sleazy?'

'A bit,' Mum said.

Dad looked at her a moment longer. 'All right,' he said.

The dog was barking again, out in the lane.

'I do love the benchtop,' Mum said.

'Good.' Dad gave a sudden laugh. 'Stop going on about it then!'

~

They had hamburgers and chips for dinner that night, and then Dad went back into the kitchen. Daniel disappeared into his room and began playing his clarinet. Freya sat with Mum on the couch watching television.

'They have their similarities, don't they,' Mum said.

'What?'

'The men in this family. They both like their space.'

Freya laughed.

Mum leaned towards her, lowered her voice. 'He has depth, that's why.'

'What?' Freya said.

'Your father. Remember how you asked me what I must have been on, to have ended up with him?'

'I didn't mean—'

'He's interesting and passionate and very charming when he wants to be. People are complicated.'

Mum settled back into the couch. They fell silent. *Sale of the Century* was on. When it finished, there was a news bulletin. Freya rose from the couch.

'Look at that,' Mum said.

Freya saw grainy images of a wall, a huge mass of grey concrete, people on top of it, celebrating, jumping up and down.

'The Berlin Wall,' Mum said. 'They're knocking it down. When I was a child, that wall was always there, right through Berlin. People got shot trying to cross it.'

'That's great, Mum.'

Mum turned to look at her. 'What?'

'I mean, you know, that they're knocking it down. That people don't have to get shot trying to escape.'

Mum nodded. 'Plenty of them would have outlived that wall.' She turned back to the television. 'If only they'd waited.'

'Yeah, Mum,' Freya said softly. 'All they had to do was wait.'

A new story came on.

'The thing is, though…'

Mum looked up at her.

'How many people,' Freya went on, 'do you think died waiting?'

Then she was at the front door, and there was something wedged in the letterbox, a package. *Happy birthday*, it said. *From Josh*. She peeled away the paper and there was a tape inside, the label scrawled with the names of songs. She smiled to herself, and thought about going over to his place to talk to him, clear the air between them, but she didn't know what she'd say, not yet. She went and found her Walkman, and inserted the new tape. 'I'm going for a walk,' she called down the hallway.

The cicadas were making a racket, their song swelling from the bushes. She walked down the street to where the buildings ended and she could see part of the harbour, and the Norfolk pines on the other side where Stockton began. A gnat wafted against her cheek. She couldn't tell where the sun was anymore. How long ago was it now since the girl in the year below her had died? Less than a week. Six days. Six mornings, six evenings. Try adding up the minutes. Somewhere on that other side, in the saltbushes, on that windswept expanse of beach that stretched off up the coast. And her killer was still out there too, living life, getting on with it.

She thought of something Josh had said to her, about this town, the way the water connected it to everything out there in the world, but all you got was the ripples. She found herself smiling, thinking of him, the things he said, and then her smile faded. She put her headphones on and pressed *play*. The comforting hiss of the tape balanced the noise of the insects, then the music kicked in and that was all there was, and she turned her back on the harbour and what lay beyond it and began walking towards the beach.

~

235

'Every year they seem to start it earlier,' Mum said.

'Start what?' Dad grunted.

'Christmas.'

They had been to the shopping centre out in the suburbs, were heading home, but they hadn't got far. There was an accident up ahead somewhere.

'It must be a bad one,' Mum said. 'Look at all the cars.'

The boot was full of groceries. They were crawling at a snail's pace, Dad hunched over the steering wheel, Mum beside him. All the windows were wound down, but the air coming in was hot and dry.

'Now look at this,' Dad said.

'What?'

'This stupid idiot wants to get in front of me.' He thrust his chin towards a car trying to edge in ahead across a give-way line. 'Look at him, being a fuckhead. That's what we need right now, a fuckhead.'

Mum put a hand on his forearm. 'Just let him in—it won't make any difference.'

Dad shrugged off her hand. 'That's your answer to everything—give in. Let people off. I'm the only one you have to disagree with. You save it all for *me*. Has it ever occurred to you that's half the problem with your life?'

As he turned to look at her, a horn blared. Freya could see the man in the other car waving his arms, shouting. Dad wrenched on the handbrake. The car jerked to a standstill and he was out on the road, slamming the door behind him.

The other man got out of his car too. As Dad approached, the man lifted his hands—whether to talk or to fight, it wasn't clear. Dad's fist made a blur. The man crumpled. Dad hit him twice more as he fell, sharp, precise blows, then he stood over him and spat on his hair. Another man got out of his car further down the road.

Dad turned. 'Come on. *Try* something!'

The second man kept his hands down, backed away. Dad laughed. His face loomed in the rear window. Freya scrambled around in her seat to face the front. Daniel did the same.

When Dad got back into the car, his breath filled the cabin.

'You do that,' he said, 'you should at least put up a fight.'

'Roy,' Mum breathed through her fingers, 'for God's sake.'

He lifted his hand, examined the knuckles. 'He had it coming. I was just the one to give it to him.'

'You're a real man, all right,' Mum said.

He looked at her. 'Don't you start.'

'Or what?' Mum said quietly, staring back at him.

The whole car was shuddering and vibrating against the engine. The muscles in Dad's face were tight, the colour gone from his cheeks, his lips. Mum turned away first. Dad grunted, dropped the handbrake and shifted the car into gear, the taut line of his neck damp with sweat. A solitary car horn lifted across the stationary line of traffic. They rolled forward.

'He shouldn't have got out of the car,' Dad murmured.

Five minutes later they started to speed up again, and not long after that they passed the scene of the accident, the police cars and the ambulance and the tow truck. There wasn't much to see, no bodies or anything, just a lot of glass, a stain that might have been blood or oil or water, and two cars by the side of the road, or what used to be cars, crumpled together in a twisted embrace of metal.

23

Sunday passed without Freya really noticing. She went for a walk late in the afternoon to Fort Scratchley, with its views out over the ocean and the coastline. There were surfers out off the point near the ocean baths, hunched in the water over their boards, paddling effortlessly for lines of swell that turned into waves as they rose to their feet. She wondered if Mr Hind was down there among them, or maybe Tim. Every now and again, very far off, a needle of lightning splintered across a horizon murky with rain that wasn't coming any closer. The storm looked so peaceful from this distance. Staring at it, she felt as if some part of her were coming undone, peeling away from the world—she couldn't describe it better than that.

That night was broken up by feverish dreams and odd

moments of thought that floated in the gaps between waking and sleep. She woke at some strange hour. Her alarm clock was flashing twelve, as if there'd been a power surge, and it occurred to her that she'd forgotten to go to work that day, that Patrick had been expecting her. It didn't matter. She thought about school. She didn't want to go to school. She didn't want *not* to go to school. Not that it mattered either way.

The murdered girl in the year below her came into her mind. Her death hung like a pall of smoke over the last weeks of the term, the last weeks of the whole school year. That pale freckled face and the broad, toothy smile. Standing there, in the shade of the fig trees, talking to that boy. Walking along the school corridor with a couple of friends, bag slung over her back, the top button on her white blouse undone. There was a rumour that she'd gotten too drunk to stand up that night, that she'd been surrounded by the boys from Stockton, that they'd spat on her and kicked her and poured beer over her head until one dragged her off into the saltbushes that separated the beach from the houses nearby. Most of the boys had lost interest then. The party had gone on.

~

'So have you dumped him then?'

Always these conversations in maths, because it was only Ally who asked, and only in Mr Hind's class, where they could get away with talking as much as they liked. With school nearly finished for the year, the class was out of control. Freya squinted down at the numbers on the page in front of her. They looked more pointless than ever. Why was she doing it to herself, coming to school when everything inside her was telling her not to?

'We weren't even going out.'

'That a yes?'

A fierce westerly was howling outside. She could see trees bending and swaying with each gust, thick branches shuddering, their leaves like out-of-control thoughts. It was the middle of the day, cloudless, bright, all the shadows shrunken by an overhead sun.

Freya chewed on the inside of her mouth, blinked to make the numbers on the page stop their drifting. 'We weren't going out, I told you.'

She shouldn't have come today. She'd hesitated at the sight of the bus bearing down on her. There'd been no sign of cloud or rain, the wind just beginning to stir with the first hint of violence. The sick feeling in the pit of her stomach had only grown stronger after she got on the bus. All she was doing was waiting. Josh hadn't been at the bus stop, but he was there at school—she'd seen him from a distance. Had he walked?

The noise of the classroom boiled around her now. She made a circle with her pen, circled again and again until there was a wet blue spiral ingrained in the page, the ink coming off on the side of her hand. She flicked the ring in her lip back and forth with her tongue, her teeth digging into the soft skin around it until it felt raw. Mr Hind was there up the front, talking.

Ally was chewing that gum of hers, the sickly fake berry smell all around her. Freya watched her take it out, balance it on her thumb and then press the wad under the desk.

'I'm glad you ditched him,' Ally said. 'He's a weirdo. All that metal in his face. Yuck. I mean, like maybe what you've got, that's fine. But he's definitely got too much. You're better off without him.'

Freya slapped her pen down. 'Jesus, you don't know anything, Ally.'

Mr Hind's voice rose above the classroom murmur. 'Freya, I'm trying to explain something here. Can you stop talking for a little bit, at least while I do?'

'Why don't *you* stop talking for a little bit?' She snapped it out without meaning to. Or maybe she *had* meant it. Someone chuckled behind her.

Mr Hind turned to stare at her. 'Pardon?'

The class fell silent. Everyone was looking, waiting, the noise in the room almost snuffed out. She stared back at him and felt the blood rushing to her face, her right eye twitching as if there were something caught in it.

He walked towards her. 'Are you having trouble? Do you need a hand?'

'No, I don't. I'm not having any trouble. Are you?'

'Let me see.'

'*No.*'

'Go, Freya,' one of the boys called in a mocking voice. 'You tell him.'

'Poor Hind,' another voice snickered. 'Are you breaking up with him?'

She didn't turn around.

'Okay, okay.' Mr Hind scanned the classroom. He looked exposed, uncomfortable, standing there in the aisle by her desk. 'Everyone back to work.' He looked down at her. 'Let's have a chat outside.'

'Leave me alone.'

'Someone's on her rags.' The whisper sent a bunch of them behind her exploding into laughter. Other students—the good ones, she supposed—were looking at her with appalled fascination, like she was from a different species.

'Freya,' Mr Hind said.

She could feel tears brimming. 'Just stop looking at me! Do your job! Just do your fucking job!'

'Outside, please, Freya.'

'Fuck off.'

His voice hardened, but still he didn't raise it. 'Outside. Now.'

She fixed her gaze on her desk. A moment—a moment was all she needed to calm down. She was sure of it.

Mr Hind stood in front of her, a piece of chalk clutched tightly in one hand.

'Freya,' he said, in his measured tone, but there was a tremor in it now, threatening to break through the surface. 'You're wasting everyone's time. Out.'

She stood up. Her chair caught behind her and toppled with a crash. She hadn't meant to push it over, but there it was, and Mr Hind's startled expression made her angrier still, and she couldn't think straight, and everything was a blur around her.

She wanted to punch him, punch him right in that stupid triangular nose of his, smash it in half. The urge to do it, to damage him—she'd never wanted to punch anyone in her life. Not ever. And the voice coming out of her mouth wasn't even hers.

'This is all shit—none of it matters. You're the one wasting people's time. Just like you've wasted your own stupid fucking life doing a bad job of'—she tossed her head, looked around the classroom—'this.'

She picked up her bag and walked out, the class dead silent behind her.

~

The bell went for recess. No one had come for her. Among the spill of bodies rushing into the quadrangle, she found Josh.

'I have to get out of here,' she said. 'You want to come?'

He didn't ask. He just nodded.

They walked into town, to the mall.

'Did you see her?' she asked as they walked along the pale, uneven pavement between the shops.

'Who?'

'Your mother. After she jumped. At the funeral, I mean?'

'No. They kept the coffin closed.'

'I'm sorry,' she said.

'I didn't want to see her,' he said eventually. 'Not like that.'

'I know. I wouldn't.'

They kept walking in silence until they came to a shop full of glass vases and crystal sculptures and stainless steel things, including a cabinet full of fancy lighters, like miniature Bunsen burners and tiny jet engines. The woman at the counter looked up at them and said hello in a clipped tone that held no welcome or warmth, only a dangerous recognition, and Freya knew it was a bad idea to stay here. Josh caught her eye after a moment and walked out again, but then several other customers walked in, and with a wild, sinking sensation in her gut, Freya decided she'd try anyway.

She didn't even bother being discreet—just reached across to the glass display shelf when the lady at the counter was talking to someone else. She knew she was being watched, but it was like falling, like she couldn't stop now she was in motion, like it had already happened. The silver lighter felt cool and heavy in her hand, and she nearly dropped it, but then she turned, letting it slip into her pocket, and walked away. She was almost at the door, almost free, before someone was calling out, asking her to stop. She bowed her head and kept going, but slowed despite herself, like some part of her was used to giving in, used to surrendering to the inevitable. Then a hand fell on her shoulder, and Freya whirled, angry, panicked at last, lifting her hand to slap the woman away, and found her wrist caught in a surprisingly strong grip.

'Where do you think you're going?' The woman looked at her with a tight, unforgiving smile. 'Don't even *think* about running.'

~

And now she was sitting in Mrs O'Neill's office, staring out at the world beyond the window while the old bag looked at her, bemused, from across the desk.

'Why did you even take it?'

'To smoke.'

Mrs O'Neill leaned forwards in her leather chair. 'You need an eighty-dollar lighter to smoke? Goodness. Maybe *that's* where I've been going wrong.'

'I thought a good lighter would help me get the last bits of pot out of the cone.'

The lines on either side of Mrs O'Neill's mouth deepened. 'I'm going to pretend I didn't hear that. Do you even listen to a word I say in class? I give you the smoking talk at least once a week.'

'*You* smoke.'

'Yes,' Mrs O'Neill conceded. 'I'm also a teacher. And a deputy principal. It's stressful. Don't get into teaching, whatever you do. But times have changed, little lady. *You* shouldn't be smoking. Anything.'

'Are you going to call my parents?' Freya asked.

Mrs O'Neill nodded. 'That's already happened, yes. And we'll have to talk about all of these absences with your parents too. Now is as good a time as any. And the incident this morning with Mr Hind. Poor Mr Hind, of all people. He really does think the best of you, Freya, and he's genuinely upset. As for anything else you might have done or said, well, there's only so many hours in a working day. But don't worry about that right now. I want to know why you'd do it in the first place.'

'Do what?'

'The lighter. Steal something like that, something you don't even need. I don't care about the question of right and wrong. Steal as many lighters as you like—but that's not what you're really doing. Do you know what you're doing?'

Freya glanced at her and then went back to staring out the window.

'You know,' Mrs O'Neill went on, 'your reports from your last school are terrific. You should be near the top of every class, but you're not. This year has *not* been a success for you. You're making problems for yourself, creating turbulence. I don't know why. Do *you* know why?'

'No.'

'Is there something going on you'd like to tell me about? At home or at school? Anything at all?'

Freya shook her head.

It was quiet in the office. A tennis ball made a hollow, repetitive sound against a nearby wall. The noise of the other students outside in the quadrangle was muffled by layers of brick and glass.

Mrs O'Neill was the one who finally spoke. 'What is it you want?'

Freya met her eyes. 'I don't know.'

'Oh, Freya, that's not an answer. Think about it. I'm not talking about right now. I'm sure right now you just want to get out of here. But where do you want to go? What do you want to do? I'm talking about your future. You're heading towards it as we speak. Full throttle. Can't you tell? You need to take charge. Make some decisions. Maybe one decision is all you need to make, and the rest will fall into place.'

Freya stared past her at the grey sky outside the window.

'Freya, are you listening to me?' Mrs O'Neill clicked her fingers in front of Freya's eyes. 'What is it you want?'

She swallowed. 'I want to get through this.'

'Through what?'

'This conversation, for a start. It just doesn't mean anything to me.'

Mrs O'Neill walked around the desk and put a hand on Freya's shoulder. 'You have more control than you think. That's what you have to remember. *You have control.* No matter what anyone tells you. It's yours, if you take it.'

They looked at one another in silence.

The phone rang. It was a relief.

Mrs O'Neill picked it up, listened and then nodded. 'Bring her in.'

The rest—Mum coming in, the jerky motion of her head as she spoke to Mrs O'Neill, and then the three-way conversation— was all a blur, and then she was sitting on the bus next to Mum, and neither of them said a single word as it turned from one street to the next and wound its slow, stifling way home.

'I don't want to talk about this with you now,' Mum said without looking at her as they got off the bus. 'Except to say that you've let me down. You've let the whole family down.'

She began walking.

Freya stopped behind her and laughed. 'The whole family? Do you really mean the *whole* family, Mum?'

'I'm trying hard here.'

'Are you going to tell Dad?'

'I haven't decided.'

'I guess that's what you *do*, right?'

'What are you talking about?'

'You decide what you do and don't want him to know.'

'I can talk to him if you like. Let you sort it out with him.'

'So can I.'

'What do you mean?'

'I know about that guy at the hospital. He has white hair. I guess he's good-looking, for an old guy. I saw you and him together.'

'When?'

Freya just stared at her.

'You have no idea,' Mum said. 'You really don't.'

'Don't I? You're cheating on Dad, right?'

Mum's neck tightened. Pink patches of colour rose under her eyes. 'Don't push me into a corner, Freya.'

They walked on in silence for a while, past the park and up the road.

'What *happened* to you?' Mum said suddenly.

'What?'

'In spite of everything, don't I look after you? Aren't I a good mother?'

Freya realised that Mum was crying without making a sound, only her flushed face and the tears running down her cheeks to betray it. Mum was always crying these days—as if that would solve anything—but this time it filled Freya with pity and guilt. She wanted to say something, then, tell her that Dad was the last person she'd ever talk to, that she was just saying things, she didn't even know why, hurling out words to see which ones would stick, but they were turning the corner into their street and Dad's station wagon was parked out the front.

~

'How was your day?' Dad asked Mum over dinner. Freya felt the heat rise into her cheeks and didn't dare look up. It was warm and stuffy in the dining room, the air unmoving. The television was on in the corner. On the other side of the world, a news presenter was talking about how the communists in Czechoslovakia had bowed to weeks of protests and given up their power without a fight. She'd only been half listening, thinking about how school was nearly over, just a week and a bit to go, but she'd have to go every day, with Mum and Mrs O'Neill both breathing down her neck.

'It was good,' Mum said.

'No news?'

'None.'

Dad put down his knife and fork. 'Have you been crying?'

'No.'

'You have.'

Mum looked distracted, not quite there. 'I'm just...I was thinking about my mother.'

'What about her?'

'Just the pity of it, our relationship. I wish it were different.'

'Are you thinking of getting back in touch with her then?'

'No,' Mum said.

Daniel poured himself a glass of water. He used only one hand, and the neck of the bottle knocked against the glass.

Dad gave him an irritated glance, then turned back to Mum. 'You sure?'

'What's the point?'

'Well,' Dad said, 'you've done it before.'

Mum didn't say anything. Daniel noisily gulped down his

water and reached for the bottle again. Freya took it and filled his glass for him.

Dad watched her pour, drumming the thick fingers of his right hand on the table. 'Get in touch with her if you like,' he said to Mum. 'I'm not going to tell you what to do.'

'I don't want to get in touch with her.'

Dad nodded and pushed away his plate. He rolled himself a cigarette, put it in his mouth and lit it, keeping his eyes on Mum as he pulled back and then released the smoke. 'That's probably for the best. Some things you just have to leave behind.'

Freya kept eating. Daniel had arranged fragments of his macaroni and cheese around the edge of his plate, to make it look like he'd finished.

Dad's eyes swung towards her. 'And how was your day, Freya?'

'It was fine,' she said. 'Nothing to report.'

24

And then school was over, and she had survived a year of it, and that was doing better than some people. Freya lay in bed, listening to the sound of Dad's station wagon driving off down the street. She had been awake for ages, waiting for him to go. A bird started up outside, the one she'd heard for the first time nearly a year ago now, when they'd just moved in and the house was still a wreck and she'd woken every morning on her strip of foam in the dining room. Another summer, another world. It was summer again, but a cool, strange day that hardly wanted to admit it.

The bird threw its warbling, full-bodied cry out into the distance, its voice rising to a higher pitch, a more frantic rhythm, and another, further off, called back with the same melancholic frenzy. Freya got out of bed and went to the window. The outside of the glass was covered in a faint film of grime—salt, whatever else filled the air—and through its grey filter, she could see the harbour, and Stockton, and the yellow arc of sand that curved towards the distant wreck of the *Sygna*. She frowned and looked back around her room—at her books crammed into the bookcase, and the surface of her desk, littered with make-up and hairbands and cassettes with peeling labels, and her clothes strewn across the floor. She got back into bed, pulled the cover to her chin and lay there staring at the slanted ceiling a while before getting up again and going downstairs.

She spent the rest of the morning and the early afternoon stretched on the couch watching daytime television. Daniel wandered around, playing with Lego in his room, bringing some of it down and quietly building and dismantling objects on the thick patterned rug Mum and Dad had bought second-hand for the living room, and then disappeared back up to his room. At one point she heard a strange thumping noise, as if her brother were playing hopscotch upstairs, then the sound of his clarinet. He was still practising 'The Final Countdown', his notes closer together now, more convincing, even sounding pretty good at times.

Mum wandered around the house too, sweeping away the dust like it wouldn't come back in a few days, putting new flowers in the vases in the living room and the dining room, arranging them and rearranging them with jerky motions of her hands until she stepped away with an air of not quite having succeeded.

For a while Freya read a book while the record player was on—the Mamas and the Papas, then Neil Sedaka and, a few times over, *The Very Best of Don McLean*, and then Tim Buckley, then the Smiths. Every now and again Mum would come in, and if their eyes met she'd give Freya a bright smile, but at other times there'd be a look on her face like she didn't see anything around her.

In the midafternoon, someone knocked at the door and Mum answered it.

Richard's voice filled the hall. 'Maryanne, what are you up to?'

'Not much. Just cleaning,' Mum said. 'It never seems to end.'

'Tell me about it. I'm going for a walk. Want to come along?'

'The kids are home. They've started their holidays.'

'They can come too.'

'I don't know.'

'What else are you going to do, Maryanne?'

'I don't know.'

There was silence, as if Mum had asked rather than answered a question, one that Richard couldn't answer.

Freya got off the couch and walked into the hall. 'Hi, Richard.'

'Hey, gorgeous. How are you?'

'Good,' she said, suppressing a yawn.

'That's you all over,' Richard said. 'Steady as a rock.'

'I probably should do a few things,' Mum said, 'before Roy gets home.'

'Oh, come on.' Richard put his hands in his pockets. 'There won't be many days like this before it gets into the ugly part of summer again.'

Mum laughed. 'Okay, we'll go out—but just for a little while.'

Soon they were walking, one narrow street, then another, heading towards Nobbys Beach, and the way out to the lighthouse. Richard was whistling as they walked.

'Why are you always so cheerful?' Mum said.

Richard laughed. 'Me? When I'm not cheerful, I'm drunk. I'm a sad drunk, and then you won't see me at all.'

'So that explains why I haven't seen you these last few weeks,' Mum said.

'It hasn't been pretty,' Richard murmured.

'What's a sad drunk?' Daniel said.

'Nothing you need to know about,' Mum told him.

'You've probably seen one without realising it,' Freya said to Daniel.

Mum glanced at her. 'What?'

'Nothing,' she said.

'Freya has real sass,' Richard said. 'I love that.'

'She has her moments,' Mum said.

They had left the road and were walking along the causeway that ran behind the beach. To their right, on the other side of a ridge of low, saltbush-covered dunes, waves were peeling from the ocean and striking the sand in clean rippling sheets. To their left, a breeze feathered the grey-brown waters of the harbour. The causeway divided up ahead—one part continued on and became the breakwall, while the other part, blocked off by a boom gate, veered up towards the lighthouse on the top of the headland.

'You know this wasn't always here,' Richard said as they made their way towards the fork in the path.

'What wasn't?' Mum asked.

'Any of it. The causeway. Nobbys Beach.' He swept one arm back the way they'd come. 'A hundred and fifty years ago, we'd have been walking across water. The headland was an island— they kept convicts on it for a while—and this was a channel.'

'Right here?' Daniel asked.

'Yep. Maybe right beneath our feet. They started building it to protect the ships coming into the harbour, because it was so dangerous. Ships used to sink here all the time, so they lopped the top off the island and used the rocks for the causeway. Convicts did the hardest part—the poor bastards had to work day and night, even during storms, on the edge of a raging sea.'

'Where'd the beach come from then?' Daniel asked.

'The beach is just the sand that has been washing up against the causeway ever since.'

'And the ships didn't sink anymore?' Daniel asked.

'No,' Richard said. 'They kept sinking. There were still lots of shipwrecks until they built the two breakwalls either side of the harbour. The worst was a steamship called the *Cawarra*. It went down just as it rounded Nobbys Head. It took hours—crew and passengers getting washed into the sea and drowning while everyone just stood on the shore, watching. There was only one survivor.'

'They didn't try to save them?' Mum asked. 'If they were that close?'

'The harbour rescue boat didn't come out—there was some kind of scandal, not enough men on duty or some of them were drunk—and you have to imagine how dangerous it was back then, the deep water, the powerful currents, oyster banks, rocks like teeth, huge waves.'

The distorted, nasal tone of a lifesaver came to them on the wind, carried from the beach, directing swimmers back between the flags.

Daniel climbed up onto a rock and stared over the saltbushes towards the sea. 'Is the ship still in the water?'

Richard nodded. 'Not just that one—dozens. They built them into the breakwalls. The *Cawarra*'s over on the Stockton side.'

'Wow,' Mum said. She shielded her eyes, stared down the length of the beach, caught Freya's eye and grinned at her, a wild, open smile.

Freya smiled back. 'Ships still sink, though,' she said to

254

Richard. 'Like the *Sygna*.'

'That's true,' Richard said. 'Human error. When people are involved, you can't get rid of the risks entirely—you just manage them the best you can.'

'Yes,' Mum said. 'I know about that.'

Richard chuckled. 'Anyway.' He pointed at the headland. 'The local Aboriginal people used to say that there was a giant kangaroo sleeping in there. Every now and again it shakes its tail and the whole place shakes.'

'Like an earthquake?' Daniel asked.

'I guess so. Might have been like ten thousand years ago, when it happened the last time. The locals think about time differently to us. The real locals, I mean.'

'Will it happen again?' Daniel asked.

'What?'

'The kangaroo?'

'Probably,' Richard said. 'I'm sure we'll be long gone, though.'

They reached the boom gate where the path divided. Richard crouched to get under it.

'The sign says keep out,' Mum said.

Richard smiled. 'Yeah, well—bit rich coming from them.'

'From who?' Freya asked.

'You know, the family that live here now to look after the lighthouse. How long do you think *they've* been here?'

Freya didn't know.

'The blink of an eye,' Richard said. He was on the other side of the boom gate.

'You sure about this?' Mum said.

'Oh, *live* a little, Maryanne,' he laughed.

Freya went under the gate. Mum followed, and then Daniel. They all started walking again, up towards the lighthouse, breathing a little heavier against the steepening incline.

'I know the family, anyway,' Richard said. 'They won't mind.'

'I don't believe a word of what you say,' Mum said.

'Oh good,' Richard replied. 'Now we're getting somewhere.'

They stopped as the path came to an end near the lighthouse, and turned to look back at the city. It was deceptive, the height they'd climbed—far higher than Freya had imagined. She could see the buildings surrounding the mall, and above them, the steep hills around the cathedral. Further off was the obelisk, a white needle pointing straight up at the sky. Before all of that lay the harbour, narrow at the neck and broad in its belly as it forked into two grey-brown rivers that twisted their way inland between the factories and coal terminals.

Looking north, across the harbour, she could see the Stockton breakwall, with its hidden bones of long-dead ships, and beyond it the long, isolated curve of beach where the girl from her school had been murdered. Much closer, a coal ship was gliding towards them, heading for open water. She looked down across its deck, imagined standing on it, watching the land slide past until there was no land left, only water, and water, and water.

They began walking down again, back towards the causeway.

'They were going to blow all of this up in the end,' Richard said, 'so that sailing ships would be able to get into the harbour without losing the wind. They ran all of these tunnels underneath where we are, and through the centre of the headland. They were going to fill it all with dynamite.'

'Why didn't they?' Freya asked.

Richard shrugged. 'Maybe they realised they were being stupid. Maybe they realised it was important, what they were destroying. Funny, isn't it. That headland's millions of years old, and they'd have destroyed it for ships that became obsolete a few decades later. Idiots will sometimes tell you that Aboriginal people have no sense of time. But it's us. We're the ones who don't. We're the ones who don't learn from it.'

Maryanne sighed. 'Is there a place in this entire town that isn't riddled with holes?'

He laughed. 'Not likely.'

A couple of old women walked by. One of them took in Daniel and then smiled at Richard.

'He looks just like you,' the woman said.

Richard and Daniel glanced at each other. Both had a slight stoop, their hands clasped behind their backs.

'He could do worse,' Richard replied.

After the women had passed, he made a show of hooking his arm through Mum's and walked several steps in a way that reminded Freya of *The Wizard of Oz*, then Mum pushed him away with a laugh. Daniel had stopped walking and looked at them in silence.

'Don't worry,' Richard said looking back at him. 'I won't steal her away.'

'More's the pity,' Mum said.

They kept walking. Freya pushed Daniel gently on the shoulder. 'They're mucking around.'

'I wasn't worried.'

'Okay then. Good.'

They didn't go straight home, but kept following the shoreline south until they had passed the baths and come to the esplanade overlooking Newcastle Beach. They stopped in at the ice-cream shop opposite the brothel. It smelled of waffles inside. Richard insisted on buying them all an ice-cream. 'What else am I going to do with my money?' he said.

When they turned into their street, they saw Dad's station

wagon parked out the front of the house. They slowed down, finished their ice-creams.

'Were we out that long?' Mum asked.

'Only an hour or so,' Richard said.

'He must be home early.'

They fell silent as they walked the last stretch to the house.

Richard hesitated as he reached his front steps, watching as they went past him and up their own steps to the front door. 'Goodbye then,' he said, and gave them an awkward nod before he took out his key and disappeared from sight. They stood there, Freya, Mum, Daniel, each on a separate step, all of them fixed on the quiet sound of Richard's door closing. Then Freya looked at Mum and waited.

25

Maryanne shook herself and opened the front door into the house. It was surprisingly dark inside. The only light came from down the hall, in the kitchen, but the thick, low sound of a throat being cleared came from the dining room as the lock snicked into place behind them.

Without needing to be told, without saying a word, Freya and Daniel went up to their rooms. Maryanne stood at the foot of the stairs, her hand on the bannister. The sound of their feet overhead and the closing of their bedroom doors made her feel abandoned and relieved at the same time.

She walked into the dining room, her eyes still adjusting after the glare outside, dark blotches swimming in her vision and coming together to make Roy's shape, hunched forward over the dining table.

She flicked on the light. 'You're home early. I thought they had a full day for you.'

Roy lowered his head. 'They did, but it doesn't matter.' There was a little grey, she noticed, in the dark, thick sprawl of curls that ran from the nape of his neck up into the close-cropped tangle at the base of his skull. His hands were clasped together in front of him, resting on the table. 'Where have you been?'

'Just out for a walk,' she said.

'Oh,' he said.

'What's wrong?'

He held up his left hand to show a bandage around his thumb, soaked with blood, a dark line of it dried along the inside of his forearm, halfway to his elbow.

'Let me see.' She pulled out a chair next to him, her knees either side of him, took his hand, unwrapped the bandage.

'It's deep,' she said. 'How did you do this?'

'I wasn't paying attention.'

'So that's where Daniel gets it from.'

He didn't smile. 'I was thinking.'

'It'll need a couple of stitches,' she said.

'I'll be fine. Just bandage it properly for me.'

'Okay.' She went and got the first-aid kit and came back to sit beside him.

He flinched a little as she took his finger and swabbed it clean with alcohol.

'Who,' he said, 'was that you were talking to outside?'

She kept her eyes on his hand. 'Just Richard.'

'Richard again.'

'He was just going for a walk,' she said. 'He asked us along.'

'Right.' His other fingers curled a little, and something

tightened in the fleshy part of his hand. 'So you go for walks with him now. Why didn't you say that in the first place?'

'Does it really matter what *order* I say things in?'

Maryanne focused on his hand. She put disinfectant on the wound, pressed it together and wrapped it firmly with clean white gauze. The dog was barking in the lane outside, in that rapid way it had, as if it were trapped inside a burning house. She tried to make her voice light. 'You know, we should walk together more. I like walking. It's easy to get out of the habit.'

He put his left hand on hers, closed it around her fingers and pressed her hand against the table, the bandage rough against her skin. The gesture made her feel oddly naked. He was studying her, waiting, his chin and mouth making a jagged cleft of shadow. She smiled—a stiff, false smile—and waited too.

'Okay,' he said. 'We'll go for a walk sometime.'

'I'd like that.' She pulled her hand out from under his and rose to her feet. 'I'm going to have a shower, then I'll cook dinner.'

'You've just been with a man,' he said, 'and now you're going to have a shower.'

For a moment they faced one another in silence.

'Go on then,' he said. 'It was a joke.'

He rolled a cigarette and brought it to his mouth. She could hear him flicking at his lighter as she walked up the stairs.

'We'll go, though,' he called softly after her. 'Soon.'

~

A week later they were walking, just as promised, Maryanne and Roy, and Daniel, the three of them on an outing like any family, but sometimes promises like this weren't the ones you wanted kept. Freya had refused to come. She'd already gone that way, she'd told them, her jaw set in a defiant line as she'd looked from Maryanne to Roy. They weren't going to force her, and so they'd gone without her. Somehow that refusal of Freya's, the knowing manner of it, had affected Roy, Maryanne sensed it, like some small fuse had been lit inside him and was burning its way through his nerves. He kept his head down as they walked.

Where the causeway divided they veered left, out along the breakwall. It was a strip of concrete only a few metres wide that jutted from the headland, separating the ocean from the harbour. Daniel ran up ahead and swerved against a gust of wind. He flung his skinny arms either side of him for balance, then recovered and slowed down.

'He doesn't run like a boy,' Roy said.

She ignored him. A week. A week since they'd gone for their walk out to the lighthouse with Richard, a week in which the weather had turned on its head the way it did on the coast, everything—the warmth, the calm, the clarity—thrown away, rain coming over at unpredictable moments, on again, off again, pummelling in fists against the windows and the roof, then fragments of blue stumbling across the sky, a sudden burn of intolerable sun, before the clouds locked back into place again and it was all humidity, and waiting, just waiting, for something to break.

The shelter of the headland was behind them, and they held hands as the wind buffeted them. It was like they were on a ship out at sea, Maryanne thought, one of those long container ships that queued up on the horizon, carrying their cargo, coming and going from this place to the next—but this one was carrying nothing and going nowhere, and only the water moved, beating the shore the way it always had, and always would, until none of this was left. Up ahead, the red warning light mounted on its wooden platform blinked through the hazy air.

To one side was the harbour—grey, impenetrable, almost calm—but on the other was the ocean, wild and windblown, booming against the concrete blocks that lined the breakwall, hissing through cracks and crevices between them, clouds of spray drifting across the path with each wave.

'Let's turn back,' Maryanne said.

Roy glanced at her, his dark face flushed, teeth bared, everything in his eyes moving. 'Where's your sense of adventure?'

'Back home,' she said. 'That's where it is.'

They kept walking.

'You know why I hurt my thumb?' Roy said, raising his voice to keep it above the wind. 'I was distracted. I was thinking. Do you know what I was thinking about?'

'Daniel!' she called. 'Not too far ahead.'

Her son ran on without stopping.

'Why is it,' Roy said, 'that you never mention anyone from work?'

She hesitated. 'I mention people. All the time.'

He cut her a quick glance, dense with calculation. 'Not the men.'

'Where did that come from?'

Maryanne wasn't sure if he was serious. He often said things in an offhand way at first—it was how he followed them up that counted, how the conversation dropped from one moment to the next, like the lurch you felt going down in a lift. Perhaps it hadn't been Freya's words that had lit the fuse, set him smouldering, but this thing, this other thing.

'Just tell me,' he said.

'Don't be—' she began, and regretted it straight away.

'Don't be what?' he said. 'Crazy? Stupid? Ridiculous?' His

voice was bitter, accusing, but eager too.

They kept on walking, leaning a little against each gust of wind, a couple, like all the other couples out for a stroll along the breakwall.

She shook her head. 'I wasn't going to say that.'

'What then? What were you going to say?' She hadn't noticed his grip getting tighter, but now it hurt. She didn't know how to take her hand away without making a scene, without starting something.

'Not *that*. I wasn't going to say that.'

He jerked her to a standstill, turned his back to the ocean to face her, still holding her hand, like he'd forgotten he was holding it, tugging her slightly off balance. 'What then?' It was almost a snarl.

A couple walked by just then. She didn't look up, her face full of heat, but she saw the waves rolling in from the horizon strike the breakwall and burst into spray, wetting their legs and feet as they hurried past. She recalled what Richard had told her, the ship going down there in the mouth of the harbour, all the passengers drowning while people gathered on the shore and looked on, in horror or maybe just because it was the most interesting thing that had happened to them in a long while—a story you'd think back on years afterwards that let you know with a grateful shudder that, yes, you were still alive, even if sometimes you felt dead.

The hours it took for the ship to go down. One survivor.

Another couple were walking towards them, arms interlocked, leaning into one another. It wouldn't do them any good if a large wave hit, but Maryanne envied their closeness. Roy, with his back to them, turned to see what she was looking at, his face rigid. Neither the man nor the woman acknowledged him, and neither spoke as they walked past.

Roy turned back to her. 'Never the men. *Never.* You only talk about the women.'

Daniel was way ahead of them now, alongside the blinking red eye on its wooden platform near the end of the breakwall.

'Let's go back,' she said. 'Please.' She raised her voice, threw it down the length of the breakwall. 'Daniel!'

Did her son even hear her? She was about to call out to him again, louder, but Roy wrenched at her hand, still gripped tight in his fist, pulling her back around to face him.

'Never,' Roy repeated. 'So why?'

'I'm sure I have,' she said, but she couldn't remember. She couldn't—she just couldn't. Maybe she hadn't. And what if she hadn't? She tried to pull her hand free. The feeling was welling again inside her, the mad, relentless feeling of wanting to be away from him at any cost, of wanting to pull the pin on everything she'd been trying to hold together—and why not? Why had she come back to him, again, after everything, come here with him, come back for *this*?

'I want an answer,' he said.

She looked towards the bulwark at the end of the breakwall, the concrete slabs stark against the boiling grey sky surging above. Daniel looked so small, sheets of spray slicing through the air, soaking him as they splattered and fell. He was no longer running, but had turned and started back towards them, his head bowed, as if he were looking for something on the ground. The red light blinked atop its platform in a mute warning or reminder.

'And don't give me the silent treatment.'

'I'm not—'

'Talk then. Talk. Or do you only talk when you go for a stroll with Richard?'

'Listen—'

'No.' He finally released her hand but then took hold of her chin so that she couldn't look away. 'You're keeping something from me.'

An answer, fierce and reckless, stirred inside her. It was like standing on the edge of a cliff and wanting to topple forward. Except she *had* fallen before, too many times. And there was nothing you could do once you were falling. All the decisions were made.

Whatever thoughts were in her head, she had to guard them. Maryanne took a breath, made everything quiet inside her, and was about to answer when the air slapped around them in a booming roar and, as she wrenched free of Roy's grip in wild panic and turned towards her son, she was in time to see a foamy white wall of sea water explode around him.

Then she was screaming, Roy was running, the water tumbling in frothing torrents into the harbour on the other side of the breakwall. Roy was there ahead of her, ankle deep in water, his back turned, then he lifted a bundle and came stumbling back towards her, hugging Daniel's pale, bloodied, distant face to his chest.

~

They did not slow down or exchange a word until they got home, Roy clutching Daniel against his bare chest, holding his shirt, wet and bloody, to their son's forehead. He walked with his head down, not meeting her eyes, and a fury built inside her as she kept pace beside him. When he pushed through the front door, Maryanne was right behind him, and as he carried Daniel through to the living room, she snatched the blood-stained shirt from his hand.

'You're not holding it right,' she snapped as Roy lowered him onto the couch. Daniel's head slumped against the armrest, his face drained of colour, as she pressed the shirt against his forehead, but he was conscious, and his eyes, she noted with relief, were alert. The wound was nasty, but more of a graze—he'd only scraped his forehead.

'What happened?' Freya was standing behind them, in the hallway.

'A freak wave,' Roy answered in a thick voice.

'Show me your eyes again,' Maryanne said, peering at her son's face.

'He'll be okay,' Roy said. 'Boys get scratched up. It'll be fine.'

Maryanne stood up, focusing still on Daniel, but aware of Roy there in the doorway, bare-chested, hulking, with that air of sullen defensiveness, like an overgrown child, like it was her job to reassure him that he hadn't done anything wrong.

She turned her back on him, blocking his view of their son, some part of her daring him to be upset. She pushed the hair away from Daniel's forehead. 'Can you see everything clearly?'

'I think so,' Daniel mumbled.

'Go and get some ice,' she told Freya. 'Wrap it in a tea towel.'

'The water makes the blood run,' Roy said. 'Makes it look like more than it is.'

'We can't afford to take chances with him,' Maryanne said, and she could feel the edge creep into her voice, the dangerous contempt that must have betrayed itself in her expression as well. 'The specialist said that. Do you remember? When he was in hospital with his injury? Do you remember that?'

Roy's voice was soft behind her. 'Is that a joke?'

Freya returned to the room. Maryanne took the tea towel from her, sat beside her son and put it gently against his head. 'We owe it to Daniel to be more careful.'

Roy scratched his cheek, nails scraping the hard bristle, as if his hand needed something, anything, to do. 'You were calling to him and he wasn't listening. That's what happened. He has to learn to pay attention to what's happening around him. He needs to take some responsibility.'

'Responsibility?' Maryanne couldn't contain herself anymore. She was up on her feet, facing him. 'Take responsibility? Like you do, Roy? Like you do?'

He actually took a step back, a startled look in his eyes. Then he recovered. 'Boys get hurt, Maryanne. They're meant to. It's normal.'

'What happened to him is *not* normal! You, Roy, are *not* normal!' Maryanne pushed him in the chest with one hard finger. 'What made me leave last year was not some fucking accident!' She pushed him again. 'It was not you being careless.' She pushed him again. 'You did it! You nearly killed him! It was *not* an accident. You aren't some freak fucking wave. You aren't a force of nature. You are a fucking man with a brain and you *decide* to do things!'

She went to push him again, but he caught her hand. He gave it a sharp, hard twist that made the bones in her wrist grind into one another, and then he tossed it away.

'And you?' he snarled. 'What about what *you* decide to do?'

Water dripped from his chin and glistened across his hairy chest. His hands had curled into fists and he stepped forward so that his face almost touched hers, something hard and endless and inviting in his eyes.

'Go on,' Maryanne said quietly. 'Show us your self-control.'

Every breath lifted and dropped his shoulders, his whole body taut, ready, straining towards her. Then he loosened, turned towards Freya and gave a strangled laugh. 'I'm not the one calling the shots, am I, Freya?'

'Leave her out of it,' Maryanne said.

'She's a part of this,' Roy said. 'We're all part of this. You'd better remember that.'

He walked out of the room, Freya stepping back to let him pass. Maryanne stared after him. His heavy tread lifted into the house above her. Their bedroom door slammed shut. She had wanted something from him, she realised. She had wanted him to snap one last time, so she could take the children and walk out, do it when her anger was larger than everything else put together, when it filled the space inside her that had been carved out by exhaustion and anxiety and doubt, when it all became worth the risk.

'Mum?' Daniel stirred on the couch.

Freya was watching her too.

Her racing heart. The sudden trembling that surged up from her knees, the wash of adrenalin that had nowhere to go, and the heat in her wrist, now a dull, aching throb. She stood there between her children in silence, knowing that they were waiting—they were always waiting for her. Then she sat down again, put the ice against her son's head and stroked his hair with her other hand.

'It's okay,' she said eventually. 'Everything is okay.'

~

Whenever something like that happened between them, a fight like that, if it remained unresolved by the time they went to bed, they would end up having sex. It was something she couldn't really understand, as if the energy that had erupted needed an outlet, one way or the other. He'd be insistent, urgent, vulnerable and aggressively sexual all at once, not so much apologising as offering himself, and wanting something in return. To say no to him then seemed inconceivable, like breaking a law of nature. And the truth of it was, when she gave him what he wanted, no matter what her mood had been before then, she *enjoyed* it on some level, that sense of being anchored, of being consumed by something vital and fundamental. God, it didn't even make sense to her, let alone anyone else, but there it was.

Afterwards, Maryanne took a deep breath as Roy rolled off her. Her body felt sticky, her pubic bone tender, her chest hollowed out. Her wrist still hurt. Her pulse was losing its urgency, a strange, frozen clarity settling over her thoughts. They lay on their backs, the sheet drawn across their waists, his hand slung like an anchor across her belly, those thick, heavy fingers splayed.

'That was good,' he said.

She didn't say anything. She wanted to, but she couldn't. He repulsed her all of a sudden, his nearness, the weight of him.

The curtains were flapping softly in the wind, by turns clinging against the window frames then snapping into the room. She got up to go to the bathroom. The light was on in the landing. Daniel's door was ajar. She stepped under the shower and let the water run across her body, enjoying the feeling of the water, so hot it was almost painful, burning into her and spilling away. Roy. She thought of him, there on the other side of that wall, in the bedroom. She thought of him on the day their son had nearly died—how long ago was it now? Almost two years, *two years*. She turned off the taps, tightened them, but they were still dripping as she stepped out onto the cold tiles.

She hoped that he would be asleep, and when she walked back into the room she thought at first that he might be, lying there with the white sheet bunched at his tanned side like a wave that had washed up against a hard coastline, one arm over his head. But then she lay down beside him and he shifted his arm, put his hand back on her belly, settled those thick, rough fingers into her skin.

'Yeah,' he said, as if they had just finished, as if he had taken a single breath since she had gone and come back. 'That was definitely good.'

She lay there and did not speak.

'You know, it's pretty much done,' he said, staring up at the ceiling. 'This house. We set out to do it in a year, and we did. No wonder we're on edge, hey? There's a few things to do still, bit of work on the bathroom, and outside, but really nothing that'll take too long. I can see to that after Christmas. Then we can think about what to do next—if we're going to sell it, or maybe hang on to it. What do you think?'

She didn't answer.

He turned his head. 'Are you even listening to me?'

'Sorry, I was—'

'What?' He raised himself on one elbow. 'What?'

'Thinking.'

He was silent, something working on the other side of his eyes. 'About today?'

'Just thinking,' she said.

'I'm sorry I hurt you,' he said. 'And about what happened. Let's move on.'

'Because that's what we *do*,' she murmured.

He made a sound somewhere between a laugh and a grunt, his mouth closed. 'You just can't help yourself, can you,' he said. 'Look at all the good it's done you, all this *thinking* you always do.'

'Maybe I'll learn.'

'What's that supposed to mean?'

'Nothing. It means nothing, Roy.' She curled into herself with the blanket around her.

He lay down again too, and the room became quiet and heavy until she heard him begin to snore. She shut her eyes, floated in a waking dream alongside him, and in the noise of his breath she heard that wave on the breakwall, saw it over and over again, Daniel caught and swept away from her, felt that feeling, that terrible feeling, wondering why her voice had not been loud enough to call him back or if she had even called him at all.

26

Without realising that she was going to do it, Maryanne picked up the phone and dialled her mother's number. Her mother picked up after two rings.

'God,' Maryanne said. 'Were you just standing there waiting for me to call?'

'That's what I do,' her mother answered.

Maryanne wondered if calling her had been a mistake.

'Well?' her mother said. 'What's happening?'

Everything was arranged in her head, pressed in there, waiting to explode out of a single, compressed space—the things she would tell her mother, the man Roy had beaten in front of the children, the walk on the breakwall, the wave, Daniel, the way she had faced Roy afterwards and been sure that he was going to snap—all of that waiting to burst out of her.

'I just wanted to see how you were,' she said.

'Well, good. The new medication they've got me on is working beautifully.'

Did her mother mean that she was good, or that it was good that she'd rung? A pause lengthened between them. Maryanne imagined her mother adjusting her hair with one hand.

'How is Roy?' her mother asked.

'Fine,' Maryanne said. 'He's done a great job with the house. You didn't see it when we first moved in—'

'And how are the children?'

'They're well. Daniel had an accident—'

Her mother's voice tightened. 'An accident?'

'A wave,' Maryanne said quickly. 'He was hit by a wave.'

In her head, all she could see was Roy afterwards, in the living room, his bare chest heaving, the whole of him a coiled spring, his eyes unrecognisable.

'Is he okay?'

'He's fine. He cut his forehead, but he's okay.'

Her mother pressed on. 'It *was* a wave, wasn't it? Were *you* there?'

'Yes,' Maryanne said, feeling the back of her neck prickle with irritation and something else more desperate. 'Of course I was there. Why do you have to make everything so difficult?'

When her mother spoke again, her voice was cool, formal. 'Is there something on your mind?'

Maryanne wrapped the cord of the phone around her fingers, pulling it tight. 'I just wanted to talk, really, just to hear your voice.'

'All right,' her mother said. 'Well, I'm good, and you're good, and I'm glad Roy's behaving. I suppose things have fallen into place for you.'

'They have,' Maryanne said. She was glad her mother couldn't see her face.

Her mother sighed. 'God, Maryanne. You should be with someone who treats a woman properly.'

Maryanne laughed sharply. 'Like Dad?'

'Well, why not like that?'

'You never said anything when *he* hit me.'

Her mother drew an exasperated breath. 'Don't go confusing what he did once or twice with what Roy does. No one back then gave a smack a second thought. Things are different now.'

'For you, maybe.'

'Well,' her mother said. 'It's Christmas coming up. I'll be thinking of you and the children. I hope you'll be able to enjoy it.'

'I have to go,' Maryanne said.

'Of course you do.'

'There's someone at the door.'

'Well, that's convenient.'

Maryanne held the phone at arm's length. She stared at it, and then she pressed the plastic receiver to her cheek again. 'I love you.'

'So you should. I'm your mother.'

As Maryanne started to put down the phone, her mother's voice came back at her.

'Maryanne, wait.'

'What?'

'Your father wasn't perfect. I wasn't either. But it's your life now. You're at the wheel. There are people depending on you.'

'Yes, so you've told me. I have to go.'

'The door,' her mother said. 'Yes. Well, you know how to reach me, and I guess I'll just be waiting until then.'

Maryanne returned the phone to its cradle and walked down the hall. She opened the front door without knowing why, almost as if she had to, as if opening it would somehow make what she'd said to her mother less of a lie. As she looked out, the neighbours across the road were getting into their car. The man looked up at her and smiled and then, still smiling, got into the car and drove off. Her heart was thumping in her chest, as if it were about to burst through. How could the world not hear it?

~

Maryanne left Daniel with Freya and walked into the mall alone. She wanted to walk, to keep walking, until there was nothing left inside her to think about. She wanted to see people, strangers, but she did not want to talk, and she avoided anyone she recognised. There were always plenty of people from the hospital bustling around at all times of day. The harbour came at her in glimpses between the buildings, framed by the wires and fences and iron structures of the railway line.

David Jones was full of people and laughter and animated voices, the escalators carrying a constant flow of shoppers up and down from the higher floors. She drifted around the ground floor in the narrow channels between shelves and racks, looking at hats and bags and gloves as if she were making decisions, but she didn't really see any of the things that passed through her hands. She had a splitting headache. She rummaged for Panadol in her bag and swallowed three.

She wasn't looking where she was going and almost collided with an older man, who leaned back to let her pass. He was well dressed, a salt and pepper beard shaped around his jaw. He gave her a smile and a wink that emptied from his eyes as swiftly as water tipped from a glass. It made her think of her father.

Her father. The way he'd always opened the door for her mother, or pulled out her chair when they went out. The way he'd sat there in the years before his death, slowly deflating, in his favourite chair or at the dining table. He had been pleasant enough as an old man, sitting there with his pipe, holding court for brief moments, easing off, letting Freya and then Daniel clamber around him, giving a soft chuckle if they misbehaved, shaking his head, but never saying anything much. She could still see it—his hand coming to rest on Freya's head, then lifting away, the bemused look on his face when she gave his leg a sudden hug. A benevolent vagueness had filled him up by then, only flashes coming through of what he'd been like before, when Maryanne was growing up. He had mellowed, like so many men did, better at being a grandfather than a father.

When she was nine or ten she had often played with the boys and girls on the street after dinner during summer, with the days winding away into long, sullen sunsets. One time she'd found herself in the diminishing tail of some long, worn-out summer afternoon, at the end of their street, beside a derelict house, in a hollow surrounded by several dense bushes, with a boy from the neighbourhood.

The other kids had all gone home, but they remained there, whether by pure chance or intention or the rhythm of the day or something more instinctive. Daring each other into something neither of them wanted to talk about. They'd been facing one another on their knees, almost close enough to touch, twigs and seeds digging into her knees. The smell and the taste of burnt leaves and blossoms hung in the air, the watchful sound of insects blurring the more distant sounds of the neighbourhood.

The boy had his shorts and underwear pulled down past his

thighs, which were pale and smooth and surprisingly not so very different from her own. She had her skirt around her waist. He was touching her very gently with a dry length of grass. Perhaps it was the heat that softened the world outside even as it sharpened theirs, or perhaps their intense fascination, but neither of them heard the approach of her father until the bushes nearest them were violently shoved apart and he stood there looking in. She had probably dropped her skirt in time, but the boy's pale genitals were on full display. The boy stayed there on his knees, staring up at her father with a blanched, stunned look.

She did not even remember her father's face, only that he picked her up by the hair and dragged her back towards the house without ever letting go, and that when she tripped, she felt a hot pain ripple through her skull, and all she saw looking up was his broad, implacable back. Inside the house, he threw her down and kicked her. It was the first time she remembered being kicked by anyone. The shock of it was worse than the sensation—being on the floor, her bladder emptying, her hands not knowing where to go, once or twice catching the hard tip of his shoes, her mother hiding somewhere, in some other part of the house, until it was over.

Her back and buttocks had still felt hot and bruised when she sat at the table for dinner.

Her father did not look at her. 'Maryanne should stay inside more after school,' he said as her mother handed him the gravy dish. 'Help you around the house.'

Her mother had nodded and then asked a few questions about his day.

When he'd finished eating, her father dabbed at his mouth with a napkin and leaned back in his chair while her mother cleared the table. He appeared thoughtful—sad, somehow. Her mother paused near him as she walked out with the used dishes, to rest her free hand on his shoulder, and her mouth pursed, her eyes flicking for a moment from Maryanne to the top of her father's lowered head.

And there was a clarity in that gaze, like all the parts in her eyes had shifted for a brief instant to show the thoughts on the other side clear and unfiltered, and her mother knew exactly what. Then she lifted some loose fragment of hair or lint from his jacket in a way that was both tentative and affectionate, and walked off into the kitchen.

Maryanne saw the boy from the bushes around a few more times, but they never spoke again, as if any words at all might resurrect between them the humiliating and shameful shape of her father.

~

After she'd taken the Panadol, Maryanne headed in the direction of the house, but she turned right before she came to their street and wandered instead to the beach. It was wild again today, the heat in the sun magnified through high grey clouds, but the wind that swept in off the water was cool, the red flags warning people away from the surf whipping and snapping with each gust. She found a pack of Valium in her handbag and took a couple of those as well.

Walking south along the esplanade to the end of the beach, she came to a set of crumbling concrete steps and followed them up to the narrow road beneath the cliff that led towards the terraced park overlooking the sea. She was sweating, could feel it dripping along her ribs and down the small of her back. At the top of the park she took another road back down the hill, back towards the sea, not stopping to look around her or take in the view. She followed the road as it dipped down past the squat bunker-like structure of the police station, and past the hospital and the people there leaning on the balconies stacked up against the sky.

She lit a cigarette and smoked as she walked. It was strange how often, when her mind was free of other things, her thoughts now turned to Roy, the thought of leaving him. Just thinking of it, being immersed in the thought of it like some sort of dream, was exhilarating—living in a house that was empty of him, just her and the children—but then there was always the anxious tumble of decisions to be made, actions taken, the impenetrable valley of cause and effect, and finally the bleak tension of wondering what it would mean to set all that into motion, the counting of what would be destroyed, what would be left standing—and above all what *he* would do.

Eventually she reached the street that intersected theirs and carried on until she reached their back alley. The dog was barking, the sound echoing down the length of the narrow lane. Its home was a small courtyard out the back of a terrace a few doors from theirs. She came to a halt beside a gate as high as her head, dropped the smouldering stub of the cigarette and ground it under her foot. The gate shuddered against the dog's weight and the scrabble of its claws. Through a gap in the wood, she could see it, a chocolate labrador with large, black, shining eyes.

'Why don't you just shut up!' she hissed. 'It's not getting you anywhere!'

The dog kept barking. Maryanne wanted to wrench open the gate and send the dog running down the alley and out of the neighbourhood forever. She wanted to hit the dog with her bag. She wanted to fill a piece of meat with poison and shove it into the animal's mouth.

There were tears in her eyes. Her vision was all blurry with them. She wiped her face with the sleeve of her shirt and got her first clear look at the dog. It was watching her intently now, without making a sound. Crouching beside the gate, she pushed her hand through the gap. The dog came forward, its head lowered, silent. She stroked its muzzle, its wet nose. Her rage was gone and she felt only pity.

'It's okay,' she told it. 'Everything's okay. I understand.'

The dog pressed its nose against her hand, and then she felt the warm, wet rasp of its tongue.

By the time she got home and closed the gate of the courtyard behind her, the dog was barking again.

Daniel came out as she walked into the kitchen.

'What is it?' she asked.

'Nothing,' he said.

She pulled him in close, his warm, thin body, ran her hand over his forehead and the bandage there. 'Does it still hurt?'

'No.'

'Good. That's good.'

He was studying her. 'Are you sad?'

'No.'

'You are.'

'No, sweetheart.' She gently pushed him away. 'It's just my day off. I just want to have a day off.'

'Do you want to hear my song? I've been practising.'

'I wouldn't be a good listener right now. Maybe later.'

'When?'

'Tonight. After dinner.'

'I want to play for you now.'

'Just…let me be for a while, okay?' She put her hand on his head, touched the edge of the bandage again, ran her fingers through his hair, but he walked away without a pause.

It was one in the afternoon. Hunger gnawed at her stomach, but she didn't want to eat. She took more tablets. Valium barely seemed to touch her—it hadn't for a long time. She lay down on the couch, her heartbeat flicking like a whip against the inside of her ears. Her eyelids sank down for a moment, and when she opened them, it was two-thirty. Roy would be home soon. The mountain of everything she would have to get through before she lay down again that night in bed reared above her.

She imagined him getting into his car and driving home from work, in towards the city, towards her, guiding the car along with one hand on the steering wheel, a cigarette hanging from his mouth, one hairy elbow resting on the edge of the wound-down window. She pictured another car coming in the other direction. She pictured the two cars crumpling into one another. She sobbed. For grief, for loss, for something that had long since been dug out of her.

She went down the hallway and picked up the phone. She dialled. Her mother did not pick up this time. 'It's me,' she said to the answering machine. 'I need to talk to you. We need to talk. Mum, are you there? Can you pick up? Please pick up.'

She put down the phone, wiped her face with the back of one hand, and stood there staring at the phone, willing it to ring. She could remember it all too clearly, her mother's hand on her father's shoulder, that look in her mother's grey eyes, and the way it had been buried with that small, controlled gesture of affection. It wasn't fair to think of it now, but she couldn't help it. She could see her mother sitting in her chair by the window, staring at the phone too, that same look in her eye, and giving a slight, almost imperceptible shake of her head. As if to say, you can wait. You can wait a little longer.

27

And then it was full-blown summer, and the year had dwindled to a few last restless days. Christmas had come and gone, and Freya was glad it was over, all of them stuck there together in the stifling heat and gloom of the house, and who cared about presents, and her and Mum both thinking of Nan but not talking about her, Dad veering between bursts of good humour and black, brooding moods, and the beach too blisteringly bright and crowded to offer any sort of relief. She was stretched out on her bed, headphones on, listening to music. Heat already radiated through the window in her bedroom and it was only morning. The forecast was for a storm today, severe weather. She was longing for it, but there was no sign of it yet. It was impossible even to imagine.

Mum and Dad were talking again downstairs—she could

hear them through the music—and after a while she realised they were getting louder. She took off her headphones and swung out of bed. By the time she'd made it down the stairs to the landing outside Daniel's room, they had fallen silent.

They were below her in the hallway. Dad was pressing Mum against the wall by the neck, his face close to hers. A step creaked under Freya's feet. He turned and saw her standing there, blinked rapidly several times and dropped his hand. Mum rubbed her neck and looked away.

'Freya,' he said. 'We were talking.'

Freya didn't say anything.

'Why don't you get out for a while?' he said hoarsely. 'It's beautiful out there.'

He stepped back from Mum, wiped his hands down his shirt and thrust them into his pockets. Mum manoeuvred past him and disappeared towards the kitchen. He glanced after her, then back up at Freya.

'Don't waste it,' he said, 'the morning.'

He took his house keys from the hook that he'd mounted on the wall near the front door, gave her an awkward nod and left the house. Freya waited until he'd gone before she came down into the hall.

Mum was in the kitchen. The tap was running and she was facing the courtyard, splashing water onto her face. A thousand thoughts ran through Freya's head, but in the end she couldn't figure out what to say, so she backed away, returned to her room and lay back down on her bed. She put her headphones on and pressed *play* on the Walkman, then *stop*, then she fast-forwarded until she found herself halfway through a song by Pink Floyd about being comfortably numb, and she wished that was her, comfortably numb, but the numbness inside was too heavy to be anything close to comfortable, and her heart beat through it like a blunt hammer.

She closed her eyes and thought of Josh's mother, standing up on that cliff, thinking—what? There was a new song on about being on thin ice, things cracking. She became aware that she was trembling, but it was not her, it was the bed itself, and as she realised this, the trembling exploded into a violent, rocking lurch that threw her from the bed onto the floor, which was shaking too, and it might have been an explosion, the way the walls wrenched into life, but they kept moving, back and forth, and back and forth, the whole structure around her drawing into a shuddering kinaesthetic groan, and she was part of the house, part of its coming apart, part of the glass shattering and objects thumping down around her, her eyes fixed on the carpet, her knees and elbows rigid, the ground beneath her lifting, rolling, as if on a wave, and her mouth open, caught on a breath, a scream that she could not release, until there was nothing, nothing around her— and all of it stopped.

She was on her hands and knees, remained there, waiting, listening warily to the sudden quiet of the house, but nothing came. She got up, slowly, and took a shaky step towards the window. A huge crack had appeared through one of the panes, right across the sky. Dust swirled up from somewhere past the houses on the other side of the road. The sun blazed down across an empty blue sky.

The door swung open behind her. Mum stood in the doorway, Daniel's arms around her waist. 'We've just had an earthquake. A big one. Let's get outside.'

Out the front, people were spilling onto the street, milling about—neighbours, Freya supposed, people whose faces were only a little familiar, whose lives seemed almost as remote from hers and from each other's as they were from life at the bottom of the ocean, but they were talking to one another now like they were old friends. Richard was on the footpath with an old woman, and they joined him.

'There won't be another one straight away,' Richard was saying. 'There might be an aftershock later.'

'But did you hear the crash?' the woman said, her eyes large.

Richard nodded. 'A big building's come down somewhere on the other side of the mall.'

The woman's red painted lips sagged at the corners. 'What about *our* houses?'

Richard shook his head. 'Don't worry, they're not going to come down. They'll be here long after we are.'

From the direction of the hospital, they heard several ambulances start their sirens, loud at first, then trailing off as they sped away into the city.

Mum looked in the direction of the hospital. 'There could be a lot of people injured. They're going to need everyone they can get at the hospital.'

'Go on then,' Richard said. 'I can keep an eye on the kids for you.'

Mum hesitated. 'Maybe just until Roy gets back?'

'Yeah,' Richard said, 'maybe until then.'

'He can't be far away,' Mum said.

She went inside and soon she was back out again with her uniform on.

'Don't go, Mum,' Daniel said.

She put a hand on his head. 'I'm only a few blocks away. People will need me over there. Your sister's here, and Richard too. You'll be fine.'

Freya put her arms about him and they watched Mum walk

286

away, her steps quick and sure, until she vanished around the corner.

'Hey!'

Josh was coming down the street towards them. He'd been running.

'Hey, yourself,' Freya said as he came closer.

He stopped in front of them and stood there, breathing hard. 'I just came to see if you needed any help.'

A faint smile crept onto Richard's face. 'You look like you need a glass of water. I'll be right back.' He went inside.

Freya stood facing Josh. 'What would you have done if we actually needed help? Like if we were trapped under rubble or something?'

He grinned and flexed his skinny arms. 'I would have used my superhuman strength to get you out.'

Richard came out and gave Josh the glass of water, and then looked around for Daniel, who was standing at the edge of the footpath, his face tilted up towards the house. 'Don't worry,' Richard said. 'You know how long these houses have been here?'

Daniel shrugged.

'You can see the years they were built along the top.' Richard pointed at the facade above Freya's window. 'See? Yours says 1905.' He winked at Freya, and then, still talking and pointing up at the houses, one hand on Daniel's shoulder, guided him away.

Freya sat with Josh on the steps. They both looked at the street, at the people clustered on the footpath, arms crossed, still talking, occasionally staring at their houses with wary expressions. Freya and Josh talked for a while too, and then they lapsed into silence.

'Listen,' Josh said then, 'I'm sorry.'

'For what?'

'For telling you about my mum. I shouldn't have. You didn't

need to know that. I wish *I* didn't know.'

'It was okay.'

He was sitting with his elbows on his knees, his chin cupped in his hands. 'Not like that. I'm over it, anyway.'

'No you're not. How could you be?'

'No.' He smiled. 'I'm not, and I couldn't. But listen. If you just want to be friends, that's okay too. We can be friends. The way I see it, people like you and me need all the friends we can get. You can't knock that back, especially not for any stupid reasons, not in a place like this.'

'Do you think it'd be better somewhere else?'

'What?'

'Life.'

'Like in Sydney?' he said.

'I don't know. Another country maybe even. Just right away from here.'

He shrugged. 'Depends. It's worth finding out, I guess. Better than always wondering.'

'You have it, you know,' she said.

'What?'

'Superhuman strength. Your mum killed herself, and you get up and go to school every day.' She laughed a little. 'Or most days.'

'Thanks,' he said, and gave a brief smile. He rested his arms on his knees, and they looked out together, towards the harbour.

Freya wanted to put her hand on his shoulder, but she didn't. She sat beside him, though, and the silence between them was at least comfortable again.

At that moment, Dad's car pulled up out the front.

Dad got out, glanced from her to Josh and back again. 'I tried to call. The phones are all dead.'

Richard came over, Daniel beside him. 'Hi there, Roy.

Maryanne's gone off to the hospital. I was keeping an eye on the kids until you got here.'

Dad grunted. 'And she just went off, leaving you in charge, did she?'

'There'll be people injured,' Richard said. 'She wanted to help.'

'She always wants to help other people.' Dad glanced from Freya to Daniel. 'Come inside with me.'

'Go on,' Richard said to Daniel. 'I'll see you soon.'

He turned to go.

'Richard,' Dad called.

'What?'

Dad walked back down the steps, so that he was standing right up in Richard's face, his arms tense, hands not quite loose. Richard was taller than Dad, just, but much skinnier. 'They're *my* children,' Dad said. '*I'm* the one who tells them what to do. Got that?'

He turned and went into the house. Freya grimaced apologetically at Richard and took Daniel's hand.

'I'll see you later,' she said to Josh.

'Yeah,' he answered.

Dad was in the hallway. He was touching the walls, running his hands over the cracks as if he were nursing a dying animal. Freya hesitated to go past him, and he didn't seem in a hurry to move.

'So much work,' he said, and she didn't know if he was talking about what had been lost or what was still to come.

28

By the time Maryanne got there, they were already bringing people out of the hospital. The North Wing, the York Wing, the outpatients building—all were being emptied. Stunned patients were walking or being guided out the doors, standing there in the park, looking up at the hospital, medical staff everywhere, bustling about, getting organised.

'We have to go up,' a nursing unit manager was saying. 'We'll need to bring down the patients who can't move. We can't use the lifts. There could be an aftershock.'

'I'm not going in there again,' someone said. 'The whole place could collapse.'

Maryanne stepped forward. 'If it goes, it goes. It's the same for us, really.'

Adrian Godfrey was rolling up his sleeves. 'There's no point waiting around, then.'

A group of them started forward, more surged behind them, and then she was clambering up the granite steps, solid under her feet, though they were hidden in near darkness, and then back out into the light of day. The abandoned wards looked so strange, cluttered with overturned trays and blankets and all sorts of debris. The only thing that felt the same was the view of the sea framed by every window they passed, and the sea breeze that came through.

Doctors, clinicians, orderlies and nurses were moving around her, anyone who could do anything, and then down the stairs she went with Adrian and two others, each of them grasping a corner of a blanket—it was all they could lay hold of at short notice—with an old man not long out of surgery slung between them, groaning softly with each step.

As they worked, bits of information came through—widespread damage, injuries, a number of fatalities, most of them where the Workers Club had collapsed, although there would have been a lot more had the earthquake struck in the evening.

It was nearing the middle of the day. Outside, ambulances were coming and going, their sirens blaring. Tarpaulins out in the park shaded patients against the blazing sun, food was being organised, and a couple of lifesavers had brought over large wheelie bins full of drinks. People were holding up blankets so that patients could go to the toilet. 'Just put the blanket over my head,' an old woman said to an orderly as Maryanne walked past. 'I don't care if people see me doing my business—I just don't want to see *them*.'

Minutes later they were climbing the steps again, making their way back into the wards. Someone had already ransacked a drugs cabinet, pulled it straight off the wall to get it open.

Maryanne shook her head. 'When did they even find the time to do that?'

'There's always an opportunity,' Adrian said, giving her a look, 'if you're willing to take it.'

Things didn't slow down the whole day. A woman was brought in from nearby in the back of a car. She'd been under an awning that had collapsed. A couple of doctors stood in the makeshift emergency ward in the park discussing what to do with her. The triage nurse looked down at her. 'It doesn't matter. She's dying.' Maryanne found herself sitting beside the woman, who was not much older than her, watching her die. She held the woman's hand, and wondered as she waited who would sit by her bed one day.

By the time the last patients were being put into an ambulance and taken off towards other hospitals, she was beyond exhausted, and the sun was gone. Workmen were setting up barriers and fencing around the hospital. Maryanne stood at the edge of the park, slid a cigarette between her lips and stared up at the Nickson Wing.

Adrian came to stand beside her. He offered a lighter and she bent her head towards it.

'Shame to think this is probably the end for the place,' he said.

She drew in the smoke and exhaled. 'What do you mean?'

'There've been people wanting to get rid of the hospital for a long time. Coastal land's worth a fortune these days. They've already got engineers talking about demolishing it.'

'Do you think they will?'

'Like I said,' he smiled, 'there's always an opportunity, if you're willing to take it.'

'I can't imagine this neighbourhood without the hospital,' she said.

He lit his own cigarette. 'I used to go bodysurfing when I was on call. I'd just keep an eye on the Nickson Wing. Someone would hang a red towel over the balcony if they needed me. I'd be up there in five minutes.' He glanced at her. 'That's not something they let you do these days. I guess everything changes.'

'My unit's being closed down,' she said, 'but they told us it was just for the time being. I've been given a few days off while they figure out where they're going to put me next. I'm not looking forward to it.'

'You'll be fine,' he said. 'They'll be happy to have you wherever you end up.'

She gave a wry shake of her head. 'I wasn't talking about that. I meant being home with Roy.'

'Oh,' he said. 'Right.'

She wiped her damp face with the back of one hand. 'Isn't there meant to be a storm coming tonight?'

Adrian nodded. 'Apparently it's already in Sydney, a big one.'

'You wouldn't know it, would you?'

He squinted at the sky. 'Not yet. They can blow in very quickly, though.'

'I'd better go,' Maryanne said, with one last look towards the hospital.

'I'll see you soon,' he told her. 'Wherever they decide to put you.'

29

The window in Freya's bedroom didn't open or close properly anymore. At night, with any sort of breeze, it creaked and rattled against its frame. So much damage had been done in less than thirty seconds—walls had ruptured, floorboards warped, pipes burst. Half the ceiling in Mum and Dad's bedroom had come down. A week had passed since the earthquake, and Dad had started on the repairs, but he hadn't got far. When she walked through the house, Freya could feel currents of air moving again through new gaps that had appeared. They were warm this afternoon, the draughts, like steam escaping from some hidden machine.

Mum was downstairs at the dining room table. Freya went to the phone without speaking to her and dialled Ally's number.

'What time do you want to meet?' Ally said.

'Six?'

'Do you want me to come over to your house?'

'No,' she said. 'Let's meet in the park opposite the police station.'

She was about to go back to her room when Mum called out to her. 'Freya?'

'What?' She paused at the foot of the stairs.

Mum's hands were clasped around a cup of tea. She was peering into the cup like she was staring into a well.

'Are you going out tonight?'

'Yeah, with some friends. Just for a while.'

'You haven't even asked me.'

'Can I then?'

Mum's eyes were red, and her face was blotchy, like she'd been crying. 'How's it going with that boy?'

'What boy?'

'Josh?'

'I don't see him much,' Freya said.

'What's going on between you two?'

Freya stared at her in silence.

'Okay,' Mum said with a weary half-smile. 'Okay.'

'Can I go then?'

'I suppose.' Mum took a sip from the cup. 'Don't drink, stay together, be safe. I'm not saying *you* would do anything stupid, but you never know what other people are capable of, right? And home by ten-thirty.'

Freya frowned. 'Since when do I have to be home by ten-thirty?'

'There's still a murderer out there.'

'There's probably still lots of murderers out there.'

'I'm not sure if that's supposed to make me feel better,' Mum said dryly.

'I'm fifteen, Mum. Isn't that how old you were when you started going out with Dad?'

'Okay,' Mum said after a pause. 'Let's say eleven. I'll be at work by then, so I guess I'll just have to trust you. Can I trust you?'

'Of course.'

Mum shrugged. 'Your father will be here anyway.'

Freya hesitated. 'Mum?'

'What?'

'When did you realise? About Dad?'

'What are you talking about?'

'You know, Mum. You know what I'm saying.'

They looked at one another in silence. Mum didn't blink. Then she smiled gently. 'When did I realise what he was like?' She shook her head. 'I could try explaining it, but I don't think you'd understand. I hope you never do. When someone becomes your world, you can't see things clearly. You can't even see *them* clearly. And before you know it…' She sighed. 'It's too late.' She put her hands on the table in front of her and studied them. 'I'm waiting for my hands to start looking like my mother's. Just waiting. If someone had told me fifteen years ago that I'd be feeling this way, I wouldn't have believed them.'

Freya went into the kitchen, poured a glass of water and drank it while she thought about what Mum had said. Mum was still sitting at the table, watching her.

'I don't regret it,' Mum said finally.

Freya looked at her but didn't say anything.

'See,' Mum went on, 'whatever else there's been between your father and me, there's also you. There's also Daniel. I wouldn't be without the two of you for the world.'

Freya wanted to say then that she could never imagine it, choosing a man like Dad, not for anything, not even for the world.

Instead she nodded and headed for the stairs.

'Freya.'

She looked back. 'Yeah?'

'How would you feel about it,' Mum said, 'if we actually left him? Like really. For good. If we never came back?'

'I'd be happy.'

'You wouldn't have a father to come home to. Maybe that's worse than you think.'

'There's worse things than not having a father to come home to.'

There was a long silence between them.

'I know,' Mum said.

Freya swallowed, about to speak, but the front door opened and closed. Dad's breath, his footsteps, came towards them. He appeared in the doorway.

'Hey,' he said.

'Hey,' Freya answered, but he was looking at Mum. As he stepped into the dining room, she slipped past him out into the hall, climbed the stairs, away from them. In her room, she studied her face in the mirror, stretched the skin under her lip taut and looked at the fine pimples there, ran a brush through her hair, listening. She wondered if Josh's mother had known on the morning of her death that she would do it, that it would happen. She wondered what the difference was between thinking it and doing it.

Below, Mum and Dad had gone into their bedroom. They were talking. Someone turned on a tap. Water throbbed and moaned through the pipes, and then there was a resonant knocking that came through the house's innards before the sound was ~~throttled~~ off. She glanced at her watch.

Ally was supposed to meet her in an hour. They would buy alcohol and walk together to the party. It was at a small beach called Susan Gilmore—named after a shipwreck, Richard had told her once—separated and hidden from the rest of the coast beneath sheer cliffs. The party had been planned two weeks ago, before the quake. If anything, the conditions were better now, better than they would ever be again. The whole inner city was dead, barricades everywhere, half the streetlights still without power. There wouldn't be many people around. The beach would belong to them.

Since the earthquake, the whole town felt as if it were being dismantled rather than put back together—like their house, like everything—but what did it matter when you were outside, and getting drunk, and you didn't really know what would happen in that dark, open-ended expanse of the evening, with no one to control you or hold you back?

It was mainly Mum's voice she could hear downstairs.

A ship's horn blasted the air like it was coming from the next room. Framed in the window, the rust-coloured hull of the ship slid past the rocks and the treetops, between the city and Stockton, where the girl had died. Freya saw the white block of the ship's cabin, a latticework of small black windows, the tiny figure of a sailor on a balcony the size of a thumbnail. She squinted and imagined the earth moving again, the amazing out-of-control feeling of it.

Perhaps they weren't fighting downstairs after all.

She sat on her desk by the window and painted her nails. It was difficult to keep her hand from shaking. She held it up, tried to force it to stay steady. It was difficult to keep anything steady.

Did it even matter? It would be dark tonight—no one would see the flaws. But *she* would know. She thought of Josh and wondered what he was doing. She touched her mouth, felt her breath, warm and vital, over her fingers. Such a fleeting thing, a breath.

An edge came into Mum's voice down below, that brittle fineness pitted all of a sudden with anxiety, then rising and sharpening to a new pitch, Dad's dogged tone hacking through it. Yes, they were fighting, no doubt about it, and this was how it would be between them until the end of time, no matter what anyone else said or did. And Mum would never, ever walk away. She would leave again, maybe, but then she would come back, and Freya had no idea why, or how she could stand it, and the thought of seeing that, of being part of it, was more than she could bear.

Catching sight of herself in the full-length mirror, she decided that her cut-off shorts were all wrong. She needed to get out into the sun more. Her upper legs were pale and thin and particularly stick-like today—she could hardly look at them. She suddenly thought of Mr Hind, the vulnerable look of his face without glasses, and when she'd yelled at him, and it made her feel a white-hot stab of guilt, like she'd betrayed someone who mattered, but how long ago was all that now? It was last year. Everything would start again soon enough. And did anyone matter, really? In the end, everyone was just…what?

Onlookers, strangers—no matter what they pretended.

She wanted some pot, needed it all dull in her head, not this busyness, this constant back and forth of thought, but she didn't have any, and she didn't want to call Josh, not for that. She opened the wardrobe door, chose a dark blue dress and slipped into it. The door creaked behind her.

'What are you doing?'

She glanced at Daniel over her shoulder. 'Getting ready. What are you doing?'

Daniel was wearing boxer shorts that looked too big and a T-shirt that didn't quite cover his belly. He walked into the room and sat on her bed, shifted around until he was comfortable.

Freya sat down beside him. 'What's up?' she said.

He looked at the floor and shrugged. 'I'm scared.'

'What do you mean?'

'I don't know.'

'There's not going to be another earthquake.'

'There was one the next day,' he said.

'That was an aftershock.'

'A what?'

'An aftershock,' she said. 'Like an echo. There's always an aftershock, but there won't be anything else. Not for years now. That's what earthquakes are really about. Just releasing tension. It all builds up underground for years and years, and then, just like that, it's okay again, and everything starts over.'

'Why?'

'That's just how it is.'

'No, why did it happen?'

'Maybe it's all those holes under the ground. The tunnels.'

Daniel stared at her, and she made herself smile at him. 'Don't worry.'

'Maybe it won't start over,' he said. 'Maybe it'll get worse. The holes are still there. Or maybe it was the kangaroo.'

'The what?'

'You know.'

'Oh, right, what Richard said about the headland? That's just a story.' She picked up her brush and began running it through her hair again. 'Nothing's going to happen now, okay?'

He nodded doubtfully. 'Okay.'

'Well,' she said, standing up, 'how do I look?'

'Pretty,' Daniel told her without lifting his head. 'Are you going out tonight?'

'Yeah.'

'I don't want you to go.'

'Why?'

'You promised you'd read with me tonight, before I went to sleep.'

Freya remembered and felt guilty. He looked so vulnerable and lonely, her brother, like he needed someone close. 'Daniel,' she said. 'I'm sorry. I forgot.'

'That's okay.'

Freya put down the brush, sat beside him again and put an arm around his bony shoulders, drawing him in towards her. He still barely came up to her shoulder, like he hadn't really grown at all in the last year—or maybe it was just that they'd both grown.

'Tomorrow, I'll read. And tonight, when I come home, I'll check in on you.'

'I'll be asleep,' he said.

She tickled him under his arms until he giggled. 'Then I'll wake you.'

He wandered off again, after that, leaving her alone.

Her parents had gone silent downstairs. There was a record playing. Freya faced herself in the mirror, frowned at what she saw. She was hungry, but she didn't want to stop to eat at home. If Mum saw her in this dress, made some comment, she'd want to change it again. With her shoes in one hand she walked halfway down the stairs. The warm crackle of the record player scraped out a song—a French voice, it sounded like, and an accordion expanding and contracting in the background.

Illuminated by the antique lights mounted on the wall, the polish of the hallway floor was so deep, the grain of the wood so fine and dark, that she could imagine walking down the stairs and stepping right into it, the wood pooling first around her feet, then her ankles, then her knees, then her waist—warm, maybe, like something living. But then she reached the bottom of the stairs and the ground was cool and hard and ungiving as it pushed against her toes and flattened the balls of her feet.

Freya paused, her hand on the bannister, her breath rapid, as if her body knew something she didn't. The music surrounded her. The woman was still singing, and the accordion beat and wavered through the subtle popping and hissing of vinyl that always reminded her of a fire burning low in a quiet room. It occurred to her all at once that maybe Daniel hadn't been talking about the earthquake when he said he'd been scared. She crept up the hallway towards the front door and paused, peering cautiously into the living room, hanging back a little. She could only see part of the room from where she stood, the soft yellow light bouncing up off the floorboards and making the white walls hazy.

Then her parents came into view, making a slow circle, Mum's long hair undone, her head resting on Dad's shoulder, her hand limp at his neck, the wedding ring glinting on her finger as they moved, his hand on the small of her back, their legs carrying them into the darkness. Then they were gone. Before they could reappear, Freya was slipping back down the hall and through the kitchen into the courtyard, out into the lengthening afternoon.

30

Maryanne heard the back door close, a furtive sound, and felt a sudden pang of loneliness. She stopped dancing, let her arms drop from Roy's shoulders.

'What?' he said.

Maryanne stared past him to the fading daylight that lingered on the wall out in the hallway. The song had ended. Another started up. 'I think Freya's left. She didn't even say goodbye. I just wanted to say goodbye to her.'

'That's Freya for you.'

'I should check on dinner.'

She tried to pull away from his arm round her waist, his hand on her back, but he didn't let go.

'Don't think we've settled anything.' His eyes flickered across her face. 'We still need to finish talking before you go to work.'

'Roy,' she said. 'Not now. Let's leave each other tonight on a good note.'

'Leave on a good note?' He frowned, made her face him. 'Is that all we do now? No, there's more I want to say. We have to work it out.'

'What is it you want to work out, exactly?'

His grip tightened. 'See? That's what I mean.'

She pulled herself free with a violent motion. 'What are you even talking about?'

'*You.*' His mouth twisted around the word. 'That's what you said. What are *you* even talking about. As if it's me and not *us*. Like I'm the one who has things to work out, like it's got nothing to do with you, like you've got one foot out the door already anyway, like you're some fucking saint. You're not, you know.'

She sighed, then walked over to the lamp on the side table beside the record player and switched it on. She lifted the needle from the record, and it was quiet. 'What is it you want, Roy? Sorry, what is it *we* want?'

The shadow of a passer-by slid across the window, across the blind still aglow with the fading daylight. The walker's crisp, light footsteps passed on, a reminder of the world stretching out beyond the house, a world in which people lived without a second thought for what happened here between Roy and her.

'What is it you want?' she repeated.

There was no pause for thought. 'Let's start with Daniel.'

'What about him?'

'You should never have brought up the police. I want you to admit that.'

'I meant what I said. You can't do it again.'

'Listen to yourself.' He took a step towards her. 'You'd call the police on me if I touched him? You'd do that—to me? He's my son, for God's sake. I'm allowed to discipline him if he steps out of line. I shouldn't have to be looking over my shoulder.'

'Isn't it enough that I let you get away with what you do to *me*?' She stopped herself, startled at her own voice, and waited for a moment before she went on. 'You need to learn to control yourself, Roy. That's not about me or Daniel or anyone else. It's not about some total stranger who pisses you off in traffic.'

'You're my wife, aren't you?'

'If this is how you treat your wife, why should I want to be?'

'We're back to that, are we?'

'I don't know *where* we are, Roy.'

'You don't want to be my wife?' He spread his arms, the gesture taking in the whole house. 'After I did all this?'

She looked back at him. 'You didn't do all of this just for me.'

'Who did I do it for then?'

She shrugged. 'I don't think *you* know why you do half the things you do. I think it's got something to do with your father, or not having a mother. You don't know how to love.'

Roy nodded jerkily. 'Sure, I don't know how to love, and you do. You've done a great job of that.'

'I've tried, Roy. It's all we can do.'

'Tried?' He spoke through clenched teeth. 'You have to make more of a goddamn effort when you're actually *trying*, Maryanne. Threatening to call the police on your husband is not making an effort. Talking to some faggot behind my back is not making an effort. Using my own son as a weapon against me is not making a fucking effort.'

'No,' she said. 'None of that is the problem here.'

He stepped closer to her, so that the space between them was gone. 'What's the problem then? Tell me.'

'Mum?' Daniel was standing in the doorway.

Maryanne pushed past Roy and went to her son. 'What is it?'

'I'm hungry,' he said.

Roy gave a soft grunt behind her.

Her pulse was thrumming against her temple. She took a breath, released only part of it. Roy was standing there still, in the middle of the room, all his weight concentrated in his stare. Even with her back to him, she could feel it bearing down on her shoulders and neck. She smiled at Daniel. 'Of course you are, darling. Dinner must be ready. Let's have some.'

A stew. The meat was tender—it had been cooking for long enough. They sat around the table, the three of them, and ate, though Maryanne only picked at it, had trouble swallowing. The news was on, grainy pictures of the long-ruling Romanian dictator and his wife who had been executed in Europe on Christmas Day.

'Aren't you eating?' Roy said.

She shook her head. 'I don't feel well.'

A bird was calling out in the gathering gloom outside, its sad cry lifting and falling above the soft burr of the television in the corner, and the dog was barking too. Get out, she imagined it crying. Get out. Roy was staring at her, and she kept a smile on her face, never meeting his eyes, while she figured out what to do next.

~

After dinner, she took Daniel upstairs. It was a relief to have an excuse to be away from Roy. While Daniel showered, she stayed in his room, then she put him in bed and sat with him, running her hands gently through his damp hair.

'You still haven't listened to the songs I learned,' he said.

'I promise, tomorrow.'

He pulled the sheet up to his neck. 'Are you going to work tonight?'

'Yes,' she said.

Daniel's expression collapsed a little. 'I don't like it when you're not home at night.'

She kissed him on the forehead. 'Close your eyes, and when you open them, it'll be morning and I'll be home. That's how you make time disappear.'

'I don't want to,' he muttered.

'It's easy,' she told him. 'I'll do it too.'

It was silent downstairs. Roy hadn't turned on the television or put on a record. She imagined him sitting at the dining table with his large, restless hands in front of him, brooding on his anger, building it. There was nothing she could do about that now. One thing at a time. She rested her head against Daniel's, let herself be calmed by his breath against her skin, its particular childish scent, and waited for her son to fall asleep.

31

The sun was gone and Ally was holding her hand in a sweaty grip as they passed a bottle between them. They crossed the barrier and set off along the path from the cliffs down to the beach, and Freya saw a fire burning below. There were moths around her, a plague of them, something strange and biblical, bogong moths, beating soft and powdery through the air. She'd never seen so many.

The roar of the sea gathered and thickened in the salt-saturated air. She thought about Daniel, the broken promise—who would read to him if she didn't? She thought about Josh, his mother in midair, plummeting towards the hard ground and away from him, away from everyone she had ever loved. Love—what was it even? She laughed.

'What's so funny?'

'Nothing. These moths. There's so many of them.'

'I know,' Ally said. 'Never seen anything like it.'

'I'm so drunk.'

'Slow down then.'

'Nah. Let's speed up.'

A pleasant fog swirled around her head, but it was treacherous too, like it was hiding something that meant her harm, and she realised that, in a way, she was afraid of herself, like she didn't know what she would do next. She shivered and rubbed her arms. Ally handed her the bottle and she swallowed another mouthful of the cheap, sweet, passionfruit-flavoured wine. It was easy to drink, went straight to your head without you hardly noticing. The gassy drink ballooned inside her and lapped at the bottom of her throat, threatening to come up.

She tried to imagine Mum somewhere like this, doing something like this. Mum must have. She must have all the time. God, she *never* wanted to be like Mum. But she wanted to figure it out—how you could end up like that, with a man like Dad, how you could stay with him and live like that for so long, longer than she had even been alive?

They were halfway down the narrow concrete path, with the cliff face beside them and the rocks and scraps of saltbush falling away in a ragged tumble towards the sand. She burped. Ally laughed at her. She saw in her mind suddenly the girl from school, the one who had been killed, standing in the quadrangle, one hand on her hip, talking to a boy, looking over her shoulder a moment, looking behind her, before laughing and returning to whatever it was she'd been saying. Like she'd known, or some part of her had, that something was waiting for her.

'It's funny how it all just goes on, isn't it?' Freya said.

309

'What do you mean?'

'Well, that girl from school got killed at a party. And here we are, at another party. And whoever did it is still out there.'

Ally looked away. 'You're being morbid.'

Freya ignored her. 'She was like this person that we knew and talked to—I mean not much, but still. And now she's just like a story we talk about.'

'Weird, huh. Anyway, that was last year. New beginnings, all that.'

'Yeah,' Freya said.

As they stepped onto the beach, the fire was burning high before them. Piles of driftwood lay heaped like bodies in its light. A portable stereo wedged in the sand was playing 'Johnny Come Home' by Fine Young Cannibals. She walked with Ally over to some of the boys and started talking. Despite the heat of the day, it was cool down here between the sea and the cliffs, and getting cooler now that darkness was falling. Only the sand was warm.

All the while, Freya kept drinking, one conversation bleeding into the next, one song into another, more and more stars filling up the sky. Mum would be heading off to work soon, off to see that doctor with the white hair, to stand around and chat and laugh with him, maybe. Did Mum think about *them* when she was at work? When she was that other person, the one who threw her head back when she laughed? Mum said she always worried about them, but at the hospital that day she'd looked like she didn't have a worry in the world. Freya thought about the girl from school again, wondered what she'd told her mum before she went out that night. And somewhere in all of that thought, she was standing alone again with Ally.

'Do you reckon she knew?'

Ally looked at her with glazed eyes. 'What?'

'You know, her mum. That girl who was murdered.'

'Are you *still* talking about that? Have you been obsessing about that all this time?'

'But do you think she knew something was wrong, that her daughter was gone, before she like found out?'

'How would she have?'

'I don't know. You know how they reckon people just feel things sometimes?'

Ally shrugged. 'I've never thought about that. You need to stop thinking about it too. No one wants to talk about that anymore.'

Suddenly Freya didn't want to talk about it anymore either. She took the bottle out of Ally's hands and swallowed a warm mouthful before handing it back. Someone was looking at her across the fire. Tim. A shiver rippled through her.

She wanted to fold her arms across her chest, but she didn't. He came walking over. He had a goatee these days, a bunch of leather necklaces draped against the taut indentation of his tanned chest, a shark tooth on display, an ivory cross. It made him look even older. Before she knew it, they were talking together, just the two of them, at the edge of the water.

'Haven't seen you around much,' he said.

'I haven't been going down to the beach that much.'

'Shame. You looked good in a bikini. Here, have some of this.'

He gave her his flask, and she took a swig. It was whisky or something like that. It burned the insides of her cheeks and her throat and made her cough. He laughed and she saw the white edge of his upper teeth as he cocked his head to one side. A muscle flexed in the line of his jaw, like he was chewing on something.

'The first bit,' he said, 'always tastes like shit.'

'After that it tastes good?'

'After that you stop noticing.'

She nodded, swallowed some more while he watched. She thought about the darkness of the water and how there could be anything under it now, anything, swimming close to the shore right where some of the others were splashing around. Anything, and you wouldn't know until it found you.

She licked her lips. Her mouth felt dry. The tape finished and then someone put in a different mix. The first song on was 'Jeane' by the Smiths. Josh had put that song on a tape for her. That line about happiness and not knowing what it meant but looking into someone's eyes and not seeing it there—she loved it.

'What?' Tim said.

'Nothing,' she said. 'I like this song.'

A couple of boys threw a heavy piece of driftwood onto the fire. Cinders flew up from the fire in plumes of heat and wafted over the sand. Within the dark boundary of rock and saltbush at the foot of the cliff, someone was hunched over and vomiting.

She suddenly noticed Josh sitting there off to one side with a couple of other boys.

And Ally was standing beside her again. 'I'm going. This party's no good. You coming?'

It was past ten already. She should be heading home soon. *Can I trust you?* Mum had asked her.

Freya felt Tim listening beside her. 'I might stay,' she said.

'Sure?'

'Yeah.'

Ally dragged her off to one side, swayed in and out of her vision. 'You're too drunk. He's like twenty-something.'

'So?'

'You're fifteen. And he's a creep. Everyone knows he's a creep. Except his stupid deadshit mates. How can you not see that?'

'Maybe you just don't know him.'

A look of disgust passed over Ally's face. 'I know him all right. You just have to *look* at a guy like that to know him.'

'Maybe that's the thing.' Freya heard herself laugh. 'You don't even know anything about *me*.'

'What?'

'Nothing. I'm staying here for now.'

Ally tugged at her hand. 'Come back with me. Don't be an idiot. You're smashed.'

'I'm not. Just go. I'll be fine. I can look after myself.'

'I'm not leaving you.'

Freya raised her voice. 'Go on. Just go.' A few people turned their heads. 'Fuck, Ally. Don't act like my mum. I've already got one. Go.'

'I'll give her a lift home,' Tim said, and something in his voice unsettled her, but it didn't make her change her mind. And then Ally was gone, walking up the narrow steps towards the city, which from this angle, down below on the beach, with the sea so close, might not have even been there at all.

32

Maryanne lifted her head with a start. Daniel was snoring softly. She realised that she had drifted off too. It was almost time to go to work. Her face felt sweaty. It was hot in the bedroom. She rose to her feet, went to the balcony door and opened it. She stood there and watched her son, lying in his bed, hardly filling it—he was still not a large boy, he never would be—with his sheet already flung to one side, his fragile-looking chest covered only in a white singlet, rising and falling with his breath. She remembered the girl who'd nearly died on the ward.

How tenuous these moments were, she thought, between life and death, those small choices you made, like making an extra phone call when you'd been told not to, or leaving for work when some instinct warned against it. She stepped onto the balcony. It was warm outside too, and humid. A moth fluttered against her, and then another. A single star shone over the line of rooftops between her and the sea. She had never noticed that star before—God, how couldn't she have? It was fierce. Nearby, lights had sprung up everywhere, from all the different windows that looked out on her, all the lives she did not know though they were so close to her own.

Moths were fluttering around her through the haze, spiralling up through the darkness against the stars, more of them than she'd ever seen, and they were crawling along the railing of the balcony too and on the glass of the window beside it. She could hear the soft, sloughing rhythm of the ocean, and she wondered about Freya, where she was right now, *who* she was right now. It wasn't her daughter's fault. The fault was Maryanne's—she'd been preoccupied, let herself be consumed by her own problems. That was why her daughter was lost. That was why *she* was lost too.

She went inside but kept the door wedged open for whatever breeze there was. The moths didn't matter—she felt sorry for them.

Downstairs it was even warmer. Roy was sitting on the couch in the living room, his feet on the coffee table, contemplating the record player, which rested in its dark corner of the room.

'I apologise,' Roy murmured. 'For everything. Your turn.'

She'd been determined to lie, to make peace between them again, to bury all of this for now, to wait until the morning at least, but at those words, the tone in which he said them, something inside her fell into place.

'I don't want to,' she said.

He stood up. 'What?'

'I don't want to do this anymore.'

'Do what?'

'Be with you.'

Roy looked at her for a long pause, then he shook his head, and every part of his body shifted as he spoke. 'You don't mean that. If you mean it, fine. But you don't.'

She didn't say anything.

'Tell me you love me,' he said. He closed the distance between them. 'Just say you love me and we'll leave it for now.'

He tried to kiss her. She pushed him away. He looked startled, let himself be pushed—looked weak, so weak that she wanted to touch him, make sure that he was okay. Wasn't that one of the things she'd fallen in love with, that vulnerability? But she didn't touch him.

'Are you leaving me again?' he said.

Pity welled up inside her, but she did not stop. 'I have to.'

He nodded again, strangely calm. 'Where would you go?'

'I'll figure it out.'

He looked away from her and sighed. 'You mean your mother. You've been talking to your mother.'

'It doesn't matter.' She reached for his shoulder. 'Roy.'

He shrugged her off, began pacing. 'It does. Of course it does! Talking with your mother behind my back. I'd like to punch her fucking face in.'

'Roy, please don't talk like that.'

He bared his teeth. 'Doesn't it matter that I love you?'

'Of course it matters.'

He frowned. 'But what?'

'We're not good together.'

'What did I do? Is it because of the other day? Because I lost my temper?'

'It's not about that.'

He shook his head. 'You're lying. It's my fault. Of course it's my fault. That's what you're thinking. You're just not *saying* it. You've just been living here with me and letting me do all this, and planning your escape.'

'You need to calm down,' she said. 'I have to go to work.'

But she couldn't go to work, she knew that, not with him like this, so agitated, not with Daniel upstairs. Maybe he'd do nothing, but she couldn't be sure—she could never be sure, there was always the thought now—and it struck her then as madness that she had managed to live with him so long, that she had made herself do it, that she had *returned* to it. No, she couldn't go to work. What she had to do was get Daniel. What she had to do was walk out of the house with him and keep walking. She would figure out the rest later. She turned to leave the room. He blocked her exit with one arm across the doorway. His white T-shirt was stained with sweat. She could feel the heat radiating from his face.

'Look me in the eye,' he said. 'Say it like you mean it. Are you sure?'

There was a way to diffuse this, she knew, some careful combination of words, like last time, and the time before, and those words would lead into their bedroom and all would be buried between them, but she couldn't bring herself to say them, not again. She had to move on—she had to.

He was breathing hard, that wounded, pleading look in his eyes, and rage too, his whole body shivering with the effort of containing it. 'Do you really want to leave me?'

She felt exhausted, alive, terribly alive, and the hallway, the house, the whole world was leaning in towards her, daring her to say it.

33

The music kept playing, the sound steadier now that the wind had dropped off, but the song itself was high and wavering. 'Silver' by the Pixies—another one Josh had put on a mixtape for her. Freya shivered and looked around. The beach wasn't so crowded anymore. Couples were wandering off among the rocks or were entwined already at the foot of the cliffs. Others still stood at a distance from one another, drinking and staring at the flames, moths fluttering between them. There were bits of clothing strewn here and there on the sand, a few shadowy figures splashing out in the water.

Tim took her by the hand and pulled her away from the glow of the fire. They stopped near the water. There was a surfer's sinewy strength in his body, no fat on him, just hard skin and hard edges, an adult's heft in his movement that startled her when he drew her in close and kissed her. His tongue pushed into her mouth, and his hands fell from her back to her bum, pressing her against him, so that she could feel his hard-on through the metal kink of the zipper in his jeans, and she did not feel good or bad, but something stirred inside her. She tasted pot in his saliva. The inside of her own mouth felt tacky. When he let her go and pulled away, she caught a glimpse of Josh over his shoulder, sitting alone on the other side of the fire, looking straight at her over a can of beer. Their eyes met and he didn't look away. Tim jerked his head up towards the path.

'Let's go, eh? I know a better place than this.'

She hesitated.

'Come on.'

'Freya!' Josh was walking towards her.

'What?' she said.

'What are you doing?'

'Nothing,' she said.

Josh glanced towards Tim. 'You're not leaving, are you? Not with him?'

Tim's hand tightened on her arm. 'Shouldn't you be in bed or something, mate?'

Josh sneered. 'I'm not even talking to you, dickhead.'

Tim bristled. 'What'd you say?'

'Let's go,' Freya said quickly. 'Let's get out of here. He's drunk. Don't worry about it. See you, Josh.'

Tim let her guide him away then, towards the path that climbed away from the beach.

'It's your lucky day, mate,' he called over his shoulder.

Josh stared after them in silence.

~

Tim had left a light on in his car. Moths crawled across the windscreen in a writhing greyish-brown sheet. He squatted down, pulled his keys out of some dark inner crevice above the tyre, opened the driver's door, and got in. After a few attempts, the engine kicked into life, and it was all she could hear. He switched on the headlights and the windscreen-wipers, and the moths scattered everywhere, some of them caught under the blades of the wipers and smearing across the glass. She could hear him laugh.

The headlights illuminated a section of the white fence that ran along the edge of the cliff. It was hardly anything, that barrier—she could easily climb over it and step out to the sheer drop on the other side, the rocks and the sand below.

The passenger window came down and he was leaning across, the shark tooth dangling from his neck, his eyes rolled up towards her.

'Are you right?'

'Yeah.'

'Get in,' he said. 'It's unlocked.'

And then she was inside, and the door was closed, the fresh air replaced by vinyl and stale smoke, and with the breeze no longer on her, she realised that she was breathing hard from the walk, and sweating. The inside of his station wagon smelled of surfboards and piss-soaked wetsuits and something else she couldn't place. She felt the slightness of her dress, the way that it stuck to her, the way that it laid bare her legs, but she didn't move. He handed her a joint and she put it to her mouth and sucked back the smoke.

'It's good bud,' Tim said. 'Concentrated like. Blow your fucking head off.'

He reversed the car away from the fence and revved the engine

320

a few times before rolling forward. The windscreen-wipers were still going, dirty water dripping down the sides of the glass, the front almost but not quite clean. As they left the car park, Freya thought about Josh, how he'd looked at her down on the beach. She wondered if she liked him more than she was letting on.

She thought of Mum then, as they got out onto the road, and everything she'd said to her in the last months, and everything that had happened. She imagined moving out, leaving for good, and she felt powerful, like she had something over Mum, had something Mum needed, and she was stronger for it, stronger at least than Mum, and that was a start. She never wanted to be as weak as Mum, and she knew that she was terrified she might be—and to think there had been a point in her life when she'd been proud to hear someone say that she was just like her.

She barely noticed as the beach slid past her on the other side of the window. And what Mum had said about not regretting being with Dad because of her and Daniel? It was an excuse. Why hadn't she left after Daniel was born, then? Why hadn't she just taken both of them with her? What had Mum said? That she wouldn't give up her and Daniel for the world? God, why did she even think she *had* to?

Tim changed gears and, without taking his eyes off the road, put his hand on her knee.

Freya blinked. Her eyes felt dry, but it didn't help to close them, like she was cutting off her one real connection to the world. She needed to talk to someone. She needed to throw up. Or maybe she didn't, but it was close. Everything was moving, coming apart. Tim put on some music, something with a man yelling and growling and a mess of instruments pounding over and through his voice, and she just wanted it to stop, but it was so far away that maybe it didn't matter. She grinned desolately, and wondered if she was experiencing the drag of her lips away from her teeth or only remembering it, if she was happy or sad or neither or both. She realised with a shock that she had no idea how long they'd been driving.

'Where are we going?' she said.

Tim glanced at her, changed gears and moved his hand a little further up her thigh.

'I'll show you. You good?'

'Yeah.'

The road veered from the beach. They were above the city. They passed the turn-off that led to Ally's house and came onto the highway. Through the trees to one side she could see the suburbs, the lit-up factories piled up beyond them and the arching line of lights that marked the bridge to Stockton.

Tim turned up the volume and returned his hand to her leg. She pressed her knees together, but his hand had moved up to the hem of her dress, and she couldn't seem to slow down her breath, as if there were nothing in the world she could control, not even her own breath, and her whole life was just motion that she didn't control, even when she thought she could. She thought of Mum again. She thought of Dad with his hand tight around Mum's neck, looking up at Freya on the stairs and giving that smile, as if to apologise. She thought of the girl who had been murdered. She thought of Josh's mother on the cliff.

'I want to go home,' she said.

He turned down the music. 'What?'

'Home. I want to go home.'

'Why?'

'I don't feel so good.'

He laughed. 'I'll make you feel good, and *then* I'll take you home.'

The confidence in his voice filled her with rage. 'Let me out.'

'You're kidding, right?'

'I'm not kidding.'

He turned his head and looked at her narrowly. 'What'd I do?'

'I want to get out.'

Something tightened in his jaw. He looked back at the road. 'I don't get it.'

'I just want to get out.'

'Listen,' he said. 'You don't know *what* you want. Why'd you jump in the car with me, then? And why the fuck get out here?'

'Let me out. Now.'

He laughed again, but it was a different laugh, tight, angry. 'No. I don't think so.'

He leaned his head closer to the steering wheel, turned off the highway, bushland now on either side of them, the headlights washing into murky tangles of trees, pebbles snapping up from the tyres and rattling against the body of the car, a sensation of sliding. He didn't slow down.

'Let me out,' she said.

'Sweetheart.'

'Let me out.'

'You're not getting out!' he said. 'Pricktease. Stuck-up cunt. You *cunt*. I left that fucking party for you. I could've stayed. Let me have a feel of your tits at least.'

'No.'

'You don't act like a fucking tease and get away with it. You're going to show me something before we leave. That's why you got in the car with me and that's what you're going to do. That's how it is.'

'Let me out.'

'You dumb bitch,' he said through his teeth. 'What are you going to *do*, all the way out here?'

Freya began screaming. It felt good to scream, good to see the boy next to her—because he was still a boy, no matter what he pretended—shocked out of his confidence. She reached for the door. The car swerved and slowed down. His hand locked around her other wrist.

'Stupid fucking crazy bitch!' he snarled. 'All right! Fucking stop, all right?'

Freya pushed. The road was a blur beneath her.

34

An hour later, with all of that still coursing through her, she was alone, walking along the road that led up the coast towards home. The sea, its noise, its smell, filled the air around her, beat into her with the breeze, the great dark expanse of ocean crunching and rippling against the beach to her right. She trudged on until the sea disappeared from view to her right, the city opening up below her to the left—its long, straight roads and suburban streetlights, the bright smoke-plumed industrial zones, and the glittering swathe of the industrial harbour. At night it was beautiful.

Both her knees and hands were bloody, and with the alcohol wearing off, she was beginning to feel the damage she'd done jumping out of Tim's car. There was a long, deep scratch along her arm where Tim had made a grab at her. Though he'd been bringing the car to a stop, the impact when she hit the road had torn open her knees and jolted both her wrists. She'd jumped to her feet, and when he climbed out of the car and came to get her, tried to pick her up, she'd shaken him off. She would walk, she'd screamed at him. He'd returned to his car and driven alongside her for a while, by turns pleading and hurling abuse. She was fucking crazy—yes, she was a mad, stupid, stuck-up bitch who just needed a good fuck, like everyone said—but she'd cried back with savage abandon, 'So fucking what?' and he hadn't dared anything more.

She turned a corner and the obelisk came into view. She couldn't see the bottom of it, but she could picture that place in a smooth dip of her memory where she had lain back with Josh, their feet on the stone, the grass against their necks, their fingers almost touching. When she'd walked on a bit further, she paused and glanced back at it once more, the obelisk a luminous white path set against darkness, a bridge into nothing. Ahead was the hospital, and the headland from which the lighthouse cast its brilliant, sweeping beam. Everything she saw held some memory now, and maybe that was all there was to a place, the memories that started to fill it so that it became yours, even if you didn't want it.

To her right, as she kept walking, was the path that led to the Bogey Hole, and she did not go towards its damp, hidden darkness but followed the road as it swung down towards Newcastle Beach, which was lit and empty, and past the huge old hospital on the left, half of it shrouded, all of it surrounded by wire fencing—where Mum had worked until the earthquake— and into the last streets that separated her from home.

And then she was standing on the back wall and staring into her house.

There it was, home.

She did not know why she had walked towards it with such purpose, did not know what to do now. She could hardly bear the thought of going inside. There was a light on, not in the kitchen, but past it, perhaps in the hallway. She felt slightly sick and almost sober.

Her knees were throbbing, blood still welling up through the grit raked into her skin. Trickles of it had hardened around her ankles. It was late. She had been walking for so long, hours maybe, all of the emotion slowly seeping out of her. The stars crowded bright and fierce overhead. Still standing there on the brick wall, she swayed. Everything looked hazy, indistinct, like she wasn't really seeing it, as if the world, like her thought, was only half formed.

The smell of Dad's cigarette smoke carried to her. He was awake then. The thought filled her with a sudden anxiety, and she knew that she was frightened of him, had always been frightened of him, though she was the only one he had never turned on. It was so much part of her, that fear, that she'd always just thought it was the world, the way things were. She dropped into the courtyard, took off her shoes and approached the kitchen door. It was open. She slipped inside. The bitter cigarette smell hung thick in the kitchen, as if Dad had just been there. The tap was dripping. She crept on her bare feet across the room, to the door between the dining room and the hallway, leaning out until she could see all the way to the front door.

There, ahead of her, down the hall, exactly where she'd expected to see him, sat Dad, on the front steps. He was facing the street, hunched over in a light that must be coming from the living room. Smoke from a cigarette curled past his ear. And halfway between Dad and where Freya stood, flung across the floor, lay Mum.

It took her a moment to understand what she was looking at, to know what it meant. It was not how the hair covered Mum's face. It was not the turn of her head. It was not the blood she saw spattered across the dark wall, and on the floor around her, half cleaned up, and soaked in a towel heaped just past her body. And it was not how little room that body took up in the hallway. It was her father, the way he sat there facing the street with that slumped, indifferent posture, like none of it had anything to do with him.

A tremendous thumping started up in her chest. She turned, nearly lost her balance, and then focused on just one thing—putting one foot in front of the other, as quietly and quickly as she could, until she was out in the courtyard, where she bent over and vomited.

And what she thought of then was Daniel.

Freya wiped her lips with one trembling hand, straightened in the darkness and stared at the house. She felt as if she were going to vomit again, but nothing came out—her belly had gone hard. All of this, she told herself, has already happened. You are remembering it. You are alive. Mum is dead. Dead, dead, dead. She knew that she could say that a thousand times over and not believe it. But her brother? What about him? The door to the balcony was open. She could see it angled inwards into darkness, the edge of a white curtain drifting out, Daniel's bed just beyond it. Something filled her then, some strange, distant determination to see it through. No matter what happened to her, no matter what she found, she needed to see him. She hoisted herself back onto the wall, and from there up onto the balcony, where she stood by the door looking in.

A faint glimmer of light from the landing shone through the gap beneath Daniel's bedroom door. She saw only dim outlines of the things in his room. She stepped fully inside. Her heart was beating so hard that she could hear nothing else. She took a breath and waited for her eyes to adjust, waited to see what was in front of her. And there he was—she had come too late. Her brother lay on his bed, the sheet on the floor, his body motionless, his face turned towards her, unseeing, darkness pooled over his eyes. She crouched down, touched his cool cheek.

And with that he awoke. A sob of relief shook through her.

'What is it?' he murmured. 'An earthquake?'

She put her hand on his mouth, leaned in close. 'Listen,' she breathed. 'Do what I tell you. Don't talk. Don't make a sound. Understand?'

He nodded, his face pale in the dark room.

She pulled him to his feet. 'We have to leave,' she whispered. 'As quiet as you can. We can't stop for anything.'

From the hallway down below there came a creak of floorboards. They went onto the balcony. She climbed over the railing, clambered onto the wall, then held out her hand for him.

Daniel just stood there on the balcony. He didn't take her hand, didn't reach for her. 'Where's Mum?' he said.

She shook her head, held out her hand again.

'Are we going to find her?' he pressed.

'Yes,' she said. 'But only if you come now. She's waiting.'

His hand found hers. The balcony door creaked softly, but it was only a breeze. Bracing herself against a drainpipe, she helped him get onto the wall and then guided him along the top of it until they reached the alley. She jumped down first, turned, held her arms up. Daniel squatted on top of the wall, then hesitated.

Dad's voice came from inside the house. 'Freya? Is that you?'

There was something mournful and hesitant in that voice, a yearning.

'Jump,' she hissed at her brother.

In the alley, out of the wind, the whole world seemed trapped, welded into place by the heat of the day. Daniel looked down at her and then back towards the house.

'If you don't jump,' she said, 'I'll leave without you.'

'Freya!' Dad called again, nearer and louder now, his voice filling the night, and she knew he was on the balcony.

Daniel jumped, and she caught him, and then she was pulling him along, guiding him around shards of broken glass that littered the ground.

They were almost at the end of the alley when Dad roared out into the darkness, fury in his voice. 'Freya!' She heard the gate to the courtyard shake. 'Freya!'

They kept walking towards the sea.

'Why aren't we going back to him?' her brother asked. 'Won't we be in trouble?'

Freya didn't answer. She was walking more quickly now, almost running, pulling him along behind her, gripping his hand as tight as she could. The night was full of small noises, but their footsteps echoed alone.

'Freya,' her brother said. 'You're hurting me.'

'Sorry,' she panted, but her grip didn't loosen, her pace didn't falter. 'Just be quiet for a little while.'

Was he following them? She couldn't turn to look. There were no lights on in any of the houses they passed. They followed the road up until they reached the hospital, most of which too lay in darkness. She paused there and gazed back the way they had come. The streetlights spilled down onto emptiness. She looked up at the dark, abandoned windows of the hospital, and her hand went slack and dropped his. They stood there in silence, side by side.

'Why are you crying?' her brother asked.

'Don't,' she answered. 'Don't talk.'

They broke into motion again and followed the road beside the bluff overlooking the sea. The drop on the other side of the white fence was steep, the crumbling, dizzying heights plunging down to the rocks below. She knew, standing there, that this was as close to saying goodbye as she would ever come, that nothing else would come as close as this. In the darkness it felt as if they might walk straight out to the distant ship whose lights seemed as fixed as the stars, neither rising nor falling ahead of them.

'Are we going to see Mum?' Daniel asked.

'Yeah,' she said.

He nodded and gave a small smile, but then his expression shifted. 'Why didn't we stop when Dad called?'

'Did you hear anything?' she said. 'Tonight?'

'Dad was calling us.'

'Before that. Before I woke you up. How could you not hear anything?'

'What do you mean?'

She didn't answer. They were still heading up, along the coast, towards the highest cliffs that overlooked the ocean, and here the breeze blew stronger, coming from somewhere over the water, and there was the noise too of the waves worrying around the rocks, but then they turned in sharply, away from the noise of the sea and the wind and towards the police station, the grey bunker set against the hill on the other side of the hospital, and Freya paused again, let Daniel pause too. The whole world was different now. Her brother was still safe from it, for seconds, minutes even, but not forever. She wanted somehow to preserve this for him. Oh how precious to still be safe from it.

A car cruised on down the hill past them. The driver's head turned to follow them as it passed. She saw a man's face for a brief moment with surprising clarity, a pale expression floating in the dark interior of the car, curiosity or fear or hunger, perhaps, and then it was gone, and they set off again.

The glass doors of the police station slid apart at their approach, the waft of air conditioning enveloping them. Distant radio voices drawled through static. The policewoman behind the desk looked at them.

Freya spoke, and her voice was loud and flat and strange. 'Something's happened.'

The policewoman rose to her feet. 'What do you mean, love?'

Her brother's hand slipped out of hers. He stepped away from her, was looking up at her, his face frozen, contorted, like he didn't know who she was, like he was afraid of her. She kept talking and she knew that she was destroying it, everything in him that was already crumbling within her. The policewoman came around the counter, took Freya in her arms. Someone came with a blanket. The phone was ringing. No one picked it up. It rattled on while they asked questions—How long ago? Where? Are you hurt? She told them everything she could. She did not cry. It was like giving a speech in school, knowing the words and saying them precisely, one after the other, but not feeling them in a way that made sense. Minutes had elapsed. Already police officers were leaving.

Now they were looking at her brother.

'I slept,' he said. 'I was sleeping.'

Then he wet his pants.

After

Again. Richard finds himself awake. God, he's awake. His heart is racing and his eyes are sore. The red numbers on the clock dance and dissolve and come together. Two-thirty am, he reads at last. The windows are rattling in their frames, the curtains billowing towards him, the air that moves across his skin warm.

He holds a hand against the sodden swirls of hair on his breast, feels the incredible beating of his life. He draws breath and shudders, pulls the sheet from his legs and swings around onto the floor. He rises and hunches over again as he begins coughing—wracking, convulsive coughs that come from deep within him and bring nothing up—an anxious cough, his boyfriend has told him.

He straightens, takes several steps and looks back at his bed. There is a residue of panic still inside him, a leftover from sleep, from dreams he tries not to think about once they are gone. He could use a cigarette right now. The cravings occasionally come when he sees someone else lighting up, but mainly at these times, when his body feels frail, like paper stretched around a brittle frame, like all he wants to do is burst into flame and be done with it. There are no cigarettes in the house, though. He stopped half a year ago, at the time of the trial, just when the stress of all of that should have made him want to smoke more than ever.

The curtains spill and gather around him and he steps through them to the window, to confront the breeze, the sky, the street, the harbour, the world. His hands resting on the sill, he stands there and lets his gaze drop back to the street. It is quiet and empty, but there is more to it than that these days. Beyond the street, beyond all of the houses, he can see the lighthouse, and beyond that, much further out, grey clouds that appear in the darkness with the quick, nervy flickering, from place to place, of a distant storm—like there is a battle being waged out there, artillery going off in rapid exchanges. Somewhere the noise must be deafening. He thinks he can hear the growl of the thunder, even here, but the sound, stretched over all that distance, is too subtle for him to be sure.

He steps back through the curtains, pulls on a bathrobe and goes down into the kitchen. While he waits for the water to boil, the lonely rumble of it building into his thoughts, he stares out into the courtyard. He can see the thick, high brick wall that separates his courtyard from the next one along, where he used to sit with Maryanne, laughing and smoking and drinking cups of coffee—then his gaze drifts back inside, to the kitchen, and finally to the paper that still sits on the benchtop. He picks it up and looks at the front page, the last thing he read before he went to bed.

There are two stories, both of them from this city.

One is about the rape and murder of the girl from Freya's school. Richard has followed the story from the beginning—he supposes that most people in Newcastle have. There is something murky about the details, the evasive statements of witnesses. An eighteen-year-old man has confessed to murder and sexual assault. Two others have been convicted of lesser offences. Still others were involved, onlookers to the initial assault, participants, but they will not be charged. All of them are students, or former students, of the same school.

The other story is about a man who killed his wife.

He has been convicted of murder, sentenced to a minimum of ten years. Richard skims across the words, finds the judge's comments and reads them again: hard worker, stress, provocation, no premeditation, devotion to family, remorse, still young enough to make something of his life.

Ten years. One of those years is already gone.

~

It was the lights that woke Richard that night, a year past, the wash of blue and red against his ceiling, the stop and start of a siren, then the sound of car doors opening and closing, and the crackle and murmur of police radios. Straight away then, it came, a sickly awareness of possibility, of all of his fears of the past months mounting into that pause when he had not yet known, had still had room for hope, but he'd known—some part of him had known. He'd gone to the window, looked down and saw them there, three police cars. A fourth pulled up as he watched, and by the time he'd put on some clothes and gone outside, there was an ambulance. The gurney being wheeled past had a body on it, hidden from sight.

He'd stumbled out into the hot, still night in a daze, without his bathrobe, just a pair of boxers and a singlet. The neighbours were coming out of their houses to stare, from a distance, at the scene, all of them stunned, curious, talkative about the family they'd barely gotten to know. He'd ignored them all.

'Who is it?' he'd asked a policeman.

'Are you a friend?'

'Yes. A neighbour. Both. I'm *her* friend.' His voice cracked a little when he said this.

The policemen's expression altered in some minute way. 'I'm sorry then.'

'Was that her?'

The policeman's hand was on Richard's chest, partly in comfort, but also preventing him from stepping forward, from getting closer to the house. Past the policeman's shoulder, the polished floorboards gleamed in the hallway light. Bags were being taken out by people wearing gloves. They did not look in his direction.

'Could you wait for us in your house?'

'Are the children—are they?' Richard couldn't finish the question.

'Only the mother.'

'Dear God,' he said. 'Where's Roy?'

'Who?'

'The husband.'

'In there.' The policeman nodded his head towards one of the paddy wagons.

Richard couldn't see anything, though. The back door of the paddy wagon concealed its occupant. But he imagined Roy sitting there on the other side of the metal. Every paddy wagon he saw after that, for the rest of his life, he would think of Roy or someone like him, sitting in there, waiting.

Later, and again in the trial, they asked Richard lots of questions. What had he heard? Fighting, yes, an argument, but that wasn't unusual, and then nothing, just nothing. He hadn't thought anything of the silence when he'd gone to bed.

Now he thought about it all the time.

~

A couple of weeks after the trial, a car had been out the front of their house when he'd gone out to his doorstep with a cup of coffee. Freya had come walking down the steps, followed by Daniel. She looked older, as if it had been years since they'd been here, her hair cut short, her stance a little straighter. Daniel looked the same as always.

What was he supposed to say to them? He'd put down his cup, walked across and, without a word, hugged them. That was a start.

'It's good to see you,' he said then in a voice that did not sound like his.

Freya nodded.

'How are you?' He ruffled Daniel's hair.

'I'm good,' Daniel said, smiling vaguely, as if he believed none of it.

The last person out of the house was an older woman, slim and well-dressed, grey hair pulled back in a ponytail. 'Who are you?' she asked.

Not hostile but not friendly either.

He put out his hand. 'I'm the neighbour,' he said to her. 'We were friends.'

Were. It still seemed strange to say that.

The woman's grip was slack within his own. 'I'm her mother.'

That, he supposed, never changed. You didn't stop being someone's mother just because they were gone.

'She talked a lot about you,' he said. 'All good things.'

Her smile reminded him of Maryanne's—self-deprecating, an ironic glint in the eye. '*All* good things?' she said.

'Well,' he said. 'Mainly. I'm Richard.'

'Alice,' she said.

He wanted to say then that he was glad to have finally met her, that he had always liked her, from the stories he'd heard from Maryanne, that he'd always thought her complex and interesting and funny, but he didn't.

'Gosh, you look like her,' he said.

A small smile crossed her face. 'Not as much as Freya does.'

Alice put a hand on Freya's shoulder, then let it fall.

'No,' he said.

Alice turned, looked up at the house.

'So this is it,' she said. 'I didn't know what to expect.'

'I know,' he said.

'To think there'll be people living here again one day,' she said.

He didn't know what to say to that.

'I remember her talking about it, the first time. She hadn't even seen it and she came anyway. And look at it—it's just a house.'

'I guess so,' he said.

'I wish they'd demolish it,' she said suddenly, with a great deal of feeling.

'Yes,' he said. 'Me too.'

Alice looked back at him, her eyes red.

'I'd better get on with it,' she said.

She went back inside. Freya and Richard and Daniel stared after her in silence.

'You're a strong girl,' Richard said, turning to Freya. 'Your mum always used to say that.'

Freya looked away and nodded again.

'I'll never stop thinking about her,' he added. 'I promise.'

'I know.' She smiled, her lips tight, a dimple in her chin, a quick, firm nod.

'Any time you want to give me a call,' he said, 'now or in ten years' time or whenever, I'll be here. Think of me like some weird good-for-nothing uncle. I don't have much family myself, and you're always welcome.'

Freya smiled at that, a flash of the old humour breaking through the sadness in her eyes, like a spark that ran from the grandmother to Maryanne to her daughter.

'Don't worry,' she said. 'You're weird, but so am I.'

Daniel laughed.

Richard picked up his cup again, lifted it in a half-salute, went inside and paused a moment in his living room. He heard a voice outside. It was the boy from down the street, the one who stood there so often out the front of the house since that day. Richard parted the curtain and saw him talking to Freya, the two of them standing a few metres apart. He wondered what was passing between them. He felt as if he were intruding on something and yet he remained frozen in place, unable to resist taking it in.

The boy stepped forward, pulled Freya into an embrace, she with her head bowed and resting on his shoulder, he with his head against hers. It looked natural and simple and complete, as if they might stay there forever, but then he stepped back, a boy again, and Maryanne's mother came out, and the boy stood there watching with his hands in his pockets as they got into the car. After the car had gone, he turned and walked slowly out of sight.

~

Ten years. One gone already. He puts the paper down again.

Still young enough to *make* something of his life.

Roy will be out in another nine years, if he behaves. And what of those children? What has Roy made of *their* lives? Where will they be in nine more years? Freya will be twenty-five. Her brother will be nineteen. At least they will be alive. At least they will have each other. At least they will be able to choose what happens next.

He takes his coffee and goes out onto the front steps. There are stars overhead. He can hear the roar of the sea, the booming of waves collapsing against the coast. There is no telling where they began, those waves, but they have ended here, the noise of their breaking filling the space between all the hard, straight angles of the houses. Soon the summer will be gone again. He sits, looks across the dark, empty length of the street and sips his coffee, thinking of Maryanne, of Freya, of Daniel. Like he is waiting for them to arrive, like it is daylight, and he knows they will be here soon.

ACKNOWLEDGEMENTS

I am grateful to the many people who helped me see this novel to completion. To Rebecca Starford, for her belief in the first draft when I was full of doubt, and the many ideas she gave me in its development, one of which was her early suggestion of shaping it around the perspective of a fifteen-year-old girl. To Elizabeth Cowell, who stepped in at a crucial moment and worked incredibly hard and with great insight to help me achieve the novel's final shape. To Michael Heyward, for the tremendous confidence he has shown not only in the novel, but in me as a writer, and to everyone at Text for supporting my work—I feel so honoured to be on your list. Also to Martin Hughes, for your generosity of spirit.

A huge thank you to Charlotte Wood, Hannah Kent, Kathryn

Heyman and Fiona McFarlane not only for taking the time to read my novel, but also for saying such wonderful things about it. And also to Sandy Cull, whose cover design captures my novel so perfectly.

Thank you to my wife, Kimiko Yoshinaga, for being an amazing mother to our children—and for the inspirational example you set in so many aspects of your life.

Thank you to my readers, Ryan O'Neill, Dael Allison, Peta Cullen, Scott Brewer and particularly Patrick Cullen, who all read drafts at various stages and provided invaluable advice, and to my agent, Benython Oldfield, for taking me on. Thank you to my mother, Nici Sala, for encouraging me, always. Thank you to both Pam Yoshinaga and Mum for sharing their nursing experiences with me. And of course, to Ben Matthews, who hasn't read any of it yet, but knows anyway—twenty years on from that first creative writing class, our brilliant friendship continues, as does my memory of the snake that ate the pony.

To all of those who have supported me at the University of Newcastle, from my mentor and champion, Keri Glastonbury, to the head of our school, Cathy Coleborne, to all of my colleagues— it is a privilege working with you, learning from you and being able to share my enthusiasm and passion for the creative writing program in English and Writing.

Lastly I wish to acknowledge the generous support of the Australia Council for the Arts. Without that initial grant for new work, my journey would have been a lot more difficult.